CRYSTAL BLUE

JOHN H. CUNNINGHAM

Other books in the BUCK REILLY ADVENTURE series
by John H. Cunningham

Red Right Return
Green to Go

Praise for John H. Cunningham and the Buck Reilly Adventure series:

"*Red Right Return* is a high-energy romp through the streets of Key West and the skyways of the Florida Straits. Cunningham's treasure-hunting, amphibian-flying hero, Buck Reilly, could be a reincarnation of Travis McGee with wings. RRR is the first in what will surely be a series of classic Florida adventure novels. Great fun, highly recommended."

– Robert Gandt, author of the Brick Maxwell series

"*Green To Go* is a rip-roaring, lock-you-to-your-seat adventure that careens through the Caribbean with the momentum of a crash landing. Great characters, excellent suspense, just enough romance, and lots of action, all bound together with the author's crisp writing style."

– Michael Reisig, author of *The Road To Key West*

"John Cunningham's *Crystal Blue* will make you a Buck Reilly fan, if you're not already. Cunningham's ability to take tropical Caribbean islands and turn them from sandy beaches and bars of Paradise to a precarious locale whenever Buck Reilly shows up is unique. Along the bumpy and exciting ride, you can expect Reilly's eclectic group of friends and miscreants to show up, along with his nemeses FBI Special Agent T. Edward Booth—who is not above blackmailing Reilly to get what he wants.

"Of course, Reilly ends up in a misadventure that threatens his life, his seaplane, a charity rock concert and a beautiful woman. As he tries to sort out what's happening, deal with Booth, and protect his plane, Reilly has to say alive to accomplish it all. He finds out it's not as simple as sippin' a mojito on a barstool in Key West. You'll be reading all night because the page-turner of a book will keep you wondering until the last pages."

– Michael Haskins, Author, Mick Murphy Key West mystery series

CRYSTAL BLUE

JOHN H. CUNNINGHAM

CRYSTAL BLUE

Published by Greene Street, LLC

Book design by Morgana Gallaway

This edition was prepared for printing by
The Editorial Department
7650 E. Broadway Blvd.
Suite 308
Tucson, Arizona 85710
www.editorialdepartment.com

Print ISBN: 978-0-9854422-4-8
Electronic ISBN: 978-0-9854422-3-1

www.jhcunningham.com

For the peacemakers

Acknowledgments

Thanks to Matt Hoggatt who wrote a great song and got a record deal on Mailboat Records, followed me on Twitter and we struck up a friendship and have co-written a song together. He also introduced me to Mike Ramos (where's the hidden track?) who connected me with Nina Avramides of HK Management, who kindly got me permission to feature Jimmy Buffett in *Crystal Blue*. Where and when? Read on and find out.

Songwriter and friend, Dave Miller, who connected me with Thom Shepherd, who along with Key West-based musician, Scott Kirby, both agreed to appear in this yarn.

For their help in scouring the Virgin Islands for great locations and facts to include in the story, thanks to Valentine Hodge on Tortola (who agreed to have his name used, but everything else about him, or his family in *Crystal Blue*, is pure fiction), and Captain Jay Rushing of St. John.

John Thedford, thanks for your support of Foxcroft School by bidding on and winning the use of your name in a Buck Reilly Adventure.

Thanks also to my publicist, Ann-Marie Nieves of GetredPR, Tim Harkness, illustrator extraordinaire, the team at The Editorial Department: Renni Browne, Ross Browne, Peter Gelfan, Shannon Roberts, Morgana Gallaway, Jane Ryder and Chris Fisher. Also to John Wojciech of C-Straight, my webpage designer, webmaster, Internet guru and all around solid dude. Thanks to Darcy Woessner for her research into adoption, unplanned pregnancy and the subsequent choices. The Seaplane Pilot's Association and Captain Chester Lawson, technical advisor on Grumman amphibians, world renowned seaplane instructor and owner of the beautiful 1946 Widgeon I'm leaning on in my picture on the back of this book.

And as always, to my lovely ladies Holly, Bailey and Cortney; my brothers Jim and Jay and their wonderful families.

Never give up on your dreams, some day they may actually come true…

The world breaks everyone, and afterward,
some are strong at the broken places.

Ernest Hemingway

CONTENTS

My Inner Voice is on Mute

1

THE AIR WAS TURBULENT OVER THE LOWER KEYS, BOTH IN AND OUTSIDE THE Beast. Towering cumulus clouds had built throughout the day, and now squalls caused me to zig and zag my way toward my charter customer Goodspeed's destination of Fort Lauderdale.

"When I heard you were running a charter service in Key West," Goodspeed said, "I expected something first class. With as much money as you ripped off at e-Antiquity, I figured you'd be living large."

I bit my lip.

He'd started the verbal attack right after we took off out of Key West. Rather than watching the turquoise water and islands pass under us like most charter customers, he stared right at me.

"Hell, the engines don't even match the wings. What'd you do, build this thing out of scrap?"

He was a big man, probably a former high school or university sports star who'd gone soft but still had the big frame. A bully all his life, I'd bet on it. He had money—or at least he dressed to make sure you thought he did—and wore his generation's symbols of prosperity: golfer's tan and a bulky gold watch. Judging by the wrinkles around his downturned mouth he'd never had a kind word for anybody, certainly not me.

I gripped the wheel and glanced down to my left. The seven-mile bridge was below. On and on he yapped.

"Are you going to keep this up the whole way to Fort Lauderdale?" I said.

Goodspeed smiled. "I've only just got started, boy. You cost me several hundred thousand—"

I shoved the wheel forward and added 20 degrees of flap. The Beast nose-dived toward the thin strip of land below.

"What the hell're you doing, Reilly? We're going down—"

I flicked off the intercom.

Halfway up Marathon Key was the small airport where I set the Beast down hard on the tarmac, military style, which bounced Goodspeed in his seat. His arms were crossed now, his mouth a thin line. We taxied to the small terminal, a hundred miles from his destination, where I reduced the RPMs and pulled off my headset. He stared at me, squint-eyed.

"This is your stop, *Mr.* Goodspeed."

"I paid for a round-trip flight—"

"You should have read the fine print in the contract."

He just stared at me. I took off my sunglasses and quoted from it word for word. "'*The pilot has the authority to deviate from, or alter the flight plan at any time, for any reason, if in his sole judgment the aircraft is in danger, in which case the pilot can terminate the charter.*'"

I unclipped his seatbelt, pulled him up, and all but tossed him out of the hatch.

"This charter's terminated."

Once he had both feet on the ground, he scurried to the wing tip, turned and shook a fist at me. "You'll regret this, Buck Reilly!" Something else about how he had a contract this time and he'd have my ass, but I didn't hear the next threat because I'd slammed the hatch shut.

Airborne and headed south, I envisioned the deserted island out in the Marquesas. I'd be there tomorrow, alone, camping for as many days as my water would last, or at least until Lenny Jackson's first political debate next week.

I was done with charters. Time for some snorkeling, spear fishing, and solitude under the starry skies above the little no-name Key out in the Marquesas.

As I flew over the old Bahia Honda bridge, I remembered jumping off the lower section as a teenager when my family vacationed here. We'd rent old conch houses in Key West and drive the thirty-odd miles north to picnic at Bahia Honda. Legend had it that a fifteen-foot hammerhead shark cruised the channel. My brother and I would walk out along the bridge's old rusted spans, twenty feet above the waterline, and jump in. We convinced ourselves there was safety in numbers. Until the time, a couple hundred yards from shore, when we counted to three and jumped into the gin-clear waters and I surfaced to find myself alone. I searched a terrified few seconds before Ben's laughter sounded above me.

"Better get your ass moving before that hammerhead eats you!"

I swam as hard as I could, convinced the shark would rise from the depths and rip me in half. With what strength I had left I chased Ben down the shore and throughout the campsites until I caught and pinned him in a patch of briars. He was still laughing, and before long I was too. But I never again trusted him to jump with me below that bridge.

A noise my engine shouldn't have been making brought me back to Goodspeed's bad-mouthing my old amphibious Grumman. Yes, this 1946 era Goose was a work in progress, and no, maybe I shouldn't have agreed to the roundtrip flight—the first since the Beast was deemed airworthy—but dammit, I needed the money. It didn't happen often, but every now and then a former investor in e-Antiquity, my bankrupt former treasure hunting business, showed up and dug at my scar tissue.

Nearly back to Key West, a familiar voice sounded in my headset and called out my N-number.

"What are you doing in the tower?" I said.

"Got an important message for you," Ray Floyd said. As the head mechanic at Key West International Airport, he was usually banished from Air Traffic Control, but Donny the controller was a friend known to bend a rule.

"Such as?"

"How does your customer like the Beauty?" Ray said.

"He didn't."

"*Didn't*? You can't even be to Miami yet—"

"Let's just say he was a little too critical of the Beast's comforts. I dropped him at Marathon."

I imagined Ray's shoulders sagging. He'd worked hard to get the Goose back into condition, and even with the new seats, the in-depth aesthetical renovation had yet to commence, thanks largely to the fact that I was broke.

"There goes the money for the paint job," Ray said. "How's Last Resort Charter and Salvage ever supposed to be profitable if you leave customers stranded?"

"I'm done with charters, Ray. Pompous assholes like Goodspeed are too hard to swallow. I just want to go—"

"Done with charters? What, you're now just Last Resort Salvage? How will you afford—"

"What's so important, Ray?"

He was silent a moment, then cleared his throat.

"There was a beautiful woman here just now, looking for a multi-day charter to the Virgin Islands."

"The only reason I'll end my camping trip will be to witness the release of Lenny Jackson's political aspirations on his unwitting competitors in next week's debate." The thought made me smile. Conch Man was primed to give them hell. "When I get back, I'm heading to the La Concha to get my stuff together. I'll be back at the airport bright and early tomorrow, just like we agreed."

"She was sexy."

"I don't care—"

"Even her name's sexy—Crystal. Said a famous musician referred her to you and that it was for a charity—"

"No charters and no charities!"

Mechanical genius, social philosopher, and video game ace, Ray had become a close friend in the time I'd been living in Key West. Eccentricities aside, he didn't give a rat's ass about my past, and he provided ballast to my occasional overly aggressive endeavors. But he could also be a pain.

I'd made a plan and I was sticking to it, even if I couldn't afford to blow off a call for a multi-day charter. I deserved a break. The stress of pouring my energies into fixing up the Beast had taken its toll. I needed a deserted island—alone with my snorkel gear, a Hawaiian sling, and hammock—a lot more than another charter customer.

Even a beautiful one.

2

Back in Key West, and after a quick exit from more of Ray on the subject of dumping my charter, I was stuck in stop-and-go traffic. In an old Rover 88 like mine the gear ratios, indelicacy of the clutch, and rigid suspension make for a jarring ride. Key West is now a 365-day-a-year destination, but in winter it gets even more crowded. Cruise ships, snowbirds, bikers, zillions of tourists—more people, more traffic.

Duval Street was lined with pedestrians sporting garish outfits and bright colors along with lots of exposed, sunburned skin. Once the swell of oncoming mopeds and pedi-cabs passed, I turned left at the La Concha hotel. When I first got to Key West a couple years ago, I thought I'd stay here a few weeks, then figure out something more permanent. But I worked out a deal with management for one of the suites, long-term. Plus it came with maid and room service, a pool, and was on the middle of Duval Street.

In my room on the sixth floor, I exhaled a long breath. I was 98% mentally checked out, ready for a break. The remaining 2% was focused on deciding what to take with me.

The phone rang.

I reached toward it, hesitated. But it might be Ray with some concern about the Beast, so I picked it up.

"Hello, is this Buck Reilly?" Female.

"That's right."

"This is Crystal Thedford, I left you a few messages on your machine and at the airport."

I noticed the red light blinking on the box next to the phone.

"Sorry, just got in—"

"No problem, but I'm pressed for time. I need to charter you and your plane for a few days to fly to St. Thomas, then around—"

"Sorry, Ms. Thedford, but Last Resort's closed next week."

"Please, call me Crystal. Is there a problem with your plane?"

I considered lying.

"No, she's fine. I'm taking a few days off to clear my head. It's been—"

"Perfect!" she said. "What better place than the Caribbean!"

"Sorry, I've already—"

"Buck—I hope you don't mind me calling you that, Jimmy said you marched to your own beat and not to get my hopes up, but also that you were the perfect guy to help."

"Jimmy?"

"My husband and I are putting on a big charity event in the British Virgin Islands—"

"Who gave you my name?"

"One of the performers participating in the event—there are quite a few—that's the problem, we need to shuttle them around and don't have enough planes or boats. It's a big deal, especially for us as we've got everything riding on—sorry—" I heard her take in a deep breath. "I'm rambling."

"Miss—ah, Crystal, I don't—"

"You see, I need to be in St. Thomas tomorrow afternoon. I could fly commercial, but once I'm there, I'm stuck. The other plane charters are full with our participants, and the ferry boats we've chartered are slow and can't do what I was hoping you could."

Why had I answered the damn phone?

"You said this was a charity event, right?" I said. "I'm not in a position to donate any—"

"Oh, gosh no, we can pay you! And you'll have plenty of free time to chill out on the world's most beautiful beaches, but you'll be getting paid while you're doing it!"

A sudden image of my ex-wife splashing in the waters of Peter Island during our honeymoon took me back to one of the happiest times of my life: e-Antiquity had been on a roll, the Wall Street Journal had just dubbed me "King Charles," and I'd just married supermodel Heather Drake after a globe-trotting whirlwind romance.

Times had changed.

And an all-expense-paid trip to the Virgin Islands suddenly sounded good. I'd have to pass through Customs on Tortola, and the memories from my last visit there were far from pleasant. But I'd been allowed to leave, eventually. And that was a long time ago.

"Please, Buck?"

I could always go camping in the Marquesas, right?

"Okay, Crystal, I'm listening."

As she spoke, images of flying down-island clicked through my mind. I explained my rates. She reiterated that she and her husband would pay all the expenses but said they were on a tight budget.

"I'm staying at the Casa Marina tonight," she said. "Why don't we have dinner and I'll tell you about the event and our schedule?"

"You have business here, too?"

"No, I just figured it would be easier for you. Let's meet at Louie's Backyard at seven." She paused. "Thanks again, Buck. This'll be a great week."

I put the phone down. She had already flown to Key West on the assumption that I'd accept her charter? Pretty confident lady. Good taste in restaurants, too.

Damn! Lulled by turquoise waters, flour-soft beaches, and some of my favorite beach bars, I'd forgotten about Lenny's debate.

3

I SHIFTED MENTAL GEARS AND DUG OUT MY OLD CHARTS. PLOTTING A COURSE to St. Thomas made me smile. I had personal history there from my e-Antiquity days. Treasure ships had passed through those waters in the 1500 and 1600's, imported and exported wealth from sugar plantations, and colonialism followed for centuries thereafter. So did wrecks, piracy, and opportunity.

What would happen when I sought to clear Customs in Tortola? Would my arrest for suspicion of murder still be on the record?

I shook my head. It *had* been four years.

Stanley Ober, the Hole Town eccentric who claimed to have a map of a sunken privateer flush with gold and silver stolen from a Barbados rum plantation had disappeared after a public meeting with me. The map I'd bought was bogus, but e-Antiquity's reputation, along with my then recent moniker of King Charles, made me the natural suspect. The legal bills racked up in that month I was incarcerated in Tortola's hell-hole of a prison had eclipsed all of Last Resort's revenues since I formed the company.

I hadn't been back to Tortola since.

I planned the route: 1,162 nautical miles, refueling in the Turks and Caicos, flight time nearly eight hours. The weather called for clear skies and light winds. Perfect.

That done, I packed shorts, flip-flops, and t-shirts into my duffel. I pondered whether to take any fishing or snorkel gear and decided against it. My stash of old maps, letters, and clues to lost treasures was nestled in the new compartment built below the Beast's left seat, newly equipped with a lock, but I didn't expect to have time to sniff out old prospects. Crystal's charter sounded active, shuttling people to and from wherever her event was being held. Still in survival mode, just trying to keep up with the bills, I couldn't afford the luxury of treasure hunting.

I set out to the airport to stow my gear and give the Beast a quick once-over before my dinner with Crystal Thedford. Our flight time would come early tomorrow and I wanted everything ready for a quick departure.

But I had to make another stop first.

I was exiting the elevator into the La Concha's lobby when I heard my name called in a deep southern accent—Frank, the concierge, with a smile on his lips and a cocktail in his hand. Well connected around town, and I don't think I'd ever seen him when he wasn't smiling.

"Buck, I'm glad I bumped into you."

"New uniform, Frank? Shorts, polo and Jack Daniels? What's up?"

"Off the clock, Bubba." Smile. "Been busier than a raccoon on trash night. Family of four staying here at the hotel want to go on a tour of the outer islands around Fort Jefferson, said they like adventure. That being the case, I suggested you for a full-day charter." Big smile. "They're available day after tomorrow—"

"Sorry, Frank, I'm headed out on a week-long gig." I patted his shoulder. "But I sure appreciate you thinking of me."

"Sure, Buck. Next time." Smile.

My old Rover took me down Whitehead and I parked on Thomas, near Petronia. I walked along the fenced area at the back of Blue Heaven, entered the gate and walked through the half-full outdoor dining area. Ahead was a crowd around the bar, which meant Conch Man was on duty. Ever since word got out that he was going to run for the Town Council, his daily pontification at the bar had attracted an increasingly larger audience. Best thing about Lenny, though, was that he wasn't playing to the crowd. He'd always espoused his opinions on what had gone wrong in Key West and what he'd do to fix it. When his uncle, Pastor Willy Peebles, finally rounded Lenny's rough edges and got him on the ballot, Lenny's homegrown rants gained immediate traction.

I made my way back to the rear corner of the bar.

"Yo, Buck, Barbancourt on the rocks?" Lenny said.

"No, I'm on my way to meet someone." Not wanting to yell over the backs of his patrons, I pointed toward the back corner of the bar. He nodded and met me there a second later.

"What's up man?"

"Change in plans. I booked a charter to the Virgin Islands."

"Sweet, brother! Wish I could join you." His bright smile was a relief.

"I'll miss your coming out party—"

"Poor choice of words in these parts." He grinned. "Yeah, guess you'll miss the ass-kicking I'm going to lay on those crackers Tuesday night." He laughed, a vision of total confidence.

"You worried?" I said.

"You crazy?"

"Fletcher's been on the Council eight years, Lenny. He has a pretty strong—"

"Shit, boy, he won't know what hit him. Be like that time Bruiser knocked your ass out here." Lenny nodded to where the occasional boxing ring had been set up since the days Hemingway had boxed here.

I had to laugh. Conch Man had always been the epitome of cockiness, unless he was in my plane, where he shook like a leaf and prayed like a monk. Pastor Willy and the political consultants he'd hired had really focused him. He was primed and chomping at the bit to launch his new political career.

"Just don't drop too many f-bombs while you're going after those boys," I said. "That *won't* have mass appeal."

"No shit, Sherlock. I'm not fucking stupid." Lenny put on a serious expression. "Why yes, Mr. Reilly, excellent point, but allow me to counter your observation with what I've learned from eight generations of Conchs, family members who've lived here since the earliest history of Key West." He burst out with a laugh. "I'm gonna kick their asses, Buck, shame you'll miss it."

I gave him a high-five, wished him well, and made my way back to the Rover. I was sorry I was going to miss it too. Lenny set loose on career politicians would be fine entertainment.

I drove down past the Southernmost Point, where even in the dark, cameras flashed to illuminate the old red, yellow, and black marker that proclaimed Key West's location ninety miles from Cuba. I turned left and continued along to Reynolds, past the Casa Marina, where Crystal was staying, and down past Higgs Beach and White Street Pier. Atlantis House was on the left. I longed for a piece of Kayla's Key Lime pie, or to go fishing with her husband Steve. More luxuries I could no longer afford.

The airport was quiet, the recent arrivals already armed with rental cars, carried away by the Five-Sixes, or received by friends and loved ones. Ray Floyd was seated in a folding chair outside the private aviation terminal holding a conch shell. When he spotted me, his eyes lit up.

"What's with the shell, Ray?"

"I've realized the conch shell is a metaphor for the human experience."

"Island existentialism?"

"The bottom of the shell flares in a cone-shaped angle up to where the bold protrusions jut out, which is like birth up to the teenage years. Those juts are like stress spikes, most dramatic in early adulthood." Ray rolled the shell over in his hands and rubbed each section. "Where the spikes begin to taper off—as life settles—the cone tapers back to the point, and while more frequent, the spikes are smaller, more rounded and subtle as life winds down toward death."

Classic Ray Floyd.

"What about shells that have a second set of jagged spikes? How do you explain them?"

"Midlife crises or trauma, of course." He rubbed his fingers along the surface. "The outside is hard and coarse like your external persona, but the inside is pink and smooth like the essence of your soul." Ray was staring at the shell while he talked. "If you count the protrusions and nubs, there's usually around forty on a good-sized shell. I'm still contemplating how they correlate to life years."

"Did you just come up with this epiphany?"

"I call it the Conch Paradigm."

"Interesting," I said. "I have a change of plans."

Ray looked up from the conch. "I heard you agreed to take Crystal Thedford to the Caribbean."

"How did you—"

"She came into the FBO and asked Stephanie a few questions about you."

Stephanie Baldwin and I had a lukewarm relationship, she being the manager of the Fixed Base Operation, me being the trouble-magnet who flew the bucket-o-bolts and was always late paying bills.

"Crystal asked, so I took her out to see the Beauty."

Ray and I had different points of view about the old Grumman Goose.

"And?" I said.

"I explained that she's a work in progress but very sound mechanically. She was happy it had nice new seats and was big enough to hold several people. Wait till you see her, Buck. She's hot!"

"Wipe your chin, Ray."

He brushed his hand across his chin, stopped, narrowed his eyes and grimaced. "And smart, too."

"She's married."

He deflated a little. "Since when has that stopped you?"

I spun on my heel to face him.

"I have *never* knowingly gone after a married woman."

"What about that blonde at Fantasy—"

"I said *knowingly*, Ray. And when I found out she was married, the fun and games were over. Not my thing, taking another man's wife." I didn't add that since my ex-wife Heather had left me for a fat-cat Hedge Fund guru, it pissed me off if a married woman came on to me.

He followed me out to the Beast where I stowed my bag, checked the lock under my seat to make sure the stash was safe, went through my storage compartment to check the anchors and supplies for the flight, then the fuel supply. Ray followed me around, spinning the conch shell in his hands like it was a football.

"Can you do me a favor and ask Flight Services to vacuum her out tonight, put a shine on the seats and top off the tanks?"

"Want her spic-and-span for your beautiful charter customer?" He pumped his eyebrows.

"Don't let your imagination go where I won't." I checked my watch. "I've got to run."

"How come you can't ask Flight Services to do that stuff?" he said.

"Because I'm meeting Crystal for dinner at Louie's."

"I knew it!"

I left with Ray's Conch paradigm in the back of my mind. I speculated where was I on the journey—still in the midst of the "stress spikes?" Or did my increasingly frequent experiences have me closer to death?

Thanks, Ray.

4

I NEVER TIRED OF DINING AT LOUIE'S BACKYARD. SET ON THE WATER AT A QUIET notch of the island, the outdoor patio provided an expansive view of the straits looking south. From there I'd seen waterspouts in the distance and watched meteor showers at night. And the people-watching was just as good.

I'd arrived early and was savoring some Zacapa rum on the rocks when Georges, the maître d', escorted a stunning brunette from inside the dining room down the stairs that bifurcated the patio. Even from the distance it was clear that Ray hadn't exaggerated. I enjoyed watching her come toward me before she knew who I was.

"Here he is, Mrs. Thedford." Georges pursed his lips. "Buck Reilly."

I stood and took her firm hand. Our eyes locked in a confident connection.

"Thanks, Georges," she said.

He raised an eyebrow and pivoted away with a half-smile on his face.

"Ms. Thedford, a pleasure to meet you."

"Crystal, remember? I'm not the formal type."

Her smile was warm as she slid into the seat that faced the water. I wanted her to enjoy the view.

"It's nice to finally have this day just about over," she said. "I've been on the move since four-thirty this morning."

"Why so long?"

"Had some details to handle in Miami, but I started out in Bethesda, Maryland."

I mentioned that I used to live in Virginia. Her mouth tightened.

"I'm familiar with your past. My husband used to be a federal prosecutor before he quit to start I Support Adoption. That's the name of our nonprofit." She must have seen my eyes flinch, because her lips pulled into a smile.

"I have no problem with your, ah, previous line of work. As a matter of fact, my parents invested in e-Antiquity when you first went public."

Oh jeez, not another—

"Don't worry." She patted my hand. "They sold at a nice profit a year before your troubles began."

"Always nice to meet a *happy* former client."

She held her smile. Her candor felt genuine. She could pause, look into your eyes, and make you feel as if you'd known her forever.

"Adoption? Children, I assume."

"That's right. We're a global nonprofit focused on adoption." She paused. "And what we're doing down in the islands may lead to major changes—social changes, that is. But we'll have plenty of time to talk about that on the flight to St. Thomas. And I'm sure you've heard about the event on TV."

"If it's not on the Weather, History, or Discovery channels, I wouldn't have seen it."

"There's a lot of celebrity participation, so the networks, newspapers, and magazines have been hyping it—plus we have a great publicist."

The waiter appeared with menus, took our drink orders—another Zacapa for me, sparkling water for Crystal. We'd be leaving early, so this would the last rum for the night. As of tomorrow, I was working.

She explained her background in fund raising and executive management for the City of Hope in Los Angeles, a large charity organization focused on cancer. She'd been in Washington addressing a congressional panel on cancer care when she met her husband.

"I guess you'd call it love at first sight," she said. "I know that's cliché, but we were married four months later. And no, I wasn't pregnant."

The smile never left her face. Not only were the corners of her mouth always turned upward, her amber eyes sparkled when she spoke and fixed squarely on yours when you spoke to her. She had to be a great fundraiser.

"How long have you been living in Key West?" she said.

"A little over three years now. It's been a nice change of pace."

"e-Antiquity must have been a fast-lane lifestyle—scouring the globe for lost treasures, darling of Wall Street, on the cover of magazines..."

"Those days are long over. I used to be somebody, and now I'm somebody else. It's just me and my airplane, the...the Goose."

"I saw it at the airport. Charming old bird."

I studied her eyes for sarcasm.

"She's a work in progress, but sound," I said.

"That's what the mechanic said. I'm not worried."

"No?"

"If you're comfortable risking your life, than I should have no concern for my own." She winked. "Even with King Charles Reilly at the helm."

I took it as a friendly jibe. Ray was right about her being beautiful, but I already knew she was also intelligent, considerate, and—

A sudden movement up by the door caught my attention: Georges, rushing down the steps and headed our way. Now what?

"Excuse me." Nearly breathless, he said, "Ms. Thedford? I'm afraid you have a call."

She looked at her cell phone, which had been face down on the table. Its red light blinked.

"An *important* call." Georges glanced around him as he spoke. My alarm bells went off. "If you'll come with me?"

Crystal's smile was gone. She pushed her chair back with a loud scrape and stood.

"You can take the call in the office."

We followed him toward the small office by the bathrooms. Crystal didn't meet my eyes before she turned and closed the door in my face.

I realized Georges' bronzed face was awfully pale. What in hell was going on?

That's when I heard Crystal shriek.

5

I PUSHED THE DOOR OPEN AND FOUND CRYSTAL WITH A FIXED STARE AND THE phone on the floor.

"What's wrong?" I said.

She continued to stare through the opened door, past Georges and me.

"It was the police," Georges said. "On St. Thomas—the Virgin Islands."

Crystal's eyelids fluttered and her chest heaved.

"What did they want?" I said.

Georges gave a quick shake of his head and shrugged his shoulders.

"They wouldn't say, only that it was—"

"John's missing," Crystal said. "My husband."

"Was he out on the water?" I said. "Was there a problem?"

My questions hung in the air.

She pressed her palms together and held them to her lips, but her eyes were wide open. What else was that in her expression? Not fear or sadness. Resignation?

"I need to get back to my hotel." Her voice was brittle.

"I can take you."

She nodded once and walked out.

Georges and I exchanged a glance. His lip was trembling.

I took off after Crystal and guided her out of the restaurant and toward Reynolds, where my Rover was parked halfway down the block.

"Did they give you any details?"

"I didn't believe any of the hype." She shuddered. "John had warned me, but he's a worrier so I laughed it off."

"What hype?"

"He said there could be trouble, but—" She made a fist and raised it like she intended to hit the dashboard but stopped mid-air.

The Casa Marina loomed ahead.

"What kind of trouble, Crystal—you mentioned social changes? Like what?"

She turned toward me and bit her lip. There was a tear on her cheek.

"Choice issues—I'm sure John's just off with one of the guests—attending to details—getting things ready."

We pulled up in front of the hotel. She had the door opened before I even stopped.

"Crystal." I grabbed her arm and her head snapped back toward me. There was fear in her eyes. "What kind of trouble could John be in?"

"There'd been some threats, about our event—"

"Threats? For a charity event?"

"It's nothing to worry about." Her voice dropped to a whisper. "If you don't want to take me down, I'll understand."

"Of course I'll take you, but what else can I do to help?"

"Just get me to St. Thomas." Her eyes had turned cold.

"I'll be here at seven. The flight time—"

She nodded and slammed the door. I watched her hurry into the hotel lobby, glancing down at her cell phone as she went.

Crap! Missing? What did that mean? And threats—by whom? I'd never heard of their charity, but adoption didn't strike me as a contentious issue. Who would have threatened them, and why? Choice issues?

Back to the La Concha. I vaguely heard Zeke call out to me from the moped rental hut, but I was in the elevator before it registered.

When my computer booted up, I searched for I Support Adoption and found a modest website with pictures of both Crystal and her husband, John. He had movie star looks, no surprise there, with determined eyes and perfect white teeth. I read through his brief biography. He and his two brothers had been adopted at birth by a loving couple unable to have children themselves. The rest was as Crystal had described him.

Crystal's biography was almost as skimpy vague, mentioning her past as an executive with City of Hope and her bachelor of arts and law degrees from NYU.

I had the impression that she must come from an established family but there was nothing in her bio to base it on.

There was a link to a brief article in USA Today describing the upcoming event, to be held at Foxy's on Jost Van Dyke. There would be many celebrities in attendance, but the names hadn't been released yet.

Foxy's? There was a small concert venue behind the famous waterfront bar, built for a millennium party intended to feature the Rolling Stones. I couldn't recall if the concert ever happened, but I'd enjoyed a painkiller or two there in the past. Odd place for a charity concert.

Elsewhere on the website I read some stats on abortion and adoption...nothing controversial...some photos of happy moms with kids...all straightforward. I clicked the "In the News" tab and found several links to stories about adoption from newspapers all over the world. More statistics, stories of new adoption laws... If there had been threats, I couldn't imagine why. Adoption was a choice, yes, but not a controversial one.

I sat up, stretched, ran my fingers through my shaggy hair and looked out the window over Duval Street.

I was just the charter pilot. Just deliver the woman to St. Thomas, see what else she needs, and find some time to relax. John Thedford will probably turn up before morning and be waiting for us at the seaplane base in Charlotte Amalie.

With that thought I closed my laptop, shut off the lights, and fell asleep to scattered recollections of the gin-clear waters, powdery white beaches, and colorful buildings of the Virgin Islands... and a glimpse of the cell where I'd spent a hellish few weeks in Hole Town, Tortola.

6

OF COURSE WHEN YOU HAVE A LONG DAY PLANNED WITH AN EARLY START, you sleep like crap the night before. At least I did. After grabbing a café con leche at Cuban Coffee Queen on Caroline, I climbed back in my Rover and drove down Palm Avenue. I was early, but there was little traffic and the morning was bright, the sky a clear metallic blue, so I took my time and pondered last night's sudden change in course. Hell, we hadn't even ordered dinner before the dream charter went south.

I took a sip of the hot café con leche—"Damn!" I'd burned my tongue.

The parking lot at the Casa Marina was quiet. I checked my watch—fifteen minutes early. I parked in a handicap spot and sat with a clear view of the main entrance across the entry circle. The hotel had changed hands a few times over the years but I remembered my father saying it had been an abandoned husk in the early seventies. Hard to imagine it as dilapidated given its current grandeur, but then Key West's history of boom to bust to boom had been as cyclical as Halley's comet.

A man in black slacks, white polo shirt, and dark glasses stood near the hotel entrance. He sucked hard on a cigarette and glanced back behind him toward the parking lot. Tall, muscular, hair slicked back. Having a smoke while his girlfriend slept?

I didn't think so.

I followed his gaze toward a black van parked in the passenger off-loading area, but from my angle I couldn't see if anyone was—

Crystal walked out of the hotel, two bags in tow. She had on tropical-weight khakis and a purple polo shirt that accentuated her glossy auburn hair, which was up in a ponytail. Smart dress for travel. I reached for the door handle, but what happened next stopped me cold. The guy with slicked-back hair flicked his cigarette and approached Crystal at a trot.

He said something to her and reached for her bags.

Crystal pulled the bags back. Slicked-back grabbed her arm.

I flew out of the Rover, jumped a hedge, and sprinted across the lot. The man now had hold of both Crystal's arms and was trying to pull her toward the van.

I rocketed toward them, lowered my shoulder, and speared him from his blind side. All three of us fell to the ground, Crystal screaming.

Slicked-back grunted but was on his feet, faster than me, hand in his pocket. I shoved Crystal behind me and rolled to my feet, crouched, as he popped open a switchblade.

"Help!" Crystal yelled.

The man lunged toward me, the knife slashed toward my neck—

I ducked, spun to my left, continued in a full circle and caught him with a clean uppercut to the kidney, which bent him over. He grunted something unintelligible, straightened, jumped back, and raised the knife again.

Damn!

Crystal screamed again, and out of the corner of my eye I noticed the side door slide open on the black van.

"What's going on!" a voice yelled from the hotel entry. "You men there—hey!"

Slicked-back waved the knife, glanced toward the hotel, back at me, his crooked teeth gritted—

"Buck! No!" Crystal said.

"Call 9-1-1!" came the voice from the entry. Slicked-back suddenly turned and jumped into the van, which sped off with him glaring back at us from the open door.

Crystal ran up behind me, along with an older, round-bellied bellman.

"Are you okay, Buck?" she said. "Oh my gosh, what *was* that?"

"The police are on their way, sir." The bellman was panting. "Are you all right?"

With my hands on my knees, I sucked air. My shirt was damp—had he cut me?

I rubbed my hand across my stomach—café con leche.

"Was he trying to steal my bags?" Crystal said. "If you hadn't come when you did—Buck, are you all right?"

I finally looked up and saw the concern on her face. I stood but spotted something on the ground. A handkerchief?

"I'm fine."

She was shaking, so I put my arm around her and she squeezed my shoulder. "That was crazy! I've never—what did he want?"

I bent down and picked up the cloth. It was moist. I smelled it and my eyes blurred—chloroform.

To her credit, Crystal wasn't crying or a puddle of nerves, just concerned and confused. Could this be connected to her husband's disappearance on St. Thomas? I heard sirens coming from White Street and in a moment of clarity stuffed the handkerchief in my pocket. We needed to get out of Key West and to the Virgin Islands to find out what was going on, not get held up here indefinitely.

Crystal stood close to me, quiet now, and I guessed she too had connected the dots. I took a deep breath, almost back to normal, and leaned close to her.

"We need to get going, so let's keep this simple." I nodded toward the police car that flew into the parking area, lights flashing and siren blaring.

She gave me a quick nod.

"I'm so sorry, folks!" A man in a suit had come from the hotel, the bellman who'd helped defuse the attack next to him. A moment later two policeman appeared in front of us.

"Someone tried to steal my suitcase." Crystal spoke up before a question was even asked. "Thank God Buck arrived at the same time."

The cops looked at me.

"Buck Reilly?" the shorter, pudgier one said. It came off like an accusation.

One cop took a statement from Crystal while the other took one from me. I followed her lead and made the attack seem like a robbery gone awry. I told him about the knife and the bellman coming in the nick of time, which caused Slicked-back to run. No, I didn't notice the make of the van or license plate. In twenty minutes they were finished and said they'd let us know if they learned anything. Crystal gave her cell number. I told them I could be reached at the La Concha.

The manager was still apologizing when we climbed aboard the Rover, now an hour behind schedule.

"Sure you still want to do this charter, Buck?" She looked straight through the windshield.

I shifted gears and we made our way down Atlantic Boulevard to A1A. One of my former partner Jack Dodson's sayings came to mind: *A job that starts bad ends bad.*

I swallowed.

"A paid trip to the Virgin Islands, are you kidding?"

I caught the hint of a smile out of the corner of my eye.

And wished I didn't know from experience that Jack's sayings almost always came true.

7

WE TOOK OFF FIFTEEN MINUTES AFTER ARRIVING AT KEY WEST International Airport, leaving Ray with his mouth agape after I told him Crystal's husband was missing and she'd just been attacked at the Casa.

It took nearly an hour of coaxing before Crystal opened up.

"This had always been John's dream—the charity, the celebrities, the promotional events—believe me, I had my fill of Hollywood while living there. I went along with it, thinking he'd never pull it off, but I admired his passion." She sighed. "I've learned that when John puts his mind to something, it's going to happen."

"Why adoption?"

She looked out the window, watching the water shimmer from 15,000 feet up as she talked.

"It's funny," she said. "I knew people who'd adopted babies, mostly from abroad, but I just never had any thoughts about it one way or the other. Then, when… one of my… college girlfriends got pregnant, it was an absolute given that she HAD to have an abortion. Sure, she fantasized about having her baby, but there were just no support systems, not to mention the culture of shame that surrounds an unwanted pregnancy—even pro-lifers sometime give a girl a hard time. So adoption was never discussed; it might as well not have been an option. I'm not saying she would have made a different choice, but it really hammered the point home. An unpleasant, binary choice isn't much of a choice at all."

My existence clearly put my birthmother's choice in the minority.

"That's not always—"

"Her parents would have killed her, Buck. She was going to law school, not nursery school."

I let a beat pass.

"Why hold the event in the Virgin Islands?" I could think of a hundred locations easier to accommodate travelers.

"My fundraising job taught me a lot about how to get celebrities to do things. It has to be something fun for them, or something that provides a lot of positive exposure. If you can do both, you increase the odds for success." She shrugged. "Plus I dated one of the top leading men for a while—I learned way more than I ever cared to."

Figures. Beautiful woman, living in L.A., high profile job with a well known charity organization. I wondered why it ended but didn't ask.

"So why Jost Van Dyke? I love it, but it's one of the harder islands to reach."

She sat up straight in her seat.

"Last year, John and I took a bareboat sailing trip out of Tortola, no captain, just the two of us. We'd already started ISA and were getting nowhere with our efforts to arouse celebrity interest, so we were burned out. John had just gotten out of a nasty divorce when I met him, and he didn't exactly leave the federal prosecutor's office on good terms, so he was pretty down."

"Good place to re-evaluate life, those islands," I said.

I asked Crystal if his nasty divorce could have led to the threats. She crossed her arms.

"John's first marriage was a disaster. His wife was nuts and he found solace in the arms of other women, but nothing happened that would make her want him to disappear—and if he dies, her gravy train ends, so that makes no sense."

"Sorry. You were saying?"

"We first sailed to Norman Island, then Cooper and Virgin Gorda. We took our time and didn't even talk about anything aside from what we wanted to eat, where we wanted to dive, and what we wanted to drink."

She giggled, mostly to herself. I imagined her on the boat, seeing her through her own eyes rather than her husband's—a smart, beautiful woman who had given up a successful and rewarding career for the man she loved. A pang of envy passed through me. My ex-wife had given up her modeling career for me, temporarily, but that's because I was making gobs of money. When that ended, she was gone faster than I could count the number of designer outfits she'd left behind.

Crystal was different. The real deal. Her husband was a lucky man.

"And then we sailed the northern coast of Tortola where we got into a huge fight. John was ready to quit ISA but I knew he was frustrated, scared even—"

"Scared of what?"

"Failure. He'd never failed at anything, and suddenly things weren't going as he envisioned. He just… lost it."

She again went quiet. I waited.

"It was a turning point," she said. "We'd hung out at Myetts on the Beach at Cane Garden Bay all afternoon and John had nearly drank an entire bottle of rum. He was very upset, drunk, and we both said things that cut to the bone." I caught her shudder out of the corner of my eye. "That night he said it was over—the charity, that is, but we both knew the failure could drag our relationship down with it. He slept out in the cockpit, and I was awake all night in the cabin. The next morning was our last day, and all we had to do was sail around to Soper's Hole to drop the boat."

She smiled, and even through her distant gaze her eyes sparkled.

"I'd been talking all along about stopping off at a tiny little island called Sandy Spit, northwest of Tortola. John must have been feeling guilty, because even though we were supposed to be back with the boat by noon, he steered us there. Turned out to be the loveliest little thatch of sand and palm trees, surrounded by the most cerulean blue water you've ever seen."

I'd been to Sandy Spit. An acre square, with a deep-water anchorage out front and the softest pink sand in the Virgin Islands. I recalled the feel of my feet sinking into that sand as if the island were swallowing me.

"We laughed and lounged on that beach, watched our catamaran lift in the gentle surf, and when John glanced at the boat, he remembered he'd promised to bring his former law partner a t-shirt from Foxy's on the next island over. So we swam back to the boat, took an aggressive course to Foxy's, and when we got there, the harbor was packed. Foxy's was bursting with people partying and having the times of their lives."

"The old Silver Fox can do that to you," I said.

She explained that there had been a reggae festival going on in Foxy's open-air pavilion. That was the spark for their idea. Voila! The vision they had changed their lives to pursue was resurrected.

"After that, everything snowballed. We added a diverse all-star board of directors that includes a famous movie director, politicians, and even Viktor Galey, a billionaire industrialist, so the connections we needed gelled, and here we are."

A shiver passed up my spine. I glanced over and Crystal still stared straight ahead, smiling at the memory. On the brink of failure, they'd powered through it and were now set to achieve what they had considered impossible. I'd felt equal joy at the start of e-Antiquity. Boy, had I been wrong.

A tear dripped from Crystal's cheek onto her purple blouse.

Why had the ISA event been derailed? Why had these people been targeted? There was either something going on that I didn't know about yet, or Crystal was holding out on me, or both.

I concentrated on flying, pushing aside my admiration for Crystal along with my attraction to her. Not a sexual attraction but more of an intellectual connection, something that's been rare in my life. Flying in a small airplane is an intimate experience, whether you intend it to be or not. And when there's an emotionally charged discussion with a woman like Crystal...

I checked our position on my chart, adjusted our airspeed to preserve fuel, which was getting low, and vectored toward Grand Turk.

"We'll be landing to refuel in about fifteen minutes," I said.

"That was fast." She checked her watch.

It had been three hours since we left Key West. I'd learned a lot about Crystal but had yet to learn a thing about why their event had produced threats, why she'd been attacked, or why her husband was missing.

I'd dig deeper on our next leg.

8

THE TURKS AND CAICOS POSSESS SOME OF THE MOST BEAUTIFUL WATERS I'VE ever seen anywhere. The fifty-plus island chain became very popular after the mid-1970's, and as a result, Providenciales enjoyed a high-rise condo boom that quadrupled lodging opportunities on the island, marred the beautiful white beaches, and lasted until the market crash that killed e-Antiquity. At least Provo had a great airport and FBO.

We had just enough time to refuel, use the restroom, grab a coffee, and get back in the air. Crystal didn't seem to notice the clear water, the coconut-laden palm trees, the singsong voice of the fuel jockey. But the brilliance of the light brought out the colors in her hair and made her amber eyes sparkle.

"So tell me more about the event," I said once we were in the air.

She turned toward me but her gaze seemed far away.

"I'm the guy who doesn't watch TV, remember?" I smiled. She tried to conjure one herself but didn't quite succeed.

"We're expecting about twenty celebrities to participate in the concert—if they haven't started dropping out because John's missing. We're calling it Adoption AID."

"Are they people you met while living in L.A.?"

"Some. But every one of them has a direct connection to adoption, either as adoptees, birth parents, adoptive parents, or relatives." She shifted in her seat and glanced out the side window. "We haven't announced the complete line-up yet, but the network that's televising the concert is supposed to start a heavy promotional campaign today."

"Anyone I'd recognize?"

"Faith Hill, Tim McGraw, Steven Spielberg, President Clinton, Jamie Foxx, Debbie Harry—"

"Blondie?"

"She was adopted. Also Brad Pitt, Angelina Jolie, Madonna, David Crosby—"

"Impressive."

She smiled. "Oh, there's plenty more. Senator McCain, country star Avery Rose, the rapper D.M.C., Jesse Jackson, Joni Mitchell, Stud Mahoney, Mike Dirnt of Green Day, Ray Liotta, Roseanne Barr, Rosie McDonnell, Tom Cruise, Nicole Kidman, Candy McKenzie, Chief Justice Roberts, Lilli Taylor, Susie Coelho, Justin Bigges… the list keeps going." She took a breath. "They're all connected to adoption, one way or another."

"Are they all showing up at your event?"

She laughed out loud. "I wish. But several will be there, and others too."

We talked about the precedent for concerts as vehicles to raise attention and money for important issues, swapping examples like Farm Aid, Live Earth, No Nukes, Live Aid, The Concert for New York City after 9/11, Hurricane Sandy Relief.

"I didn't realize adoption needed that kind of attention," I said.

Crystal smiled. "Fifty percent of all pregnancies are unplanned, and of them, nearly fifty percent are terminated."

Ah, *Choice*. "So this is against—"

"It's not against anything," she said. "But one of our goals is to promote adoption to increase grace for people facing unplanned pregnancies."

She'd said this was John's passion, but I didn't buy that story about her college roommate, figured she might have her own reasons too. I also had a sinking feeling that while this all sounded progressive and well-intended, it could create resentment from radical elements on either side of the Choice issue. Were any of those groups crazy enough to kidnap John and try to grab Crystal?

"You need to understand, Buck—Society judges women for their choices. So do their jobs, friends, even family. Abortion in the States outnumbers domestic adoption by twenty-to-one, and not necessarily because women prefer that. It's because you can hide an abortion—society still forces secrecy. As a choice, adoption is the path least taken."

"So you talk about changing society," I said. "How might that lead to John's disappearance?"

"Because we're calling for a social revolution."

I glanced toward her. "*Revolution*?"

"For society to accept and support women facing unplanned pregnancy? Trust me, *that* would be revolutionary."

The hours had passed quickly, and soon it was time to prepare for our approach to St. Thomas. I thought of the contraband treasure maps locked below my seat, and sweat broke out on my brow. My life's work was far less noble. I may not have resumed my hunt for treasure since e-Antiquity failed, but I hadn't totally distanced myself from the possibility. I glanced at Crystal, now watching Puerto Rico as we flew over it. Her profile reminded me of Audrey Hepburn.

Focus, Reilly.

I still hadn't learned for certain why the Thedford's efforts had produced threats, but at the moment I had a water landing to deal with. I hadn't flown to Charlotte Amalie for several years, and the sight of cruise ships and boats buzzing around the harbor like water bugs required my attention. The police were expecting us, so I hoped we'd get up-to-date news on John's disappearance.

After that, we'd see where we stood.

9

AS WE HEADED TOWARD THE BUSY SEAPLANE BASE AT THE FOOT OF CHARLOTTE Amalie I tuned out everything but our route to the splash zone. Seaborne Airlines operated several deHavilland Twin Otters on floats that made frequent daily landings, so the people operating ferries and boats around the harbor were accustomed to seaplanes. Since water landings were no longer allowed in the British Virgin Islands and St. John, the base was one of the busiest in the Caribbean.

Crystal was subdued as we made our approach. When we set down smoothly into the light chop, water flew up above our side vent windows and sprayed off the props. I'd quickly come to appreciate the weight and mass of the Goose—compared to Betty, my former Widgeon, the Beast had much greater stability and felt far more solid on the ground and in the water. Once repainted, fully reupholstered, and the renovations complete, the Beast would be a treasure to operate, but for now the mismatched paint on the fuselage and wings drew curious glances. Maybe they thought we were South American smugglers here to make a drop.

By the time we taxied up to the dock, a handful of police in blue pants and white shirts stood stone-faced to greet us. That wasn't a surprise, but I hadn't anticipated the camera crews and reporters behind them.

"We have company, Crystal."

"I hope they have some news." Her attention was on the law enforcement officers.

"I'll help you any way I can, okay?"

"Would you come speak to the police with me?"

I nodded and waited until the props stopped rotating.

"Let's go."

Noise from the traffic on the road next to the seaplane base competed with the high-horsepower outboard motors on boats around the harbor. But it was shouts from the reporters that caused Crystal to wince. One of the policemen turned and pushed the more aggressive camera crews back. A gray-haired cop walked forward to meet us as we stepped onto the dock.

"Ms. Thedford?"

Crystal nodded.

"I'm Lieutenant White of the Virgin Islands Police Department." He paused and glanced at me. "And you are?"

"Buck Reilly. I'm Ms. Thedford's pilot."

"Have you found my husband, Lieutenant White?"

The officer squinted. "Not yet, ma'am, but we're doing everything we can."

Her shoulders slumped.

"With all the other activity here—related to your show, that is—our force has its hands full coordinating with authorities on Tortola, but I want to assure you that this is a top priority for us." The lieutenant had an island accent and a habit of putting his thumbs in his gun belt, which made me think he'd seen a lot of old Westerns.

"Where can we reach you if we have news—or questions?" White said.

"We have a room booked at Frenchman's Reef."

The lieutenant glanced at me.

"And you, Mr. Reilly?" he said.

"He'll be at the same hotel," Crystal said. "Can I reach you on the number you gave me yesterday, lieutenant?"

"Yes, ma'am, same one."

They agreed to touch base in the morning, gave us their cards, and Crystal and I walked up the dock toward the camera crews waiting by the street.

She suddenly turned into the small building where Seaborne's offices were located. I followed.

"Ms. Thedford?" A tall, sandy-haired man stood up behind the small counter. "I'm so sorry to hear that your husband's missing." He extended his hand. "I'm Jerry Butler, the flight manager for Seaborne here on St. Thomas."

"Yes, Jerry, I'm here to check logistics with you. Have you been—"

"Ah, well, Ms. Thedford, we have a little problem. Actually, a not-so-little problem." He took in a deep breath. "We've grounded our fleet and won't be able to help you any longer."

"Why on earth!"

He looked from Crystal to me, then back to her.

"Bomb threats."

"*Bomb threats*?" we said in unison.

"Afraid so. Specific to your event, in fact."

The color drained from her face.

"How will the performers get around the islands?"

"This morning we had multiple phone calls stating that if any of our planes flew this week, they'd be shot down." He shook his head. "I know it sounds crazy, but they stated categorically that we were not to get involved with the Adoption AID concert or our other planes would be sabotaged on the ground."

What the hell?

Jerry Butler apologized profusely but said their insurer had threatened to cancel them if they lost a single plane, which would put them out of business.

"Grounding our fleet will cost us a fortune, but we have no choice."

Crystal and I left their FBO, Jerry following us out still apologizing.

"Is that Goose airworthy?" he said as we turned to walk up the dock toward the street.

My gut reaction was that it was a stereotypical floats -vs.-boats snob comment, but then again, the old Beast did look rough. I ignored him and took Crystal by the arm. She was silent and no doubt in shock.

The moment we got to the street, the press descended on us like a mudslide.

"Any news on your husband?"

"Will the concert be cancelled?"

"Are the bomb threats on Seaborne related to your event?"

"Ms. Thedford?"

"Ms. Thedford?"

"*Ms. Thedford*?"

I shielded her and steered her toward the Frenchman's Reef ferry down the seawall. The captain was untying the bowline to disembark, so we had to hurry or we'd be stranded amidst the reporters.

One of the newsies grabbed my shoulder.

"Who are you?"

I spun on my heel and shoved his cameraman back with a stiff arm.

"Leave the lady alone or you'll have to fish that nice camera out of the harbor." I let my glare linger until I realized the other crews had their cameras trained on me.

Lovely.

I caught up with Crystal and hopped on the ferry just as the captain revved the engine to pull away. We sat pressed between an arguing family and a snuggling couple. Crystal kept a straight face, but I had the feeling she was going to break into hysterics at any minute.

As we neared Frenchman's Reef, perched high above the point, I studied the cruise ships that filled the western side of the harbor. Massive people-freighters that slogged from port to port laden with enough food and booze to feed five times the thousands they carried. Three behemoths moored end to end, all carrying different flags. Just past them a sun-bleached old sailboat with laundry hanging from its main mast, anchored in front of a huge, sleek, metallic blue luxury yacht. One of the largest private yachts I'd ever seen. Her name was *Shaska*.

I looked back at Crystal just as she wiped tears off her cheeks.

Damn.

10

I DROPPED MY FLIGHT BAG AND DUFFEL IN MY GARDEN VIEW ROOM AT Frenchman's Reef. Crystal had rooms reserved at several islands for her guest performers and staff. We agreed to meet at one of the outdoor tiki bars in an hour. She didn't want to eat, but I convinced her she needed to. We went our separate ways to get cleaned up and clear our heads. She said she needed to check her messages.

The police in Charlotte Amalie had been no help. Between Crystal getting attacked in Key West, her husband's disappearance, and the bomb threats, there was no chance that this was all a misunderstanding.

It had been a long day of flying, and right now I just wanted a shower—

The room phone rang.

News from Crystal?

"Hello?"

"Well, well, well, if it isn't Buck Reilly."

That voice. Shit.

"And you already managed to get yourself on national television fighting with the press, hotshot. Well done."

Special Agent T. Edward Booth of the FBI.

"What do you want?"

"To help," he said. "What else would you expect?"

"This must be bigger news than I expected if you're sticking your nose into it," I said. "Are the Virgin Islands even in your jurisdiction, or are you free-lancing toward that next promotion?"

A laugh. "As a matter of fact, the U.S. Virgin Islands are indeed within my purview. We have limited support there, however, so I'm glad you're—"

"My dance card's full."

"So I saw. Looks like the lovely Mrs. Thedford is quite dependent on you. Is she aware of the list of crimes still pending against you?"

"Did you call to bust my balls, or do you have any information that might help me find Crystal's husband?"

Silence for a moment, then a quiet snicker.

"Junior detective at it again? Well, it's damn lucky you're there, son, saves me the gas money to send you down."

"Wait a minute—what do you need my help for?"

"Because the BVI isn't in my jurisdiction, and things are pretty frosty with them these days."

The U.S. and British Virgin Islands were only a few miles apart, but both were territorial and rigidly enforced Customs requirements. Neither government tolerated uninvited foreign law enforcement agencies impinging on their sovereignty. Unfortunately, I'd learned of this first hand on Tortola a few years back.

"Gee, Booth, I can't imagine you don't have a stellar relationship with your counterpart in the BVI, given your magnanimous and humble style."

"Funny. We've worked hard to maintain a cordial environment, but with the South American drug and arms trade now utilizing the USVI as a major hub, the murder stats there are the worst of any U.S. state or territory, nearly ten times worse per capita, in fact, so the Brits aren't real happy with us."

I hadn't realized that.

I swallowed the bitter reality that I needed to set my personal grudge aside and see what I could learn that might help Crystal.

"What news do you have about John Thedford?" I said.

"Only that he disappeared on St. John last night. The Park Police have a small installation there, but they're really not set up for investigative work."

"Why would anybody threaten these people, Booth? They're only promoting adoption—hell, they won't even say anything remotely adverse toward anyone who might have contrary opinions."

"You mean the bomb threat against that dink-ass airline?"

I wasn't surprised that Crystal and her husband hadn't reported whatever threats they'd received. It didn't seem their nature to let fear slow them down—even if common sense might suggest otherwise.

"That's not enough?" I said.

He paused. "Sounded like maybe you knew something."

"Any theories?"

"There's no shortage of wackos down there, Reilly. Not as flaky as Key West, mind you, but there's major gang activity—and then you have pro-statehood organizations, anti-statehood too, along with a bunch of quasi-racist activity—"

"Racist?"

"Those born in the USVI and down-islanders are at each other's throats. A real paradise, as long as you don't peek under the veil of fantasy."

Even though Booth was being more forthright than ever, I didn't relish his call for help. Crystal needed my exclusive attention.

"Here's the deal, Reilly. I have the U.S. side covered with the VIPD—"

"I met a tight-lipped cop named Lieutenant White from VIPD today."

"Right, Kenneth White, seems okay, but what I need is for you to be my eyes and ears in the BVI. No investigating, no bull in a china shop, just an observer with daily reports back to me. Can you handle that?"

I'd helped him a couple times before, under duress. Given that my old e-Antiquity partner was still in a federal penitentiary for stuff much like what I'd been accused of, I had no easy way to decline being Booth's amateur operative. Again.

The only problem was that I had a history in the BVI. Did Booth know about that? It had to be in my file, but hell, maybe it was buried under the rest of my… experiences.

"I'm helping Crystal Thedford shuttle her performers around, but I'll also be looking for information about her husband while I'm at it, so..." I had an idea. "Actually there is something you can do."

"I'll send you the credit card and cell phone again—"

"Aside from that."

"I'm all ears."

"Water landings are illegal in the BVI and outside St. Thomas. I could be a lot more nimble and penetrating if you could make a call and get them to waive that for me. Professional courtesy between law enforcement agencies and all."

Booth was silent. Given his summary of poor relations between the BVI and the USVI, would he even be able to swing that?

He sighed. "I'll work on it."

"You do that. Send me the phone and credit card ASAP. I'll be on the move in the morning."

"I'll have them couriered over tonight. Remember, one-fifty per diem. This isn't a vacation for you and the beautiful Ms. Thedford."

I remembered Crystal's tears on the ferry.

"No shit, J. Edgar."

With that I hung up. So much for a nap.

I barely had time for a shower before I was to meet Crystal, and I knew if I wasn't there she wouldn't wait. Damn Booth. But I was already up to my knees in this situation. It's not like he asked me to do something I wasn't doing anyway, and now I'd have some financial help. Of course, that help came with strings—handcuffs, you might say—and Booth just rubbed me the wrong way.

The FBI's interest in the disappearance of Crystal's husband was good news. But given that they were calling me for help, I had limited confidence it would add up to much.

11

CRYSTAL SAT AT THE TIKI BAR STARING INTO THE CARIBBEAN SEA. STEEL drums set the tone around the pool. A one-man band with three pans was perched at the far corner of the patio. Crystal had changed into a tank top, and if I didn't know her story I'd have assumed she was a beautiful woman relaxing on vacation. I even fantasized for a mini-second that she and I were here together. Then cleared my throat.

"Hey, Crystal. Anything new?"

Her eyes refocused in my direction.

"Everything's turning to shit, Buck."

"What do you mean?"

"The news about John's disappearance is getting out and it's all falling apart, fast. My assistant's been inundated with calls from the managers and agents of our celebrity guests." Her delivery of this news was so deadpan I figured she was either remarkably calm or in shock.

"Worried calls or pissed-off calls?"

"Worried, so far."

The bartender arrived with a toothy smile. I asked for a Carib beer and Crystal ordered a margarita.

"Any news on your husband?" I said.

"Nothing that will help us find him."

This while averting my eyes. I remembered I'd been hired as a charter pilot, not a private eye, and I hadn't really done anything yet to earn her trust—aside from fighting off her attacker at the Casa Marina.

"Thanks for what you did back at the harbor," she said. "With those reporters."

"I don't have fond memories of pushy newshounds."

"Given that the other planes we'd hired are now grounded, I really need you to shuttle the talent around. Otherwise, this entire show's *kaput*. We've put all our savings into this event, hoping to get reimbursed through advertising revenues, so if it fails, we're broke. Of course none of that matters if we can't find John."

"Can you postpone the show?"

She shook her head.

"It was so hard to line the celebrities up for this one date—and we've already spent the money." She sat up tall and took in a deep breath. "I have to keep everything under control and hope the authorities find John."

I thought of Booth.

"I'm sure they're doing everything possible. The VIPD works closely with the FBI, and the bomb threat brings additional attention to the situation."

Her gaze drifted back out to sea. The sun hovered over Water Island to the west, and the sky's colors elicited the standard oohs and aahs from others at the bar, along with speculation about whether there would be a green flash. It was a gorgeous Caribbean sunset and we had a ringside seat, but my mind was micro-focused on Crystal.

"They start arriving *en masse* day after tomorrow," she said. "Of course they're staying in different villas and resorts all over the Virgin Islands."

"I'll do whatever I can to help."

She turned back to look straight in my eyes. I sensed a current between us. The hair on my arms stood up.

"I appreciate that, Buck. I need all the help I can get."

"But for me to help you, I need to know more about whatever threats you've received and to be kept in the loop with any updates from the police."

She turned toward the music as the steel drummer began *Three Little*

Birds. He wasn't singing, thank God. I didn't think Crystal would agree that 'everything was going to be all right.'

"I appreciate that." She reached out, squeezed the top of my hand, and left hers there. I swallowed.

"So what can you tell me about the threats?"

She withdrew her hand. "Nothing we took particularly seriously—God, I can hardly remember what they said."

"They, as in multiple? Were there letters? Phone calls? Emails?"

"Voice mails at our office, for one." She leaned forward. "The first one was really strange—in fact I thought it was a wrong number. The voice sounded foreign. It said we should abandon our plans for the 'save the children' concert."

"That's it?"

"A few days later, John answered the phone—it was him again, the foreign-sounding guy. They had a brief conversation."

Crystal suddenly slid off her seat, crossed her arms.

I waited.

"John never told me exactly what he said, but he was shaken, I could see it. I asked him what was wrong and he said nothing, then went for a long walk. I knew something was bothering him—I was afraid the network had cancelled their plans to carry the show or maybe one of the bigger names dropped out, but I didn't find out until he got back that it was another threat."

The drummer now started a version of *No Woman No Cry*.

"He said it was the same voice and he said if we continue with our 'save the children' concert, there'd be trouble. I pressed him for more, but he laughed it off, said we should ignore it."

Not much to go on. The choice of words was odd, "save the children," but if she was right and the caller was foreign, it could have been a translation disconnect—or was it some kind of philosophical statement?

"Is that it?" I said.

She sighed. She rolled her eyes. Finally she answered my question.

"We did get some posts on our website and Facebook page by what I would describe as religious extremists."

I waited for more, but she just shook her head.

"You mean radical Christians, Jews, Muslims, what?" I'd have thought they'd support any alternative to abortion.

"Yeah, pretty much all of the above—some over-zealous types who think making it too easy to give up a child for adoption will promote promiscuity or may even threaten the institution of marriage." She shrugged.

"Good grief," I muttered.

I looked up. Crystal was signing the bill for the drinks. My beer had gone warm, but only ice remained in hers. We'd flown over a thousand miles today and I suddenly felt leaden in my seat, exhausted. Her revelations hadn't helped.

"I need to get to Jost Van Dyke tomorrow to keep things under control, or the concert will fall apart," she said. "Can you take me?"

"The BVI doesn't allow water landings, but I'm, ah, trying to get a special permit. So we'll need to take the ferry to Tortola, get our passports stamped, then take the ferry to Jost."

When she nodded I noticed the dark circles—they accentuated her eyes, but she hadn't been getting much sleep. She probably wouldn't sleep tonight, either.

An idea had been gnawing at me since I spoke with Booth.

"If you're okay with it, I'd like to stop on St. John first and see what we can learn from the Park Police about John's disappearance. The first ferry's at seven-thirty."

"That's fine."

We stood, and just as I was about to turn toward my room, she stepped up and gave me a tight hug.

"Thanks, Buck. Jimmy was right—you may not have the best reputation, but you're a good guy." She looked up into my eyes. "I really appreciate your help. See you in the morning."

I watched her walk away. She'd surprised the hell out of me, and my heart was racing. I wasn't sure what hit me harder—that she'd said I didn't have the best reputation, that she thought I was a good guy, or the hug.

I turned around and sat back down at the tiki bar, my mind swirling like the sky in Van Gogh's *Starry Night*. It was more than her need that drew me to Crystal—I'd have to push that aside. But I'd do anything I could to help and protect her.

The toothy bartender returned.

"Rum," I said. "I need rum."

12

THE PHONE RANG IN THE MIDDLE OF THE NIGHT.

I awoke with a jump from deep, dreamless slumber. At first I didn't know where I was and rolled to the left toward where my nightstand is at the La Concha. When it rang again I rolled to the right and swung my arm toward the illuminated dial pad.

"Hello?"

"Help the woman and your plane will be on the bottom of the harbor."

I shook my head. The room was pitch black. Was I dreaming?

"What?" I said.

"You help the woman with the concert, and your plane will be sunk—"

"Listen!" I shouted. "Where's John Thedford? Do you want a ransom?"

Silence on the other end, followed by a click.

The clock read 4:15

Son of a bitch!

My mind went from zero to ninety in a flash. Who knew I was here? Right—anybody who watched the news, thanks to my nationally broadcast confrontation with the camera team.

The Beast. I hadn't thought of her once since we left the dock. She was totally exposed at the harbor. Had I even locked the hatch? There was no security at the seaplane base because no planes were stored there. Except mine.

Way to go, dumb ass!

I scrambled around the room, pulled my clothes on, grabbed my flight bag—and stopped just as I was about to bolt out of the room. Crystal.

I called the front desk and asked them to relay a message.

"What's the fastest way to town?" I said. "Is the launch to Charlotte Amalie Harbor running yet?"

"No, mon, not until eight o'clock. Hang on a second?" He put me on hold and after nearly a minute returned to the line. "But the launch leaves for town at five to pick up staff to bring back."

I checked the clock: 4:52.

"If you can get there quick, they—"

"On my way," I said.

"And Mr. Reilly? There's a package here at the front desk for you."

A package?

"Fine, I'll be right there."

I grabbed my bag and sprinted down the maze of hallways to the front desk. The man there handed me a package and I took off, through the grounds, past the pool and tiki bar where I'd had a couple too many last night, down the long staircase where I nearly tripped over a massive iguana asleep on the warm stone stair, and onto the dock where a sleepy-eyed captain watched me approach.

"Catch a ride…to the harbor?" I was breathing so hard, my question was nearly unintelligible.

"C'mon, mon."

I collapsed onto the bench seat, caught my breath, and tore open the bulky envelope. Inside was a cell phone and credit card. No note.

The morning was cool and the stars faded as the sun approached the eastern horizon. The half-moon was just above the hills of St. Thomas. Between day and night I felt lost, concerned and unsure as to what I was doing. One thing was certain, I couldn't lose the Beast. The old Grumman Goose might be a work in progress, but she was all I had in this world, and given how we'd come together, at an extremely high emotional price and with all the effort, sweat, and what money I had left invested into getting her airworthy, her safety was paramount.

The launch captain sipped coffee and smoked a fat blunt on his way through the harbor. He glanced at me, took in my uncombed shoulder-length hair, and held the spliff out to me. The weed smelled good. I shook my head. I hadn't lost myself in any drug other than liquor since college.

I glanced around the harbor and saw that only one cruise ship remained at the dock. With little traffic, the launch made good time, and the half-dozen people on the dock jumped out of the way as I leapt from the bow before the captain even wrapped the line around a cleat.

I sprinted down the street and veered left onto the short pier. As I feared: no guards, no fence, no security of any kind. The Beast was there, floating high, and appeared to be at peace in the early morning light. The flat black of the old CIA paint job on the fuselage absorbed light on the port side, and the dull silver of the Alaskan replacement wing and engine glistened on the starboard side.

My heart thumped as I pulled her mooring rope toward me and scanned the port engine, wing, and fuselage. I checked the hatch. At least I'd locked it—what's this?

There was a long piece of masking tape near the handle.

There were no new scratches or evidence of tampering on the lock. I pressed in closer and saw writing on the tape. There wasn't much light, but… it was a series of numbers. I squinted and made out the words: "Call me."

It was a phone number, but there was no name. Could it be the people who snatched John? The guy who called me? Or maybe a reporter?

I peeled the tape off and placed it on a blank page in my little leather notebook. I popped the hatch open, tossed my bag inside, and climbed atop the wing. After inspecting each of the radial engines, manually moving the flaps, and double-checking anything that someone may have been able to reach, I breathed a sigh of relief.

The Beast appeared to be intact.

Before I left Key West I'd updated my information on the local airports, including the St. Thomas Jet Center at the Cyril E. King Airport. The FBO there didn't open until 7:00 a.m. It was now 6:20. If I timed it right, that would still allow me time to meet Crystal at the ferry in Red Hook by 7:30.

I climbed aboard and repeated the same in-depth inspection of the electrical systems, moving parts, and chastity of the plane's integrity. All looked good. A sudden jolt of paranoia caused a shiver to run through me. What if someone attached something to the hull?

I sat for a few moments and remembered the call that woke me and set me on this course today. The voice sounded more like an island accent than anything else. And the statements were threatening but not immediate. It wasn't much to go on, but I decided to trust my gut. And if the note were from my late night caller, why would he ask me to call him if he was going to blow up my plane?

The port engine started right up and shattered the quiet calm of the harbor. The RPMs settled down, and the starboard engine huffed and puffed before it too roared to life. I untied the mooring lines, closed the hatch, and used the light of dawn to taxi toward the take-off zone marked on my sectional chart. With little boat traffic, I was quickly up on the step and in the air. It was now 6:50, my timing, for once, perfect—provided the staff at the Jet Center showed up on time.

"Sorry, girl," I said.

I smiled. People talked to their cars, their pets, their boats—me, I talked to my plane. The Beast had risen from the ashes of the Bay of Pigs in Cuba, literally fifty-years after the fact, and had been stitched together to form a macabre craft that carried me safely back to Key West. Then, through the efforts of Ray Floyd and myself to find more appropriate long term parts, I'd developed an affection for her, quite different from what I'd felt for Betty. In some ways it ran deeper.

"You know I call you the Beast out of affection." I patted the top of the instrument panel as we banked hard to starboard for the short flight to Cyril E. King airport just to the west of the seaplane base.

The surprise wake-up call still bothered me. Could it be the same person who called John Thedford? Was it a local from the Virgin Islands? His statement was so brief there wasn't much to go on. I didn't like being on the radar, but it meant they were watching the situation closely and intent on disrupting ISA's plans. If I was being watched, it might be possible to flush them out. The note taped on the Beast's hatch was another mystery, but one I'd have to visit later. With any luck, it was the first break in this mess.

Air traffic control answered my call, and with no commercial airliners due in before noon, allowed me quick entry. I breathed a sigh of relief, more confident in the security at Cyril E. King than leaving the Beast a sitting duck in Charlotte Amalie's harbor. Now, if I could hurry through the paperwork and find a cab, I should be able to catch Crystal in Red Hook.

13

I MADE THE 7:30 A.M. FERRY BY THE SKIN OF MY TEETH. TURNS OUT THE FBO wasn't wild about unscheduled antique flying boats popping up out of the harbor and onto their radar screen. Especially when they viewed the Beast as equivalent to an aviation version of the Flying Dutchman.

Hey, she needs a paint job. Sue me.

Crystal, pecking away at her cell phone in the ferry terminal, gave me a tepid smile as I walked into the waiting area. Having decided not to mention my surprise wake-up call just yet, I simply told her I needed to move the Beast to solid ground.

Between emails, texting, and phone calls, she didn't have much to say to me during our crossing through Pillsbury Sound. She spent most of the time trying to placate yet another worried star handler.

"Everything's still set for this weekend," she said. "No, we have a private plane to meet Mike at the airport—whichever airport you like, St. Thomas is closest." She glanced at me and rolled her eyes. "No, there was no bomb threat on *his* plane—it's a really cool vintage seaplane the pilot brought me over in from Key West… Buck Reilly, Last Resort Charter and Salvage…"

Poor Crystal. Neither my reputation or the name of my company would give anyone confidence. Even if she was able to cajole the rock stars into showing up, they might still get cold feet when they spotted the Beast.

As our boat pulled into Cruz Bay, there was a new condo development up on the hill above the town that hadn't been there last time I'd visited. St. John was 80% parkland, thanks to the vision of Laurance Rockefeller back in 1956, and so far only a few hotels existed here, which made this smallest of the U.S. Virgin Islands the most peaceful. Though I guess John Thedford might disagree, since this was the last place he'd been seen.

As we disembarked from the ferry, Crystal put the phone away and looked at the beach to the right of the dock.

"That's American Watersports." She pointed toward a dozen boats of various sizes anchored close to shore. "We have a couple of their boats chartered for the rest of the week."

"Good, let's stop in to see them after we talk to the Park Police." Speedboats might be more comforting to her celebrity concert participants than the Beast, and I didn't have permission for water landings yet.

I led Crystal off the dock and through the collection of pickup trucks with elaborate benches and canopies erected in their beds—the vehicles of choice for the taxis on the island that shuttled tourists back and forth from town to the pristine beaches. Traffic was hectic along the one-way street, but we managed to get to the far side without getting flattened. There, past a parking lot, was another ferry terminal—the gateway to the British Virgin Islands—and past that, on the far side of the harbor, the fleet and headquarters of the U.S. Park Police.

Once around the small harbor we passed two center console boats and another small cabin cruiser, all with official National Park Service emblems on their hulls. The idle boats gave me a sense of angst as we entered the Virgin Islands National Park Visitor's Center, the two-story off-white building where the Park Police had their offices. We took the stairs and once we said who we were, the receptionist went to get the officer on duty. Tall, tanned, and in his early thirties, he came out dressed in a pressed white shirt with gold epaulets.

"Hi, I'm Chuck Deaver." He shook our hands. "I'm sorry about your husband, Ms. Thedford."

"Is there news?" Crystal said.

"I'm, sorry, no. We haven't found him yet."

"How big's your fleet?" I said.

Deaver walked over to the front window.

"That's all of it moored out front."

"*Three boats*?" I said.

He nodded. "Budget cuts."

"Is that just for St. John?"

"And St. Thomas. There's one more boat over on St. Croix. We're pretty understaffed these days, considering all the, ah, activity in the region. There's a Coast Guard base on Puerto Rico, but they don't mess with missing persons reports unless a boat's lost at sea."

Those three boats couldn't do squat against a well-financed criminal organization. No wonder the USVI was a hub for guns and drugs.

"Why aren't they out searching for my husband?" Crystal said.

Deaver took in a short breath.

"We've scoured the entire southwestern coastline multiple times, Ms. Thedford. Normally, if there's a drowning near Cruz Bay, the currents are pretty predictable—not that it happens that often, mind you. We've also deployed scuba divers and asked the local operators to help us dive the harbor by the ferry docks, just in case. Again, we found nothing—in that case fortunately."

Crystal, her body as rigid as a board, squeezed my bicep.

"You're familiar with the event that the Thedford's organization is hosting on Jost Van Dyke this weekend?" I said.

"I am, plus I saw it on the news last night. Pretty amazing line-up." His sudden smile revealed straight white teeth. "We've been coordinating with the police in the BVI to facilitate the Customs process and try to help them get ready for the onslaught of visitors. Last I heard you were expecting around five thousand people."

"Have you been coordinating the search for John Thedford with the BVI authorities?" I said.

"That's really VIPD's job, but we've informed them of the situation and asked that they keep a look out, let us know if they hear anything."

Crystal groaned.

"I'll be outside, Buck. Officer Deaver, please get those boats back out and continue to search for my husband. Please." With that, she hurried out.

Deaver watched her go, then turned back to me.

"Poor woman. There's not much more we can do, frankly."

"How about foul play?" I said. "You've heard about the bomb threat on Seaborne Airlines, I assume?"

"Yes, and I know the police are talking to local sources looking for any information or leads." He glanced over his shoulder. "There's a rumor Thedford may have left on a boat, but don't quote me."

"Rumor?"

"Came from a local drunk, so his tip wasn't considered reliable."

"Can I get the name of the witness?"

He shook his head. "Sorry."

Would John have left by boat alone? His history of extra-marital affairs suddenly nagged at me.

I asked Deaver about the various genres of criminal or radical groups Booth had mentioned to me. He had no idea whether any could be connected to John's disappearance, or if any of them opposed adoption.

"As for gang activity, St. Thomas and St. Croix have more, just due to population," he said, "but we've had some inadvertent killings, some shoot-outs on the island. Trafficking tends to bring that as a byproduct." He shrugged. "There are factions of Crips and Bloods here, and if you include Puerto Rico there's a bunch of Latin gangs like Ñeta, Los Huevos, and Bacalao. What with the budget cuts and the vast area of water and number of small craft, it's like Swiss cheese here. Even the DEA and Coast Guard can't keep up."

Why would any of these groups care about a fundraiser to promote adoption?

"Can you share any local gang leader names?"

"Sure." He raised an eyebrow. "But I wouldn't recommend trying to talk to them, if that's what you're thinking. One name I've heard here is Diego Francis, not sure which gang he's affiliated with. Last year in St. Thomas, there was a sweep made against one of the drug gangs and thirty people were arrested. Unfortunately, the cases were thrown out due to an illegal search and seizure ruling. The big shot amongst that bunch was a guy named Burke, goes by Boom-Boom. A real sweetheart."

I wrote their names in the back of my small leather notebook.

"Like I said, I wouldn't suggest trying to talk to them."

"How about the BVI? Any gang activity over there?"

"Nothing like here. Guns are illegal there, and the penalties are stiff. That's one reason relations are so strained between our local governments these days. They're pissed that we can't keep crime under control over here, and as a result it's begun to spread all over the islands."

Perfect. I didn't want to leave Crystal alone any longer, but had one last question.

"What about water landings? Any chance that would be allowed outside the seaplane base on St. Thomas, either in the USVI or the BVI?"

"Not a chance," Deaver said. "Given all the other challenges with smuggling these days, seaplanes spell trouble."

With that, and a request that the Park Service not give up on the search for John Thedford, I left to find Crystal.

Based on Deaver's assessment about seaplanes, I gave Booth scant odds that he'd be able to get me carte blanche landing rights for the Beast. Then again, with only three boats to patrol these waters, the Park Service wouldn't be able to do much about it if I decided otherwise.

14

WITH MY NOTEBOOK STILL IN HAND, I THOUGHT TO CHECK WHAT CONTACTS I had in St. John before I rejoined Crystal. I thumbed the pages and a name jumped out at me. Jack Anderson.

I smiled. Why hadn't I thought of him sooner?

Crystal was outside, sitting on a bench that looked out over the dormant fleet of the U.S. Park Service. I was just about to ask to borrow her phone when I remembered the one Booth sent me was in my backpack.

"That was a bust," she said. "There's no urgency to find John." She glanced up at me and squinted into the late morning sun, the circles under her eyes darker now. "Did you learn anything?"

"I got some names I plan to check out, but only because they're tied to local gangs."

"Gangs? Do you think—"

"Back when I was running e-Antiquity, I learned that those who operated outside the law often had more up-to-the-minute information than the police."

Crystal gave me a weak smile.

I'd decided to keep the "unreliable" witness who said he'd seen John leave on a boat to myself for now. I held my little leather book up.

"But there's another guy I'm hoping is on-island, because he could be a good source." With that I dug the phone out of my pack, punched in the numbers, and listened to the ringing on the other end.

"Hello?"

"That you, Jack?"

There was a brief silence. "Who's calling?"

"It's Buck—Charles Reilly."

Crystal raised her eyebrows.

"King? What do you know!" Jack's voice lifted. "How can I help you?"

"Any chance you're on St. John?"

"Sure am, got a closing tomorrow."

I glanced at my watch. "You still a regular at Morgan's Mango?"

He laughed. "Yeah, pretty much every damn night."

"Can you meet me there for an early lunch?"

We agreed to meet in thirty minutes. Morgan's Mango was right across the street, so I led Crystal to a seat in the front corner, me facing the street.

"Who're we meeting?" she said.

"Guy named Jack Anderson, a developer from New Jersey I met in Virginia. He bought a beautiful hundred acres of private land here on St. John years ago and developed the finest gated community on-island. When he was excavating one of the home sites his crew dug into a crypt of Calusa Indian artifacts. One thing led to another and he called me to help him out."

"Help him out *how*?" Crystal said.

"When any kind of old artifacts are found on a property, it stops construction projects dead in their tracks. In this case, the local government required an archeologist to come sift through the site with a toothbrush to determine what was there in order to decide whether they'd allow construction to continue at all. The schedule in the contract for the buyer had a drop dead date if Jack missed delivering it by more than three months. By the time he found me, sixty days had already elapsed and he was at risk of losing a couple million dollars."

"Were you able to cut through the red tape?"

"At that time, e-Antiquity was pretty well known and had historians and archeologists on retainer, so I came down with a renowned professor of archeology from the University of the Caribbean. We were able to make a quick determination and had one of our extraction teams expedite the documentation and withdrawal of all the pots, tools, plates, bones—everything was excavated and placed into padded cases."

"What happened to the items you recovered, Buck?"

"The government kept it all. It was one of the few instances where we didn't keep any of the recovered items, so we took a nice fee and Jack was able to meet his schedule."

"Yes I was," said a voice from the stairs below us.

Jack Anderson walked up the curved outdoor staircase to the restaurant's entrance. His beard was now fully gray, though he still had a ponytail.

"And Kenny Chesney was very pleased with the finished home," he said as he reached our table. "I never told him the cause of the delay."

I made introductions. When Crystal mentioned that she and her husband were behind the Adoption AID concert this weekend, Jack's expression turned serious.

"Can't imagine today's news is gonna help," he said.

"Was there news of John?" Crystal said, her voice shrill.

"That actor, Stud Mahoney. He's been kidnapped."

Crystal covered her face with both hands. Only one word escaped between her fingers.

"Shit."

I put my arm around her shoulder and pulled her toward me. I felt her shake, then she sucked in a deep breath.

"I'm so sorry," Jack said. "I thought you knew."

If that wasn't the nail in the coffin of Adoption AID, I didn't know what would be.

"How do you know he was kidnapped?" I said. "Was it on television?"

"The radio. Just heard it on the way over here. The DJ said there was a note asking for a ransom, and that Mahoney's production studio is offering a hundred grand for any information that leads to his recovery."

Crystal dropped her hands. I could see in her eyes that she'd noted the anomaly as well. I knew she'd be in a hurry to find out what was going on and field the inevitable barrage of calls, texts, and emails from all the star-handlers, so I got to the point.

"Jack, I apologize, but this isn't strictly a social call," I said.

"Didn't think it was."

"Given the news of the kidnapped actor, we'll need to find out what's going on, but I wanted to ask what you know about local gang activity here on St. John, and in the Virgins in general."

He rubbed his beard and I swear it made an audible sound, like sandpaper.

"Gotten pretty bad these last several years," he said. "Murder rate's the worst in the U.S." He took in a deep breath. "Along with the usual—drugs, prostitution, turf wars—"

"Do you know the names of any of the gangbangers, and particularly their leaders?"

"You kidding? Every time we started a new house we got hit up for protection money."

I raised my eyebrows. Jack nodded.

"Head honcho here on St. John's a guy named Diego Francis," he said. "Ruthless SOB. Supposedly killed his own sister for turning tricks and cutting him out—anyway, he lives in a compound over in Fish Bay." He gave me a cold stare. "If you're thinking of going to talk to him, then for God's sake watch your ass. He's a security freak. The cops won't go near the place."

I glanced at Crystal. She was already getting up out of her seat, her cell phone buzzing like an angry hornet.

"So what's his main line of interest, this Diego Francis?" I said.

"Guns. Supposed to be like the Springfield Armory over there."

Ugh, I hate guns.

With Friends Like These...

15

WE STOOD BY THE FERRY DOCK. CRYSTAL AGREED TO TURN OFF HER PHONE until we could decide what to do.

"Stud Mahoney was adopted, Buck. That's why he's here."

She fell into my arms. Sobs wracked her body as I held her close and tried to think of what to say. The situation was spiraling out of control, fast, and there was no point in feigning optimism. So I just held her until she cried herself out, her face buried in my neck.

Her hair smelled of jasmine. I breathed it in deeply, turned my head down, and gave her a soft quick kiss on the cheek.

Crystal broke free, wiped away tears, and looked away from me.

"I have to get to Jost Van Dyke," she said. "I'm so worried about John, but what can I do? I have to try to keep things together so when they find him we can…we can…"

"Carry on with the show?" My voice was a near whisper.

"Right. Yes." She was still dabbing at her eyes.

"I'll stay here and see what I can find out about John and Stud Mahoney. You focus on keeping the celebrities on board."

Her shoulders slumped.

My hand never left her back as we went inside and bought her a ticket on the next ferry. It left for Tortola in fifteen minutes. She'd clear Customs there and take the next one to Jost Van Dyke.

Back outside, I walked her to the canopied waiting area. She hadn't said a word. Confused emotions paralyzed my tongue.

"I have no choice but to try and keep this thing together," she said finally. "We've put everything on the line—" She pressed a fist to her mouth and willed the tears away. "Are you still going to fly people around if I can keep the event on track? Because the people start arriving tomorrow and the day after—"

"I won't abandon you, Crystal. But there are a few things here I want to check out—"

"The Westin!" she said.

"The *what*?"

"We had a room booked at the Westin. John was going to stay there until tomorrow." Her forehead wrinkled. "I don't recall if I told that to the police. I know he'd already checked in, he called me from there the afternoon he disappeared."

A worker on the ferry opened the gate and began loading baggage piled by the ramp. People started to press aboard.

"Okay, I'll check that out too," I said. "Now get moving—wait!" I retrieved Booth's cell phone from my bag and we exchanged numbers. "Let's touch base later today, but call me sooner if you hear anything about John or Stud Mahoney. Okay?"

"Right, and one last thing…" Crystal reached into her bag, pulled out a folder, and opened it. Her husband stared out at me. "I had this printed at the hotel on St. Thomas last night. I thought they might come in handy."

"Good thinking." It was a different photo from the one on their website, but he still had the great smile. "Now get moving or you'll miss the boat."

She nodded, then a determined expression settled on her face. She started to go, spun back and gave me a bear hug.

"Thank you so much, Buck. I know you'll call me with anything you learn too."

I stood on numb legs as the ferry pulled away. When Crystal waved from the back of the boat a shiver passed through me. I was in danger too, and not from gangs or bombs or kidnappers.

The cell phone rang and I jumped. Unless Crystal was calling me already, it could only be one person.

The screen read: YOUR MASTER. I answered the call.

"Very funny, Booth."

"What the hell's going on with this Adoption AID show? The promoter disappears, now a leading man has been kidnapped? Maybe your lady friend should cancel—"

"Get to the point—"

"The point is that you're now *off* the case of the missing promoter and *on* the case of the missing movie star—"

"I don't think so."

"Listen, Reilly, this isn't an option—hell, they interrupted regular programming on every major network to break the story about Stud Mahoney being kidnapped. Nobody gives a damn about some do-gooder—"

"Maybe they're connected, Booth, ever think of that?"

"Different M.O. altogether, hotshot. Nothing but silence followed the promoter's disappearance—"

"A bomb threat on Seaborne Airlines is silence? The phone call I had in the middle of the night telling me to stay away from the Adoption AID concert is—"

"What phone call—"

"Two people in the Virgin Islands, both here for the same reason, both disappeared, and you think it's a coincidence?"

My finger hovered above the END button.

"Reilly! Don't you hang up on me, Reilly!"

"You've got me for another ten seconds," I said.

"And why did you call that real estate developer on St. John?" he said. "You better not be doing side business with federal prop—"

"Are you going to check up on every call I make?"

"Damn straight—"

END. I stabbed the button with my rigid index finger, over and over.

Eat shit, Booth.

16

"YEAH, I WAS WORKING HERE THAT NIGHT, WHAT A PARTY," THE BARTENDER said.

The Beach Bar was at the end of the beach at Cruz Bay, past a few restaurants and behind the retail stores out on the road that paralleled the shore. It was nothing more than a bar with stools on both sides covered by a canopy, with a small seating area cum stage at the far end. According to the cops, it was the last place John Thedford had been seen.

"What was the party all about?"

"Drinking, listening to music, trying to get laid. What else?"

The bartender was pushing fifty, pudgy but tan. His beard was at least four days old, his gray hair was tied into a ponytail, and the letters B-E-E-R were tattooed on the knuckles of his right hand. Not-so-subliminal advertising to his patrons.

"That's it?" I said. "Just a typical night at the Beach Bar?"

"That, and Kenney Chesney here for an acoustic show. God love him."

I tried to remember if Crystal had mentioned him on her list of participants.

"Is he playing in that Adoption AID concert on Jost this weekend?"

The bartender glanced at me, then turned back to washing glasses.

"Let me call his manager on my speed dial and I'll let you know."

I ordered a beer, drank half in one slug, and reached into my bag.

"Friend of mine's the promoter, and he—"

"Wandered off and disappeared. Yep, know all about it. Cops came around yesterday asking questions." He looked at my hair and mustache, both due and overdue for a trim. "You're no cop."

"That's right, I'm a friend. Thedford's wife asked me to help find him."

"Like maybe he ran off with another woman? You a private eye?"

"Nope."

I drained half of the remaining beer and opened my file.

"Here's his picture. You remember him from the night of the party? Anything you can tell me that might help me find him?"

He looked up from washing glasses.

"Yeah, I remember him, he was pretty buzzed. Yucked it up with the musicians during a break, flirted with some of the babes waiting to take a shot at Kenny, then throws me a handful of cash and stumbles down the steps there onto the beach." He smiled. "Alone."

Innocent flirting or my-wife's-a- thousand-miles-away flirting?

"You see him get on a boat down the beach?"

"Nope, wasn't that interested, but heard the guy down at American Watersports saw him."

American—that's the group Crystal chartered.

"You know the guy's name?"

"Billy. Kind of a lush."

The unreliable witness?

"Thedford say anything to you while he was here?"

The bartender looked both ways down the bar, then leaned toward me, holding a glass.

"Yeah, about five times. 'Double rum and Coke.'"

I peeled a ten out of my money clip and dropped it on the bar. I was about to walk off but stopped. Given his last wise-ass answer, the question was probably a waste, but you never know.

"One other thing." Head turned to the side, he glanced at me with one eye. "You know how to get in touch with Diego Francis?"

I heard the glass he was holding drop to the floor and shatter.

On the other side of the bar, two burly black guys looked up.

"You got business with Diego?" the bartender said. "Or you just crazy?"

I finally had his attention.

"Little of both, I guess." He set another beer on the counter and leaned toward me. "That's not a name I'd be throwing around town, know what I mean?"

I held my palms up.

"I'm just trying to—"

"Help your friend, yeah, I get it, but that's not a good rock to turn over." He delivered this last part in a whisper.

Next thing I knew, one of the black guys was on the stool next to me. His friend's eyes drilled mine from the other side of the bar where they'd both been sitting.

"I hear you mention Diego Francis?" he said.

I leaned back and glanced at him. Dreadlocks, tattoos on dark skin, pupils dilated, T-shirt taut over a muscular frame.

I swallowed. Here goes.

"Yeah, you know where I can find him?"

The bartender walked to the far end of the bar and kept his back to us.

"What you want with him, man?" the black guy said.

I held out my hand.

"I'm Buck Reilly." The man stared at me, ignoring the hand hovering in space between us. I held his stare and didn't flinch, then took back my hand. "I'm looking for somebody. Thought Diego might be able to help me find him."

I glanced over at his friend on the other side of the bar, whose eyes were still laser-focused on me.

I turned back to—

WHAP!

Excruciating pain on my cheek! Before I could react, another vicious blow.

Then everything turned black.

17

I GRADUALLY BOUNCED AWAKE, ONLY TO REALIZE I WAS IN THE TRUNK OF A CAR that was traveling along a bumpy road. My hands weren't constrained, so I felt my face and winced—my jaw was sore to the touch. Damn. In the over thirty Golden Glove bouts I'd fought some dozen years ago, I'd never once been knocked out.

The car swerved. We seemed to hit every pothole the driver could find. Loud music drowned out conversation, if there was any. Had they been hanging out at the Beach Bar to see if anyone came asking about John Thedford? Or did Diego have lookouts all over town? Were they taking me to see him now, or were we headed to the far end of the island where they'd make me disappear? Hell, I only asked to speak with the guy.

I felt around the inside of the pitch-black trunk hoping to find a tire iron, bottle, anything I could surprise them with, but came up empty. The smell of sweat and maybe piss told me this wasn't their first grab and go.

As we continued to bounce along for another few minutes I wondered how Crystal was faring at Jost Van Dyke. Had there been a mass celebrity exodus? Had the police found any leads in either missing persons case? Crap—what if she'd been grabbed too?

The music stopped, then the car, and in seconds the trunk popped open. I shielded my face from the blinding sun as strong hands gripped my arms. I knew better than to struggle. Yet.

Jerked up and out of the trunk in one swift motion, I landed on my feet in front of my two assailants. The dreadlocked man who hadn't punched me held a small pistol aimed at my chest.

"Listen, fellas, I wasn't looking for trouble—"

"Shut your face, fool, or I'll give you another one of these." The man who had knocked me out held up his fist, along with a pair of brass knuckles that explained why my jaw hurt so much.

I held my hands up, slowly.

"It's cool, man."

"Well, well, well, what have we here?" A voice came from up a path bordered with tropical flowers. I glanced around. The property had lush grounds, and I could just see the corner of what appeared to be a large stately home through the palm trees. I also spotted a tall fence topped with razor wire and men dressed in camouflage along the perimeter.

The source of the voice appeared: A dark-skinned man in black linen pants and a tropical print shirt that would make Ray Floyd drool. About my age but several inches shorter and of medium build. As nice as the clothes were, he had a rough-hewn face scarred from fire or severe acne. And he was smiling—which threw me, because it seemed sincere and yet there was kind of a sneer tucked away in it.

He turned to the guy who'd cold-cocked me and held his hand up for a high-five. Brass Knuckles slapped his hand and grinned.

"Diego Francis," he said. "Always happy to meet a pilot—especially when business is hot."

"Buck Reilly."

Diego extended his hand. I felt like I'd landed down the rabbit hole, but I shook it off.

"Saw you on TV in St. Thomas. You was with that lady here for the Adoption AID concert. The one whose husband's gone missing."

I swallowed. Diego smiled.

"Yeah, that was me—"

"I know, bro. In fact, I know all about you." His face either had a permanent smile or was deformed by whatever caused his scars. "When I saw you with that honey I knew you'd come to St. John. Knew you'd sniff around at the Beach Bar, too."

Dreadlocks laughed.

"Last Resort Charters?" Diego said.

"And Salvage," I said.

"And treasure hunter before that. Yeah, bro, I know all about you, even when you got arrested on Tortola." He paused to get that smile back on his face. "But that ain't what interests me most."

"I expect you know I'm here to help Crystal Thedford find her husband and fly her guests around for the concert?"

He nodded to my abductors and turned back up the path. Dreadlocks swung the gun toward me.

"Follow the man."

I followed.

Inside, the home was spectacular, right out of *Architectural Digest, Arms Merchant Edition*. I flashed back to my suite at the La Concha in Key West, then allowed my mind to rewind further, to my former home—all right, mansion—in Great Falls, Virginia.

Damn, being broke sucks.

Diego waved his hand in the air and a uniformed maid appeared with a drink tray. Nobody asked what I wanted, but she poured two glasses of soda water with fresh lemon. I could have used a rum but didn't want one, not knowing what was on Diego's mind. I didn't think his voice matched that of my wakeup caller, but he did have an accent. He could have been the one who'd called John Thedford, but why?

He sat down in a plush animal print chair—cheetah, or maybe hyena.

"Do you know anything about what happened to John Thedford?" I said.

"I guess we're friends now, right?" Diego said. "You asking me questions and all. You must of skirted the law a bit here and there, hmmm?" There came the weird smile. "Shit, bro, you're no angel."

"Those days are over," I said. "Last Resort Charter and Salvage, kind of says it all, doesn't it?"

"See, I like people who had money and lost it," he said. "Makes 'em hungry. I like hungry. I was born fucking voracious and look what it got me." He held an arm out.

I didn't like where this was headed, but I had no leverage.

"The Adoption AID concert is a pretty innocent gig—"

"Tell that to those two dudes missing in action."

"I hope to get the chance," I said.

He laughed, then sat back in his chair, sipped his bubbly drink, and… smiled?

I glanced over my shoulder. The two goons who'd brought me here lingered in the background, watching us. Dreadlocks still held the gun and Brass Knuckles was spinning a knife.

"I want Last Resort Charter to make a delivery for me," Diego said.

"I'm booked at the moment—"

"Not any more, bro."

"But my plane's on St. Thomas, and I was hoping you could help me—"

His belly laugh cut me short.

"You were hoping *I* would help *you*, huh? That's rich, Buck Reilly. That's really rich."

"You got something against adoption?" I said.

He startled me by jumping up out of his chair.

"You fucking crazy, bro?" His eyes burned holes into mine, and his scarred face no longer even hinted at a smile. I heard the two goons behind me shuffle closer.

"You obviously haven't done your homework, have you? Before going around Cruz Bay asking about me you might of used your head first."

He pounded his index finger against his own skull.

"I was a fucking orphan, bro. My mumma was a heroin addict. Never knew who my old man was, but then she didn't live long enough to tell me shit anyway." His face was now inches from mine. "Adopted? Shit, no such luck here. No insta-family to the rescue, just a kid on the streets, doing whatever he needed to stay alive then thrive."

Interesting.

"So while you're making a buck flying that pretty lady around with some fancy singers and movie stars, don't talk to me about fucking adoption like you give a shit—"

"I was an orphan too."

Diego gave me a long, measuring look, then nodded.

"Huh, makes sense. Overachiever, pushing the rules, breaking some. Broken relationships, loner." He smiled without a trace of sneer. "Knew I'd like you, man."

What the—? Diego *had* done his homework, and he processed information fast. But what he didn't know was that my adoptive family was great and that I'd only recently learned I was adopted in the first place.

"If I find those missing men you'll owe me, right?" he said.

"There's a reward out for the actor," I said. "But if John Thedford and Mahoney don't turn up soon, the charity concert will get cancelled anyway."

Diego slid his palm down the side of his jaw, which reminded me of the pain in mine. He walked back to his chair and drained the soda. I took in the rest of the room. Latin-themed original art and sculpture, tropical paintings mixed with tribal scenes. But there were also motion sensors in every corner, cameras with red lights aglow, and bars on the closed windows. I'd seen this veneer of culture built on criminal empires in more than one place around the world.

"So you don't know anything about their disappearances?" I held my breath.

"What's the range on that old-ass plane of yours?" Diego said.

"About a thousand miles, empty."

"And full?"

"Depends on the weight."

"Heavy," he said.

"Maybe eight hundred miles," I said.

"Fly better than it looks?"

For the first time I smiled.

"So far."

"Here's the deal," he said. "An opportunity's arisen that could…well, let's just say it could take my business global." His eyes took on a distant look. "I have a vision and I need to be ready to take advantage—fast—in order to capitalize on it. Know what I'm saying? I'd hate to miss that chance when the time comes. I'd *really* hate it." His eyes focused—on me. "So when I call, you need to come or it'll be *you* that makes me miss my chance."

An argument percolated in my throat, but I swallowed it. Diego looked past me.

"Yo, Spice, take Mr. Reilly back to where you found him." Then, to me, "Gimme your phone number." He pointed to a pad of paper on the side table.

I explained that my phone was new and I didn't know the number. It was in my bag, back at the Beach Bar.

Dreadlocks, a.k.a. Spice, muttered something and left me alone with Brass Knuckles and Diego until he returned from his car with my backpack. I kept a straight face, wrote the number of Booth's phone down and shouldered my bag.

"You be ready for my call and I'll let you know when I find something about your people," Diego said.

"*When* you find something?"

The smile-cum-sneer was back.

"These are my islands, bro. Nothing gets past me for long. And when the time comes, you're going to help me step up to the next level in exchange for me finding your lost sheep."

Perfect.

"And when the concert goes down," he said, "I want a front row seat and an introduction to Jamie Foxx and Denzel Washington. Heard they'll be there." He smiled—a real one. "They some bad motherfuckers."

I took some comfort from the fact that on the return trip I was in the back seat, not the trunk.

18

THE CELL PHONE IN MY POCKET RANG AS DREADLOCKS AND BRASS KNUCKLES drove me back toward Cruz Bay. The caller ID indicated it was Crystal, but I didn't want to talk to her with Diego's goons listening in so I hit END.

The small car rocketed down a hill near Chocolate Hole toward the intersection below.

"You guys can let me off here," I said.

"The Westin?" Dreadlock said.

"No, here's fine."

The car screeched to a stop.

"When Mr. Francis calls you, be sure to answer," Brass Knuckles said. "Otherwise, we'll come find you."

I jumped out, rubbing my sore chin as they sped off. They drove a blue Hyundai, and I made a note to avoid it if I saw it again. Nice-sized trunk, though.

A steady stream of pick-up truck taxis packed with tourists spewed out of the road leading toward the Westin, the largest hotel on the island. I retrieved Crystal's number and hit SEND.

"Buck, I'm so glad you called back." She was out of breath. "Everything okay on St. John?"

"Sure," I said. "It's paradise here, what could be wrong? How about on Jost? I take it you made it there okay."

"Oh, I made it. The ferry worked out fine and Customs was a breeze, albeit on island-time." She paused. "But when I got here, I found out Scarlet—that's my assistant—was understating the amount of shit that's been going on."

"What's the deal?"

A brittle laugh.

"What's *not* the deal would be more like it," she said. "There's no new news on John or Stud, and the latest problem is protestors—Pro Life, Pro Choice, Pro-Statehood, religious groups, and some I'm not sure about yet."

I squeezed my eyes shut and rubbed my temple.

"Are they threatening you in any way?"

"No, but if looks could kill, I'd need armed bodyguards just to survive the walk from the dock to the stage." Her voice wasn't shaky but it had an edge.

I urged her to contact the authorities, then told her I'd just arrived at the Westin and wanted to check John's room for any clues.

"Good idea—no point in coming here now," she said. "I need you to pick up people in San Juan and St. Thomas tomorrow and fly them to where they're staying. And then we have to get people here for rehearsals. A couple of my board members are helping too."

A lump formed in my throat.

"I can't land my plane in BVI waters, Crystal. The government won't allow it. And there's not many places I can land in the USVI, either."

Silence.

"Crystal? Are you there?"

"I was thinking. We have those speed boats from St. John on retainer. Talk to them. The owner's name is Bill something.... Bill Hartman, that's it. Can you talk to him?"

Billy the boozer, I presumed. I promised I'd see him and she said that if John's luggage and briefcase were still in his room at the Westin, there was a schedule of arrivals and logistics for ferrying people around.

We hung up as I arrived at the Westin. After a lot of persuasion, the hotel manager agreed to give me a key to John Thedford's suite. The police had already been there but the rooms weren't sealed since they hadn't detected anything suggesting foul play. Thedford was paid up through half of next week, so all his possessions were still there.

I took in the beach-front view from the balcony. God knew how many rooms were spread out over close to fifty acres on the palm-lined shores of Great Cruz Bay. Verdant hills formed a horseshoe around the turquoise water, the masts of countless moored sailboats swaying in the afternoon breeze. Looking down I watched children run around the compound, squealing with delight as their parents watched from their deck chairs and sipped umbrella'd drinks.

Back to work.

Aside from the luggage and a few shirts and slacks in the suite's closet, nothing suggested anyone had actually occupied the room—no toiletries in the bathroom, the king bed made, everything in its place. I slid the shirts across the rack—good quality resort-style—checked his shirt and pants pockets and found nothing. No receipts, no cash, not a business card or even a pen.

I pulled out the Tumi suitcase—shoes, underwear, a belt. Damn. Now the briefcase, a leather Coach bag with lots of wear and tear, loaded to the hilt with files, paper, and brochures.

I found the mini-bar and liberated two tiny bottles of Bacardi rum, which I emptied into a glass and gulped neat. Then I sat at the desk and started sorting.

After a half-hour I had the files sorted into a few piles: logistics for the event, correspondence with the participants or their managers, bills, and ISA-related legal looking documents. None of it provided any insight into what might have happened to John Thedford. At least the logistics offered me a road map to where he'd been and planned to go—along with a ball-busting schedule of arrivals over the next 48 hours, which I had no idea how I'd manage. I scanned the list and counted a dozen different people I needed to retrieve who would've been covered by Seaborne. Then there were another half-dozen to shuttle to different exclusive resorts throughout the Virgin Islands. And the first arrival was tomorrow morning in St. Thomas.

There was no way I could do it alone, and no way I'd have time to look for John. Even if the charter boats were still willing to help, that wouldn't be enough to cover everyone.

I sat back in the chair. No clues.

I opened the sliding glass door and retreated to the balcony to think. Looked past the beach and pool area below to the bay, boat to boat, and after that dark blue all the way to the horizon. The sun was well into its downward arc.

A fat pelican flew close to the balcony and sparked an idea.

I needed help, lots of help, different kinds of help. Maybe my go-to mentor could be of assistance. I dug into my backpack and removed my notebook and cell phone, in the process spotting the piece of tape I'd found on the Beast's hatch this morning. The note instructing me to call.

Whether it was the rum, the lack of clues in John's briefcase, the aftereffects of those brass knuckles to my chin, or just overwhelming fatigue, I was for the moment at a loss—which number should I call first? I finally opened the notebook to my list of phone numbers and found the G's. Dialed, sat back in the chair, and waited.

"Harry Greenbaum here," came the familiar voice.

"Hey, Harry. It's Buck Reilly."

"You've caught me in a bit of a rush, dear boy—next block up, Percy." A car horn sounded in the background. "I'm in New York and late for a board meeting at GVI."

"What's that stand for? Greenbaum Ventures? One of your sixty-four companies?"

Harry's chuckle had the same refined British subtlety as his voice.

"That's what most people assume GVI is, and I never share what the acronym actually means. But legally the name of the company is Greenbaum Vulture Investors." He snickered. "The board doesn't even know that—and by the way, I'm down to sixty-three companies now."

Harry's candor warmed my heart. We've always been close, and even though he lost tens of millions when e-Antiquity tubed, he made many millions more and sold it off before that happened. After my parent's sudden death, Harry was the closest thing to a paternal role model I had left.

"Down one?" I said. "Not another e-Antiquity-type failure, I hope."

"No, no, no, nothing of the sort. I sold London Inks to an Indian firm and doubled my money. So today's—take a right, Percy—today's meeting is to review what next to acquire and how best to deploy the capital."

Harry's British style and manners were all the more successful given his Yiddish drive and ability to pick diamonds from piles of coal others refused or abandoned.

"Real quick then, Harry, I'm in St. John, U.S. Virgin Islands—"

"I trust you're not mixed up with that kidnapping, dear boy? The movie star, what's his name, Jugs Mengle?"

I choked back a laugh.

"Stud Mahoney, and no, not directly, but I *am* helping the promoter of the event Mahoney was here to support, and it's all unraveling—"

"Buck, I truly am sorry, but I must depart. Percy here will take notes on what you need, and I'll get back to you once I can fill the request with whichever of my companies might have insight into your current dilemma. Cheers."

With that Harry was gone, and another familiar British accent came on the line. I provided a concise query I thought Harry might be able to feed through his sources and come up with some guidance. The question was so random Percy had me repeat it three times before he rang off.

For as long as I'd known Harry, Percy had been his driver, professional to the core like most of Harry's corporate leaders—with the exception of me: his only failed investment, far as I knew.

19

I GRABBED THE FILE WITH THE GUEST ARRIVAL SCHEDULE, CONTACT NUMBERS, and other logistics, stuffed it into my backpack, and shoveled the rest of the piles back into John's worn briefcase. Who knows, maybe he'd return to the hotel. Or maybe he disappeared on a boat with an exotic island woman or a Hollywood starlet. I hustled down to the lobby and asked a bellman to call me a cab. A shrill whistle later and one of the pick-up truck taxis lumbered out of the shade of a broad royal palm.

"Ferry dock," I said. The driver just sat there.

Once on the rear bench seat, I realized he was waiting in hopes of more passengers. I leaned over, knocked on the sliding window at the back of the cab, and pointed up the street.

The driver released the clutch, which sent me flying toward the gateless edge of the truck bed.

Wise guy.

The road to town had little traffic but wound over steep hills that had me clinging to the railing, then chugged through local neighborhoods, then a basketball court where the fence was lined with spectators and players awaiting their turn. It wasn't until we were descending into Cruz Bay that I remembered I hadn't called the number on the piece of masking tape. I retrieved the phone and the tape, then dialed…

"What?" A man's voice.

"Did you leave this phone number on my plane at the harbor in Charlotte Amalie early this morning?"

"Plane? What the fuck? Who be—"

A loud noise sounded—I thought he'd dropped the phone, but a second later another voice was on the line.

"Who this?"

"Buck Reilly. Did you leave a phone number on my plane this morning?"

A deep quick laugh.

"Last night they left the number for you. 'Bout time you called, brudda."

The taxi reached the circle just above Cruz Bay and turned down the hill that led to the harbor.

"What do you want?" I said.

"What *I* want?" Could this be the person who'd been calling John Thedford? "I want to talk to you."

"We're talking now—"

"Face to face. In person."

"I'm pretty busy, what it's about?"

"Where you at? I have someone get you."

Cagey. I don't like cagey. Dammit, I wanted to know if this had anything to do with Thedford.

"If you've been to the harbor today," I said, "you probably noticed I left—"

"Right. Plane's at Cyril King now. You back at Frenchman's Reef yet?"

It had to be the guy who woke me up this morning.

"I will be later," I said. "Where can we meet?"

"I have someone pick you up at eight. Out front."

"But—"

Click.

Damn!

The taxi circled around the block and fell in behind a few other trucks, then stopped. I leapt from the back, handed the man a ten, and kept going. I checked my watch. It was nearly 6:00 p.m., I still had some things to do here, and now I needed to be at Frenchman's Reef by 8:00.

On the dock, I watched the ferry get smaller as it motored out of the harbor—I'd just missed it. The schedule on the wall showed one more crossing to St. Thomas tonight: 7:30.

No way I could make it to the hotel by 8:00.

Damn.

I jumped from the pier to the sand. At the far end of the beach was the Beach Bar from which Diego's goons had so rudely extracted me. But in the middle of the beach was American Watersports, and the crowded harbor made me guess all their boats had returned from their charters for the night. I pulled off my boat shoes and hurried over the sand toward the path next to their sign. I started down the alley—

"We're closed," a voice shouted from above me.

I glanced back and noticed a man drinking from a bottle of Carib beer, making eye contact with me from the adjacent patio bar.

"You the manager?"

He shook his head and let out a loud burp. "Owner. Want to rent a boat for tomorrow?"

I walked back out to the beach and found stairs that led into the bar. The owner was a guy about my age with a deepwater tan, shoulder-length dirty-blond hair, and a beer gut that told me this was a nightly routine if not an all-day one. I held out my hand.

"Buck Reilly. I'm with the Adoption AID people who chartered—"

"Hell, I been wondering if anyone else was gonna show up." He smiled. "We been holding the Powerplay for you, along with the Cigarette." He squinted at me. "The hell happened to your jaw there, Buck? Got a nice purple bruise—"

"Tripped on a lizard." I rubbed my palm down my tender jawbone.

Out in the harbor was a black cigarette speedboat with twin in-board engines on the back. Not very subtle, but it was certainly fast and would connect with a certain crowd.

"Things have been a little messed up," I said.

"No shit. Heard about that actor—and what about Thedford? He turn up yet?"

"No, he hasn't. Are you Billy?"

"The one and only," he said.

So far, so good. "Thedford came by here, right?"

"Stopped in the other night after he got here, before the party down the beach. Told me we'd be heading over to check arrangements on Tortola and Peter Island the next day—that'd be yesterday—and then a few other places today. Then he disappeared."

It felt like a hamster wheel was turning in my stomach. This was only the second person I'd met that had seen John Thedford here on St. John—not counting Diego Francis, but the jury was still out on him.

"Was anyone with him, or was there anything strange you saw that might—"

"Nah, man, wish there was. Already told the cops, but he came in alone, maybe had a little buzz, jolly as hell. Nice guy and boy was he excited. Who could blame him? All these big shots coming here for his show. Hell, I was pretty fired up too."

"So he didn't tell you anything—"

"No, sorry—Buck, right? He split for the Westin but came back later to the party at the Beach Bar, which was the last time—" He set the empty beer on the bar. I noticed the bartender raise her eyebrow. Cute blond.

"Two Caribs, please?" I turned back to Billy. "You were saying, last time what?"

"Last time anyone saw him, except for me."

I waited. It wasn't easy, but Billy was not a man to be rushed.

"Pretty sure I saw him get on board a red Cigarette, right out here on the beach."

"Pretty sure?"

"Well, I'd been here a few hours, but yeah, I'm pretty sure that's what I saw."

I flashed back to Officer Deaver of the Park Police. He hadn't mentioned it was a *red* boat.

"You called the cops?"

"Nah, they were going door to door asking if anyone had seen him." He smiled at the waitress. "Right, Sunny?"

She gave him a quick smile, which caused Manny to chuckle. He didn't notice her roll her eyes when she turned away.

"So they found you here and you told them he left on a red boat?"

"Yeah, but I wasn't entirely sure. It *had* been a long day and all."

"You never said if he was with anyone," I said.

"Well, there was at least one other person in the boat…"

"A woman?"

He shrugged. "Someone behind the wheel, that's all I recall."

I checked my watch. 6:45. *Shit!*

"You gotta be somewhere?"

The bartender put the two beers down and smiled at me. She had the beginnings of dreadlocks and wore a snug Red Sox tank top. I gave her a twenty.

"As a matter of fact, I need to get to Frenchman's Reef within the hour." The next part was dicey, since Billy was half in the bag. "Can you run me over in that Cigarette?"

Billy laughed and lit a Marlboro Light.

"You don't want me running a boat right now." He smiled. "But I can see if Jeremy's around, he's the one was gonna captain for Thedford."

After a draw on the cigarette and a deep pull on the beer, Billy un-holstered his cell phone and turned towards the water, and then after a couple minutes turned back to me with a smile on his face, the phone still pressed to his ear.

"Good. Get here quick." He winked at me.

I checked my watch. 6:50.

"Jeremy's on his way—"

"I'm right here," came a voice from behind me.

I turned to see a tall guy in his mid-twenties with a to-go cup in his hand and a smile on his face.

"I was next door at the Mojito," he said.

What a life these boys have…

"The boat's paid for," Billy said, "so take the man where he wants to go."

"Buck Reilly," I said. "Frenchman's Reef, St. Thomas."

"Let's do it."

Once we waded out the fifty yards to where the Cigarette was moored to three different buoys, Jeremy jumped aboard and fired up the twin inboards while I untied us. By 7:01 he was swinging the bow out toward open water.

"I really appreciate this, man," I said.

"No worries, I've just been waiting around to help your friend." He glanced both ways to check for traffic and added throttle. The twin engines pushed the sleek boat through the harbor like a knife.

"Did you meet John Thedford?"

Jeremy nodded and checked the gauges on our boat, all the while dodging dinghies.

"Yeah, when he first came in."

Once we cleared the boats, he added more throttle. The Cigarette jumped forward, but he still had a lot of throttle to go.

"Was anyone with him?"

"Not sure, but there was a chick hanging out on the beach. Looked like she was waiting for someone. Might have been your boy."

We passed the green buoy into open water.

"What'd she look like?"

"Tall with a nice rack is all I remember. No—she had dark, long hair, too."

Lovely.

"You think Billy really saw Thedford leave on that red Cigarette?"

He looked at me, zeroed in on the bruise on my face, then glanced back up at my eyes.

"That time of night? Billy Hartman can't usually see his feet."

Damn.

20

Jeremy pressed the throttle down hard and the Cigarette roared forward, splitting the sea like a scalpel. At this speed I'd make my 8:00 meeting with the mystery caller.

We bounced steadily in the mild chop, each slight turn of the wheel jerking us immediately in the direction he steered. Conversation was impractical due to the speed of the wind and the snarl of the twin engines, so I mulled over what Billy Hartman, Officer Deaver, and Jeremy had said....

What the hell. I used Booth's cell phone and texted Diego Francis and asked if he knew anyone with a red Cigarette who might have grabbed Thedford.

I turned back to Jeremy: "Have you ever seen a red Cigarette boat around here?"

"You see all kinds in these islands."

The authorities must not have believed Thedford left on that go-fast boat, otherwise they wouldn't have dredged the harbor and searched the beaches. I thought of the Beast, how the mystery man on the phone knew I'd moved her to the airport. I thought about what Jimmy Buffett referred to as the Coconut Telegraph, the way information travels so fast in the islands, especially among those whose lives depend on real-time information.

I was on my own, skipping across the water at high speed with a list of questions that just kept getting longer. The fact that Crystal needed me intensified the pressure to the point where I could feel my heart pounding.

We made the crossing in record time, at least for me, and compared to the ferry it felt like time travel. The setting sun cast a fruit juice glow on the passage between Great St. James and Little St. James islands as we approached the southern coast of St. Thomas.

"You know Diego Francis?" I said.

Jeremy whipped around to face me, his brow furrowed.

"*Know* him? Hell no. Know *of* him? You can't live around here and not."

"As bad as they say?"

"Gangsta all the way."

"Was he at the Beach Bar concert the other night?"

Jeremy shook his head, slowly. "Couldn't tell you, but he doesn't miss much. If he wasn't there, you can be sure some of his people were."

Hmmm.

"You heard any rumors about Adoption AID, like maybe anyone who wasn't happy about it?"

He glanced back at me with his brow furrowed. "Movie stars and rocks stars in the islands for a party on Jost? What's not to like?"

Right, what's not to like.

We passed the ferry I'd watched leave St. John just as it angled away toward Red Hook. Boat traffic got thicker. Commercial and sport fisherman, dive boats, pleasure craft, sail and power, all glided toward destinations like Secret Harbour, Bolongo Bay, and Bluebeard's Beach Club. My destination, Frenchman's Reef, was visible high above the water on an outcrop that jutted out mid-island, just before the coast turned north into the harbor of Charlotte Amalie.

A large cruise ship emerged from that gap and dwarfed everything else. I glanced out to sea—two more massive ships steamed toward St. Thomas, ready to deposit happy-go-lucky vacationers in one of the busiest ports in the Caribbean.

Just as Jeremy let off on the throttles I checked my watch: 7:45. I'd make it.

The phone vibrated in my pocket. For once I was glad to see YOUR MASTER on the screen, hoping Booth had some good news for me.

"Tell me something useful."

"About time you answered the damn phone. Been trying for an hour."

"Got my hands full down here, Booth. Have you paved the way for me to land the Beast—er, my plane—in BVI waters yet? I've got a hell of a lot—"

"Don't start bossing me around, hotshot, and what the hell are you doing calling known criminals on that phone I gave you?"

Crap. I'd texted Diego.

Jeremy was idling the boat toward the dock where the shuttle from Frenchman's Reef goes back and forth to town. I pulled my notebook out of my backpack and handed it to him, then waved my hand to imitate writing while I mouthed: give me your cell number.

"Reilly? I know you're there, I hear boat motors and birds chirping. I want an answer—"

"The answer is that local law enforcement haven't found dick, and if they have, nobody's shared it with Crystal or me, so I'm taking an alternative route to find Thed—"

"Stud Mahoney, Reilly! Forget about the charity case!"

"I'm hoping one will lead to the other, Booth. Now what about my plane?"

Silence.

"Booth?"

"The commissioner of the BVI's Royal VIPD is considering the request—"

"Considering? Government-time's even slower than island time. Dammit, shit's happening fast here and if I can't get from point A to point B—"

"Where's Mrs. Thedford? I have some questions for her."

Whoa. "What kind of questions?"

"Let's just say your pretty lady friend may not be as squeaky clean as her AID concert might make you think."

I swallowed.

Jeremy handed me back my notebook. I mouthed a thank-you and said

I'd call him tomorrow. Then jumped off the boat, my mind atwirl from Booth's insinuations. I considered asking him about the red Cigarette, but given his comment on the "charity case," I let it go. It was 7:55 and I needed to get out front fast.

"Text me...when you have me cleared...for water landings." I was talking and jogging at the same time. "Which better...be...by morning... for me...to be...effective."

"The hell are you doing, Reilly, jerking off?"

I hit the END button as I ran through the lobby toward the front door.

A black SUV with tinted windows was parked out front, and like a foolish mouse I headed straight for the cheese.

21

THE SUV'S PASSENGER SIDE WINDOW LOWERED A FEW INCHES. I STOPPED A couple feet away. It was pitch black inside, so I took a deep breath and moved closer to look in the window.

Inside was a face with blood red eyes. Literally. I jerked back.

"You Buck Reilly?"

"That's right."

The window lowered further. The man held a sawed-off shotgun.

"Get in back."

I may have spotted my underwear as I stood frozen.

"Nothing to worry about," Sawed-off said.

I took a lungful of air, rolled some imaginary dice, and pulled open the back door. Slid inside the ice-cold SUV and found a man next to me with a shotgun resting between his legs, pointed toward the roof.

"Let's go," he said.

The driver slowly edged out of the circular entry and up the hill, then turned left.

"Where are we going?" I said.

None of them responded. Instead, the driver pushed a button and ear-deafening music erupted inside the vehicle. I nearly jumped out of my seat, but none of them so much as flinched.

So much for conversation.

As we wound up and down the road toward the port I tried to note landmarks, but darkness fell quickly and I had nothing but the occasional lighted sign or structure to track. Three cruise ships were at the docks, and as we approached them we turned to the right and began to weave back up the hill. Even though the air conditioning was blasting as high as the music, there was a smell of perspiration inside the SUV. The three men were all dreadlocked, beefy, sunglass-wearing soldiers, and I was either their guest, or target.

Tourist facilities disappeared as we switch-backed our way into the mountainous region, which I recalled from previous visits was above Magen's Bay. A sudden turn up a washed-out gravel path resulted in a gut-busting jolt that rattled my teeth along with the SUV. No speed was lost—if anything, the driver accelerated.

But soon he slowed, then braked abruptly. The headlights illuminated a chain link gate. After a moment a man emerged from the woods—it took me a few seconds to realize he was holding the largest blunt I'd ever seen. The driver rolled down his window and the sentry handed him the huge smoldering reefer. The driver inhaled deeply and passed it to Sawed-off in the passenger seat. He did the same, then handed it back to my seatmate, who kept the ember glowing and tried to hand it to me.

I held up my hand to abstain, but his expression turned to a sneer of mistrust. The driver and Sawed-off both turned in their seats to stare at me.

Talk about peer pressure.

I took hold of the monster with both hands and tried to draw in just enough to make the cherry glow—

My lungs expanded and my throat constricted and I started to cough uncontrollably. A head rush like I hadn't felt in years hit me and I wondered what these boys were smoking—check that, what *I* had just smoked.

The men in the car and the guard outside laughed and laughed. More unintelligible statements, laughs and fist-bumps, and the gate screeched open. Gravel blasted out behind us as we launched up the hill to a promontory—even in the darkness I could tell there'd be 360-degree views. In the center of it all was an old house made of stone and block with a red tiled roof and a lot of people standing around it, all holding guns.

Even though the smoke had only been in my lungs for a second, I felt as if my head had separated from my body and floated above the scene, untethered. My backseat neighbor spoke to me, lifted the shotgun, and opened the truck door. The other men followed and I sat there a moment, unable to feel my feet. I took a deep breath and tried to gather what was left of my wits to deal with whoever I was soon to meet, for whatever purpose.

And shit, I was stoned. Not wrecked, but definitely stoned.

The others stared at me. I tried to count how many there were but kept losing track. At least ten men, many of whom had glowing cherries in the middle of their faces, which I hoped were cigarettes or blunts and not glowing red Cyclops eyes. I couldn't afford another toke, decorum be damned. I had no tolerance for the stuff anymore

I had a fleeting thought that perhaps John Thedford was being held in the house, and possibly even Stud Mahoney, which would be marvelous since he was such an accomplished action star and could help figure out what to do next….

"Buck Reilly," a loud voice came from the lit porch.

I floated toward the sound, concentrating on the crunching noise caused by each step, which sounded like chewing Wheaties. The observation struck me as funny but I bit my lip to stifle my laughter, knowing that once I started I wouldn't be able to stop. Damn weed.

"That's me," I said to the giant standing on the porch. "And you are?"

A booming laugh and hot breath sprang from his mouth and I imagined it shooting my hair backwards like in cartoons. I again stifled a laugh.

"Let's say I'm an interested partner." The man was huge, much bigger than the others, and had a shaved head. He wore sunglasses even though it was pitch black, which matched the tone of his skin. He reminded me of the alien in *Predator*, who stalked and killed everybody but Arnold Schwarzenegger, who outsmarted the creature and lived to become governor of California.

A high-pitched giggle escaped my lips.

"Something funny?" he said.

One of the three-dreadlocked men who had brought me here spoke in their undecipherable argot, then nodded toward me with a chuckle.

"Aha," the big man said. Big yellow teeth glistened in my direction.

Chastened, I sucked in a deep breath.

"Not really in the market for a partner—"

"Listen, I know all about your work as a for-profit Indiana Jones wannabe."

Damn, had everyone in the USVI researched my past?

"Which is why I'm guessing you're either the new Big Man that's rumored to be moving into town, or you're connected to him."

The new Big Man?

"Um, not really sure what you're talking about—"

His smile remained in place, but fewer teeth were showing.

"I understand, brudda, not exactly neutral ground here, but you need to know my network's the best in the islands. I'm the biggest importer, have the most control, and can deliver quality product in a steady pipeline."

I swallowed. He thinks I'm—

"And if it ain't you, which wouldn't surprise me since you came here all by yourself, than you need to tell your boss we should meet." He held out his hand. "Boom-Boom Burke."

"Swell." I took a steadying breath. "Look, I'm here for the thing at Foxy's—the charity concert. To promote adoption."

The yellow teeth disappeared.

It all came back to me in a muddled rush—the phone calls, the threats, the kidnappings. Getting caught up in the middle of the local gang leader's desire to expand his business wouldn't help, nor would it do much for my health.

"How do *you* feel about adoption?" I said.

My question caused a sudden mental image of Dr. Ruth, the tiny little sex therapist who used to be on television, and I had to bite my lip not to laugh again. I couldn't read his expression in the darkness, and my direct question was less than crafty, but under the circumstances I felt like I was doing okay.

"How do I *feel* about it?" he said. "Sounds like a good cover to me, that's what I think." He laughed. "And that plane of yours is ideal for inter-island deliveries, so I'm telling you, we could do some serious business together. From what I'm hearing on the street, you, or whoever you work for, are diversified, big time, all over the world. I want to partner with you and grow."

El crappo.

"Here's the thing, Boom-Boom, starting tomorrow I'm balls to the walls trying to run celeb—um, movie stars and singers around the islands to help with this charity concert. And, well, all the others—the logistical help—It's all been cancelled 'cause of bomb threats and other challenges, like the promoter, John Thedford, disappearing. And Stud Mahoney's been kidnapped."

I couldn't believe I'd gotten through all that. Boom-Boom was staring at me like he couldn't believe it either.

"The hell you saying?"

"This concert, it's only to promote adoption," I said. "It's a charity, know what I mean? In my personal opinion their goals are way too lofty, but hey, nothing ventured, nothing—"

"You're starting to piss me off with this bullshit," Boom-Boom said.

"—gained. So, my question for you, before we talk about any partnering with, ah, your group, is…" What was the question? Oh. "My question is if you know anything about phone calls, challenges, threats to the Thedfords—"

Book-Boom reached out like he wanted to grab me by the throat but stopped short, hesitated, and dropped his island-sized paw.

"You need to say no to weed, brudda, makes you talk crazy."

That I couldn't argue with. But my head was clearing.

"I know all about that concert, yeah, and about that dude disappearing."

"You know where he is?" I said. "Or Stud Mahoney?"

Everyone stood motionless, all their eyes fixed on us.

Stay off the ropes…

"How about this." I squinted at him in the darkness. "All bullshit aside, you help me find Thedford and Mahoney, I'll make the connection you're asking about."

"Aha! Knew you was bullshitting me, Reilly."

"But this is all tied together—I can't tell how, but if I don't hurry up and find John Thedford and the actor, bad things are going to happen. So I'll help you, but you need to help me first."

Boom-Boom stared at me a long moment.

"Wait here," he said finally.

A couple of his men followed after him and entered the building. The rest milled about and kept an eye on me. A shooting star tore across the night sky only to vanish into the blackness. I could relate. I'd gambled by telling him what he wanted to hear, which could either blow up in my face or create an urgency that might actually help.

A cell phone rang and one of my minders answered. I couldn't be sure, but based on his incomprehensible accent and mouth full of marbles, I thought it might have been the driver of the SUV that brought me here.

He glanced at me, grunted something, and walked down to where the SUV was parked. He got inside and turned it on but kept the lights off. An electrical jolt ran through my spine and down my limbs. I looked around in the darkness, my eyes having adjusted, but saw nothing except natural walls of dark undergrowth that surrounded the perimeter. Had Boom-Boom seen through my con? Should I run? Scream?

A shaft of light illuminated the building entry, then Boom-Boom and his men fanned out toward me. I sucked in a breath and held it. He moved through the darkness like a panther.

"I have your number," he said. "And I have eyes all over these islands. I'll see what I can find out."

I exhaled.

"But you tell the Big Man about me too, all right, brudda?"

I was tempted to mention that Diego Francis had referenced some new opportunity too but figured that would be pushing my luck. I was leaving in one piece and I might have Boom-Boom Burke's network working on my behalf, which could be a good thing.

But I'd owe him an introduction to someone I didn't know.

What a tangled web we weave when trying to save our asses.

22

ONCE BACK AT FRENCHMAN'S REEF I WANTED NOTHING MORE THAN TO collapse on my bed and sleep for a week. Couldn't do that without knowing Crystal's fate with the picketers on Jost. I also wanted to know what Booth's intel on her might be, but I had a feeling it would take me a while to find out, assuming I could.

The pile of papers I retrieved from John Thedford's briefcase brought back the brutal reality that I had to be in three places at once over the next few days. I ran my palm down my cheek—the pain in my jaw was still sharp from today's brass knuckle brunch. That realization led to another one: I hadn't had a meal all day. And so with a cheeseburger and cold beer on order from room service I sat back to consider my options.

I only came up with one.

After several rings, Ray Floyd's voice came on the line.

"Based on what I see on caller ID, I shouldn't be taking this call."

Damn Booth.

"Don't be silly, Ray. Would I be calling to cause you any heartburn?"

"Heartburn, no. Brain damage, yes. How's Crystal Thedford doing? Are you two an item yet?"

"She's a married woman," I said over the sound of machine gun fire and explosions in the background. By day Ray was cerebral, a true island philosopher, but by night he was Delta Force and Seal Team Six rolled into one, poised to dole out serious punishment to video bad guys. I'd actually seen him dig deep and deploy those virtual skills in real life a couple of times, which is one of the reasons I was calling him now.

"Is the Beast okay?" he said.

Boom-bam-whoosh…

"Ray! Can you pause the noise for a minute!"

Silence. "What's the problem, Buck?"

"Have you seen the news? John Thedford's still missing, and that actor Stud Mahoney has been—"

"Kidnapped, yeah, I saw that. Is it all related?"

"I think so, but in addition, there was a bomb threat against the charter airline that was supposed to ferry Crystal's guests around—"

"Seaborne Airlines? I ever tell you I turned down a job offer from them to be their head mechanic? They're grounded?"

"No, you didn't, and yes, they are. I have a couple speed boats at my disposal, but Crystal's like the little Dutch Boy with her finger in the dyke trying to keep the whole concert from unraveling, and…" I paused, not wanting to give Ray too much to be worried about.

"And what?" he said.

"And I need your help."

Silence.

"And Lenny Jackson's help too—did he have his debate last night? Did you go?"

"Oh my God, you missed it. Lenny was…well, a true island original's about all I can say. Holy smokes. The other candidates sat there with their mouths open when he got on a roll. The crowd loved him."

I'd really wanted to see him but couldn't dwell on that right now.

"What do you need me to do?" Ray said. "And why is South Region SAC involved?"

Damn caller ID. Booth's a ninny.

"Nothing hairy—"

"Sure, Buck, that's what you always say."

"Flying celebrities around the islands sound hairy to you? Movie stars, singers, all kinds of famous people are descending here tomorrow. I can't babysit them *and* look for Thedford *and* the missing action star."

"What am I supposed to fly?" he said.

"How should I know? Charter something. ISA had budgeted to pay Seaborne, they have money."

When I recited the schedule of who was arriving and when, I had him. He oohed, he ahhed, he said "This could be really fun," and promised to see if Lenny was available too.

What would he say if he saw the bruise on the side of my face?

Didn't matter, because I had no intention of putting Ray in harm's way. He could have the glory runs with the big shots while I chased my tail looking for answers.

"Tell Conch Man I really need his help. His constituents will be all the more impressed with him if he can get some celebrity endorsements."

We hung up just as there was a knock on the door.

Now what?

Room service dropped off a cheeseburger that turned out to be cold and in a soggy bun, but as hungry as I was, I could have eaten the metal tray. And as tired as I was, after eating it I fell into deep, dreamless sleep—until the phone rang.

Damn!

I grabbed the cell phone off the end table and sent half the contents from the dinner tray flying off the bed. It was 3:20 a.m. But I couldn't even be mad—caller ID said it was Crystal.

"Buck, I'm so sorry to wake you. I just don't know what—or who…"

"What's the matter?"

"We're running out of time and I'm… Let's just say the center isn't holding."

I paced around, trying to blink away the sleep.

"Has something else happened?"

"Viktor and I spoke with that detective—you know, the one from VIPD who met us when we arrived on St. Thomas?"

"Viktor?"

"He's on our Board—"

"Lieutenant White?"

"I hadn't heard a thing so I called him earlier and he finally called me back tonight. Those bastards haven't even been looking for John, all their energy is focused on Stud Mahoney. They say if they're connected, Mahoney will lead them to John, but they're not even sure they *are* connected, so that means they've given up—" Her voice broke.

I walked to the balcony window and stared out over the halos of light in the tropical courtyard while she sobbed quietly on the other end of the phone.

"Crystal, listen, I've been talking to a lot of different people. When I used to search for artifacts around the world, I found that people either parallel to the obvious partners—or in some cases diametrically opposed to them—often provided more indirect yet better information because they had an entirely different network."

"Who are you talking about, Buck? I didn't understand a word of that."

I sighed. "Let's just say I'm building a network."

I debated whether or not to let her know that her husband might have left St. John under his own power. I also considered asking for a description of her assistant, but that would lead to more speculation, not assuage her concerns.

She asked if I was ready to handle the onslaught of arrivals. I crossed my fingers, said yes, and hoped Ray would come through—otherwise, high-rolling celebrities would be stranded at airports scattered around the Virgin Islands and Puerto Rico, which would lead to the collapse of Adoption AID assuming it was still standing.

I didn't need that on my conscience.

"Did the police question you at all, Crystal?"

"What do you mean?"

"I don't know, about John. His disappearance."

"Yeah, I guess, but they do that to everyone, right? You don't...you don't think I had something to do—"

"No! Just trying to figure out what they're doing."

She was quiet.

"Have there been any issues caused by the protestors, any more threats?" I said.

"There was a fight today, between a few of them. It's tense."

"Don't give up." A lump formed in my throat.

"Thanks, Buck.... I wish you were here."

I closed my eyes and imagined her the first time we met at Louie's Backyard.

"Be safe," I said.

I tried Booth's cell phone. Voicemail.

"It's Buck Reilly. You have any news for me? And how about permission to land my plane? Call me!"

I shoved everything off the bed with a crash and collapsed, hoping for another couple hours of sleep before things got really crazy.

23

THE REST OF THE WEE HOURS PASSED FITFULLY AS I SHIFTED BETWEEN sleeping and considering what, if anything, I'd learned so far. There were some potential aggressors against adoption, but were any of them motivated enough for kidnappings and bombings? Both Boom-Boom and Diego were charged up over some new opportunity—Mr. Big, as Boom-Boom called him. Could that be a connection? I'd been focused on local possibilities. It was time to view the bigger picture.

From my flight bag I pulled out a wad of paper. Lieutenant White's card fell out of the pile. I studied it. He was part of the Criminal Investigation Special Operations Bureau Command located at Burns Field. I called the number and found out they were located just north of the airport and adjacent to the University of the Virgin Islands. Perfect.

Time to rattle some cages.

I loaded up my backpack and checked the cell phone for messages, but there was nothing from Booth and nothing yet from Ray.

After a quick shower I made my way through the hotel complex to the dining area to grab a coffee and croissant for the road. The police station was all the way over on the western side of Charlotte Amalie. I'd jump on the ferry to town, then—

"Where are you headed, hotshot?"

Special Agent T. Edward Booth was seated at a table overlooking the harbor, a full breakfast of eggs, bacon, fruit, and muffins spread out before him.

"Perfect timing, too," he said. "What's your room number so I can charge this?"

"What the hell are you doing here, Booth?"

"Sit down and let's catch up."

He poured me a cup of coffee. For once, I was actually relieved to see him—maybe his presence here meant he was taking this situation seriously.

"I trust you're here to work and this isn't some boondoggle vacation on the taxpayer's nickel," I said.

"Always the smartass. I didn't send you that credit card and phone so you could network with felons and whisper late night nothings to married women." He doused his scrambled eggs in ketchup and shoveled a load into his mouth. "What have you found out—and why's your cheek purple and yellow? You boxing for gas money again?"

"I've got your credit card for that." I rubbed my still tender cheek. "I'm doing what none of your people seem capable of—trying to find out who's opposed to Adoption AID—"

"There you go again, junior detective on the wrong trail. Why can't you ever stick to what I tell you?" The eggs caught in a gap between his teeth distracted me.

"Did you show up here to bust my balls or do you have something to tell me?"

"The FAA sent a letter of authorization to land in U.S. waters here to the hotel, by fax," he said.

"And the BVI?"

He sighed and took a bite of blueberry muffin.

"They agreed, tentatively, but that's one of the reasons I'm here." He reached into his shirt pocket. I realized it was the first time I'd seen him without his blue blazer. He removed a letter, unfolded it, and handed it over.

There was an FBI seal on top. The letter mentioned the Beast's tail number and referenced a conversation Booth had with Duncan Mather, Commissioner of the Royal Virgin Islands Police Force. It said the amphibious plane with this tail number would be allowed to make water landings in the BVI, once inspected by officials to verify that it did not contain weapons or other illegal substances. Instructions and a phone number on Tortola followed.

I suddenly felt lightheaded.

"What's the matter, kid? You just turned white as Wonder Bread."

"This is the best you can do?" I didn't want to tell him that checking in with the Royal VIPD was the last thing I wanted to do.

"They're very formal over there. Pain in the ass, really, but once you check in, all should be fine. Unless you're carrying weapons or dope. You wouldn't do that, of course."

"What have you found out about John Thedford?"

"There've been no new demands over Stud Mahoney, which is what I'm sure you meant to ask. And by the way, Mahoney's real name is Mike Kuznewski. That's what's on his passport. Guess Polacks don't make convincing action heroes in Hollywood." He stopped eating and stared at me. "Anything about Stud Mahoney you want to tell me?"

"I haven't heard a thing."

His glare lingered. "Mm-hmm."

"Tell me the details of his kidnapping. I can't do shit if I don't know where to look."

"You don't watch the news, Reilly?"

"I've been too busy doing your job."

He curled his lip. "He had a suite on Peter Island, swanky, exclusive resort in the BVI—"

"I've been there, Booth."

"Of course you have." His sneer made me smile. "Few afternoons ago he ordered a big lunch for him and his agent, hot little number doing more than just getting him movie deals, if you know what I mean. Room service shows up thirty minutes later and he's gone. Room's a mess and there's a note says he's dead if a million dollars isn't paid within forty-eight hours."

"Paid where?"

"That's the thing, it didn't specify further instructions, and there's been no follow up." Booth sighed. "His studio offered a hundred-grand reward to anyone who can help find him."

No mention of Adoption AID or the concert. Weird. Maybe they *were* unrelated.

"Peter Island's pretty isolated," I said. "Anybody see boats coming or going during that time?"

"There were a few, but the room service order was placed from his cell phone, not the phone in the suite."

"So maybe he was already gone." I thought for a few seconds. "Did he ever check in?"

"Oh yeah, the night before. Big deal, guests went crazy, he made a stink about the first suite not being big enough. Then demanded champagne and caviar on the beach. Typical Hollywood prick."

"So if he's not hidden in some other villa—"

"The Royal Police went door to door, he's not there."

"Then he must've left by boat," I said. "What about the eyewitness on St. John who saw Thedford leave Cruz Bay aboard a speedboat?"

Booth's expression didn't change. He just stared at me.

"A red Cigarette, to be precise."

"News to me, Reilly—"

"Officer Deaver from the Park Police mentioned it, and I talked to the witness."

"A drunk." Booth spoke into his food and when he looked up wouldn't meet my eyes. "Can't be taken seriously." He then launched into the semi-insider's version of radical pro-life and pro-choice fringe groups. These were the people who bombed abortion clinics at one end of the spectrum and supported late-stage abortions at the other. "Radical" didn't really cover it.

"Are there any of those types of groups active down here?" Something Crystal mentioned occurred to me. "What about anti-adoption groups?"

"Historically, no activity here," Booth said, "and the anti-adoption types have been peaceful so far, but given that this show is being broadcast world-wide, it's not limited to local groups."

"Really?" Crystal never said it was *that* big. Good grief!

"Don't get me wrong, Reilly. These islands may not have the concentration of crazies like your beloved Key West, but they've got plenty of nuts.

One such loon calls himself Reverend Hellfire and he's right here on St. Thomas." Booth laughed, but I didn't have the luxury of dismissing potential leads.

"Not your typical Christian pastor's name. Is he a sole proprietor?"

"Something like that. Even down here people start religions for tax purposes, but this guy's off the proverbial deep end."

Booth didn't look like he seemed too concerned about the potential antagonists he'd been describing. He mopped up the remaining ketchup with his last piece of wheat toast and stuffed it in his mouth.

"How about the international groups you mentioned?" I said. "Why would they be pissy about Adoption AID?"

This got me his most pedantic expression.

"Black marketeers are the biggest businesses abroad, Reilly. They don't like anything to rock the status quo. Not that I think they have anything to do with a little feel-good charity concert, but don't think the big boys sit back and allow market forces to change without being the ones to manipulate them."

I gave him a long, long look. "Market forces?"

"If adoption is more readily available, the prices for babies would drop."

Silence followed.

"Why do I feel like you're not telling me everything?"

His eyes narrowed. "What I came here to ask you, face to face, is whether Crystal Thedford has come clean with you yet."

My stomach sank. "About what?"

"About when she lived in L.A."

"Said she worked for City of Hope."

"You're a sap, Reilly. Not who she worked for, who she lived with."

A flash popped in my head. "She mentioned she'd lived with an actor." He smiled, but his eyes kept the squint.

"That's right, hotshot. Crystal Banks, her maiden name, lived with Stud Mahoney."

I nearly spit coffee all over Booth.

"Now her husband and former lover are both missing."

When Jack Anderson told us Stud was missing, the one word she'd said was "Shit."

"Watch your ass, kid."

I leaned forward. "So she's under suspicion?"

"Damn straight, but we know she was home in Maryland when her husband disappeared, and with you when Mahoney vanished." I didn't take the bait, my mind still spinning too fast. "Now go get your FAA permission slip off the fax machine, fly over to Tortola so they can laugh their way through inspecting that lobster trap of an airplane, and start island hopping until you find me something useful."

He stood. I was amazed to see him in tropical weight khakis and with his blue button-down shirt untucked. He almost looked relaxed, which bothered me.

"I have a meeting with the Task Force Against Gang Activity now, so if you'll excuse me."

I watched him walk through the patio and into the main building. He had Federal Agent written all over him, and no interest in hiding it.

Crystal knew Stud Mahoney? Lived with him?

Crap.

Based on the directions I received earlier, I knew the Criminal Investigative Bureau was somewhere on the other side of Water Island. I studied the shore, looked past the seaplane base to the west, where the University of the Virgin Islands was situated. Booth had been uncharacteristically helpful, albeit brutal. It then hit me that he said he didn't know anything about the red Cigarette, but also said they guy who reported it was a drunk. He clearly was still holding back.

I had to learn more, and fast.

Could I beat Booth to Lieutenant White?

24

THE FAA FAX DIDN'T SAY MUCH, BUT I FIGURED IT WAS A GET OUT OF JAIL Free card. I'd ask about it at the airport when I got there. The first pick-up was in 90 minutes: the country singer Avery Rose. I'd never seen her in concert, but she endorsed some cosmetics company that had her face emblazoned on a Five Sixes taxi in Key West, and in the words of Ray Floyd, she was hot—or at least she'd been airbrushed to look hot.

I hopped aboard the launch from Frenchman's Reef and we set out toward the dock in Charlotte Amalie. The sky was clear, a light breeze staved off perspiration, and laughter from those on board lightened my heart for a moment. Rather than dwelling on what I hadn't found out or what Booth had shared, I sat back on the bench and caught some rays.

Once on shore, I waved down a cab. When I told the driver to take me to Burns Field by the university he gave me a double-take. I didn't blame him. Based on my appearance, if I were headed to the police station it would more likely be in the back of a patrol car.

I phoned Captain Jeremy from the cab. He promised to be at the public dock next to the airport in two and half hours. I pulled out John Thedford's schedule and gave him the contact information for Jamie Foxx, who was coming in by private jet and specified that he wanted to be taken to Caneel Bay on St. John by private boat.

"No shit!" Jeremy said.

"After that I need you back at the dock by Cyril King to get somebody else. I'll let you know the specifics when the time gets closer." I wasn't being secretive—I could only plan a few moves ahead with so much going on.

"Got it," he said.

"Text me to let me know you made the pick-up."

The cabbie pulled up in front of the police station. The tinted double glass doors opened into a small lobby. In what looked like a bank teller booth with bulletproofed glass was a large black woman in uniform, her hair swirled up in an orange beehive. I tried my damndest not to stare. It wasn't easy—her fingernails were at least an inch long, with a different exotic design painted on each one. There was a microphone button with a sign that said Push to Speak, so I did.

"I'm looking for Lieutenant Kenneth White."

She raised an eyebrow. "Is he expecting you?"

I caught my reflection was in the glass. Unshaven, hair wild after the crossing on the ferry, skin red. I smiled.

"Just tell him T. Edward Booth from the FBI is here to see him."

Now both of her eyebrows lifted.

"Credentials?"

"Undercover, don't carry any." I kept a straight face. Feds don't smile.

She opened the mag lock and pointed to a hallway.

"Conference room, second door on the right. He'll be there in a minute, *Special Agent Booth*."

The conference room had a wood laminate table and eight chairs that had faded from mauve to a sickly pink. A picture of the President hung on one wall, facing one of the Police Commissioner for the USVI on the opposite wall. Neither was smiling.

I sat with my back to the door. White came up behind me and stopped.

"Come in and close the door," I said without turning around.

The door closed. He walked around the end of the table and saw me. His eyes changed from surprise to recognition to suspicion, all in half a second.

"You're that pilot—the treasure hunter, Buck Reilly," he said. "Where's Booth?"

"I just left him at Frenchman's Reef. He's on his way to meet with the Task Force Against Gang Activity and sent me with a message for you. He also wanted you to give me a briefing." My voice hadn't wavered, despite the serious bullshit I was laying down.

"*What*? Why the hell would he send you?"

I pulled the FAA fax from my breast pocket.

"Read this," I said.

His forehead tripled over with furrows. I hadn't noticed when we met before, but his eyes were hazel, rare in black men. He shook his head.

"Water landings are illegal outside of Charlotte Amalie and Christiansted Harbors." He sat down and handed me back the fax. "What's this about?"

"I'm assisting the FBI in their search for John Thedford and Mike Kuznewski, a.k.a. Stud Mahoney." I loved saying a.k.a. but managed not to grin.

"Why you? From what I've read, you're under suspicion for enough crimes to be locked away until you're a senior citizen."

"You're welcome to call Special Agent Booth." I pulled out the cell phone and handed it to him with Booth's name and number on the screen. "I'm not here to discuss anything sensitive, just to alert you that I'm headed to the BVI and that I'm allowed to make water landings around the USVI."

"That's fine, but has he alerted the Royal—"

"Duncan Mather's expecting me." I held out the letter addressed to Mather with the FBI seal on top. I held my breath.

"Dunk's a good man," White said. "Bit of a tight-ass, but hey, that's the Brits." He sat back in his chair. "So what can I tell you?"

"Booth's getting a rundown from the Task Force on the spike in gang activity and whether or not any of them could've been involved in the kidnappings, but I'm supposed to get your thoughts on other suspects." Sweat had started to drip down my back and I felt my forehead beading. "Are there any radical fringe pro-life or pro-choice elements?"

White rubbed his chin, shook his head.

"Things are different here than on the mainland. Not as many abortions, but nearly sixty percent of kids live in single-parent homes. Cheaper for women to have the kids, safer too I suppose, but the majority of fathers don't offer any support."

"So you think it might be a different angle?"

"There's a power struggle brewing that could result in a gang war. Not sure how that would be connected, though."

"What kind of power struggle?"

He rubbed his eyes. "We've had reports of a major international cartel making moves to overtake and consolidate criminal activities in the northern Caribbean."

Diego and Boom-Boom's comments came to mind.

"You said international. From where?"

"That we don't know, only that it's an organization with tentacles all over the world. Drugs, prostitution, human trafficking, arms, numbers—you name it. A conglomerate of sorts."

"So, what's any of that got to do with adoption?"

"I didn't say it did." He waved a hand. "There's no evidence tying these missing people to a turf war."

I didn't say anything, knew he had to have more.

"There are some quasi-religious kooks the adoption issue might have set off," White said. "But I don't see a connection to the actor."

"Ahh, you mean, like..." I closed my eyes for a second and rummaged in my brain for the name. "Reverend Hell No?"

"Hellfire." He smiled. "Yeah, he's a candidate. He's against anything he considers contradiction to God's will—"

"God as in the Christian God?"

"I'm not sure he can tell you exactly what God he's talking about. He's been known to quote the Bible, the Quran, the Talmud, Jah, and a lot of other stuff he makes up, on top of what he claims to be divine whispers 'from above.'

"Bottom line is he vehemently opposes man changing the course of what he considers destiny. Every now and then we send a plainclothes officer to one of his sermons. Last week he spoke out against abortion *and* adoption, said that if a woman gets pregnant, no matter how, there's no choice but to carry and raise the child. That's the lot you were given, he says, so you don't turn your nose up at it."

"And what does he say about people who do?"

"That they don't deserve to live."

Interesting.

"Hellfire's not his real name, I take it?"

"Nah, he was born in Christiansted to a missionary woman from Germany. Father was a native but never had much to do with him. His legal name is Randy Jaegle."

The door opened behind me. Officer Fingernails poked her beehive inside.

"Your conference call with the Task Force's starting. Do you and Agent Booth want to dial-in from here?"

My stomach clenched as if it were a sponge someone just squeezed. I wiped the sweat from my brow as White's eyes met mine.

"Shall we?" he said.

"Before you do that, have you made any connection between John Thedford and Stud Mahoney?"

"Aside from Adoption AID?"

I nodded. His face showed nothing.

"Not that I'm aware of," he said, "but we can ask Special Agent Booth."

I glanced at my ancient Rolex Submariner.

"I have to get to Tortola. Dunk's expecting me." I stood up fast and nearly caused my chair to fall over. "Give Booth my regards."

Lieutenant White had already turned on the speakerphone and was pressing numbers.

"Tell him yourself before you leave," he said.

He glanced up as the connection beeped. A number of voices could be heard on the speaker. I scooted for the door, saluted White, mouthed "I'll call you," and left.

Inside her glass box Fingernails was delicately peeling a banana, which took incredible coordination. I pulled at the handle but the exit door wouldn't open. I heard White's voice rise from the conference room.

"Do you mind?" I nodded toward the door. Fingernails slapped her hand down on the button like it was a game show and she had the winning answer. I scurried out and all but sprinted across Julian Jackson Drive toward the airport without a glance back. I dashed down the road into the airport's General Aviation driveway, managing to get honked at by a van overloaded with tourists destined for Bolongo Bay, according to the sign on the van's grill. Why hadn't Booth told Lieutenant White about Crystal's connection to Stud Mahoney? Was he hoarding clues for his own gain, as usual? Or was he telling him on the call now? I hoped I wouldn't need White's help any time soon, because he was sure to mention our meeting to Booth.

And why hadn't Crystal told me about her relationship with Stud?

I finally stopped to catch my breath and glance at my watch. I was ten minutes late to pick up Avery Rose.

25

When the cell phone buzzed on my hip, I figured it was Booth. Ready to press END, I saw the number on the screen and smiled.

"Tell me something good, Ray."

"We're refueling on Providenciales—be there in an hour and a half."

I paused outside the entrance of the General Aviation building and pumped my fist.

"Terrific! What plane did you charter?"

"Charter my ass, I borrowed it," Ray said. "Spottswell's Baron."

"The drug plane? I thought that thing was jinxed."

Ray shared details of their first leg, including Lenny's initial terror of flying, which he cured with a political rant. One debate and he already fancied himself the next Barack Obama.

I heard rustling in the background, an unmistakable voice.

"Who the fuck you talking to? That Buck? Give me the damn phone—"

By the noise that followed, Lenny must have ripped it out of Ray's hand.

"What kind of shit you getting me into, man? I got a constituency to fight for, a campaign to run—damn, Ray, you see the legs on that fine island honey? I may have to make Provo a sister city to Key West and have a junket here—"

"Lenny! I'm late to pick up a bona fide country music star!"

"You can keep all of them, Buck. I want me some adopted mothers, like Charlize Theron and Sandra Bullock. Not a bunch of boring-ass writers and Supreme Court justices, man. Ray promised me some primo honeys and maybe a politician, like Bill Clinton or John McCain. I may not agree with all their shit, but hey, I get them to endorse my ass, sky's the limit."

The grin on my face had people staring at me. It was so good to hear Lenny's voice.

"I'll leave you guys a list and a schedule at the concierge desk here at the Private Aviation terminal—some by plane, some by boat. You can split 'em up."

He handed the phone back to Ray.

"And if something goes wrong or you have any trouble at all or if you can't reach me, let's make the Beach Bar on St. John our rendezvous point every night."

"Trouble, what kind of—"

"I'm late, gotta go."

"Wait, Buck, before we left Key West we heard news reports that Islamic terrorists kidnapped Stud Mahoney." Ray went on to explain that Mahoney's captors were demanding the release of prisoners from Guantanamo. "I don't want to get caught in the middle of that."

"Don't worry, Ray. Got to run."

Good grief. I hung up, took a deep breath, and entered the Private Aviation building hoping Avery Rose's plane was late.

It wasn't. And those pictures of her on the Five Sixes taxis had not been airbrushed. If anything, they didn't do her justice. What is it about a tall woman in cut-off shorts and cowboy boots with long black hair and blue eyes and the world's biggest smile?

"You must be Buck Reilly," she said.

"Yes, ma'am, that's me."

She had to be 5'11" but with the boots came close to looking me in the eye.

She eyed me up and down. "You're cuter than I remembered from those pictures in the Wall Street Journal, King Charles."

Crap. But she winked at me.

"Call me Buck." She had three large suitcases. What everyone would need for a long weekend in the islands. "Is this everything?" I said. "We're in kind of a hurry."

When I reached for one of her bags she took hold of my forearm and gave it a subtle squeeze.

"I'm tired of flying, Buck. Don't bother with that right now."

"But—"

"I know you're busy and I don't want to throw a wrench in your schedule, but I had a concert in Dallas last night, flew home to Nashville, threw everything I own into these here bags, and barely made my flight to Miami, then to St. Thomas. I need a drink and to stretch my legs."

"I understand, but—"

She pressed two fingers against my lips and held them there, gently. Her smile was mesmerizing.

This is business, Buck. *Focus.*

She said she was going to grab lunch with her manager here on St. Thomas, then take the ferry to Tortola, where the Peter Island shuttle would pick them up at Customs. I wondered if she'd seen the Beast and was just being kind.

"But if you'd like to meet there for dinner later…"

"Sorry, Avery, but I'm swamped."

"I'll see you again, though, right?"

I couldn't decide if she was a major flirt, really sweet, or both.

"I'll be picking you up at Peter Island, unless you'd rather travel by speedboat—"

"No, no, Buck—I'll wait for you. I love seaplanes, saw yours out on the tarmac. Grumman Goose, right? I grew up in Fort Lauderdale and used to fly the Chalk's Mallards to Bimini to go fishing with my daddy."

My, oh my.

I left Avery Rose at the desk awaiting a car to take her downtown but carried with me the scent of whatever citrusy perfume, soap, or shampoo came off her as I walked out to the Beast. I was one-for-one with successful pick-ups, and since I'd assigned the rest to Captain Jeremy, Ray and

Lenny, I had more time on St. Thomas to search for clues. That was both good and bad—good because I wanted to turn over some rocks here, bad because it left me exposed to the wrath of Special Agent Booth and Lieutenant White.

A glance at the cell phone showed a missed call from Booth. The red light indicated I had a message. No reason to spoil the mood by listening to him rant. Instead I dialed Crystal.

"Buck, is everything okay?"

"So far so good. Met up with Avery Rose and we're squared away."

"Thank God," she said. "How will you get everyone from their airports to all the different resorts, then here to Jost Van Dyke? I feel so terrible putting all that on your back."

"Don't worry, under control." I explained that help was on the way.

"That's fantastic!" Her voice lifted. "We just might pull this off! Now, if they'd only find John...."

"I met with Lieutenant White, and the FBI has sent their Special Agent in Charge of South Florida and the Caribbean Basin down. I met with him, too. They're on the case, Crystal. They'll check into every possibility." I let my statement hang in the air.

She was quiet on the other end.

"Crystal?"

"I'm here."

"Anything new to share?"

"I got a phone call—it's got to be the same man who called John before. We had a bad connection but he threatened me, Buck. He said if I don't cancel the 'save the children' show, then I'd—and this where he lost me, but it sounded like he said I too would 'eat shit.'"

"Are you sure you heard him right?"

"I couldn't tell if it was an island accent, or what. It happened so fast."

I told her I had some things to look into on St. Thomas. She mentioned that rehearsals started tomorrow, then said goodbye and hung up.

I thought back over everything she'd said. It struck me that she sounded awfully calm for a woman whose husband was still missing, whose big charity event was still in trouble, whose relationship with a kidnapped actor was still (for all she knew) unknown, who'd just received a menacing threat by phone.

26

Reverend Hellfire's church was up in the mountains, near Boom-Boom's compound. I watched the taxi disappear and had serious doubts about how I'd get back to town.

The church was an old stone building that had to be at least a hundred years old. It had the look of former respectability run afoul, amplified by the overgrown tropical forest that pressed up against its walls. There was no sign out front, nor anything to proclaim the name of the Assembly. Unless you knew what it was, there was no way to identify the building as a house of worship.

Once at the rough-hewn front door, I did find a red cross painted on the wood—but it had three lines extending off the top, which reminded me of an old tattoo I'd seen on a paroled felon's hand between his thumb and index finger. He bragged about being a former gang member when he loaded my '72 Land Rover onto a flatbed truck when it broke down up on Sugarloaf Key a few months ago.

Could Reverend Hellfire have gang connections?

I tried the door but of course it was locked.

I couldn't see much through the dusty windows next to the door. I'd walk around back, but all the brush—

"Who the hell're you?"

I jumped at the sound of the voice that boomed from behind me. I turned and saw a man in shorts and a black t-shirt, medium height but solidly built with light mocha skin and the piercing gaze of a wolverine.

"Why you looking in my windows?"

And an accent I couldn't place.

"I was looking for Reverend Hellfire. Do you know where I could find him?"

"No need, he found you." His eyes eased off their squint. "Who're you and what do you want?" He made no move to approach me, shake my hand, or pass the collection plate.

"My name's Buck Reilly, and I… well, I'd like to learn something about you and your church."

He stared at me. I looked about as church-going as he did church-leading, so we were equally at a loss.

"I was just going in," he said. "Come on."

Hellfire brushed past me and used an ancient skeleton key to turn the lock. Once inside he flipped a switch and a few naked bulbs lit the rafters. A quick look around revealed no flowers, plaques, candles, or vessels filled with holy water. The only thing on the wall was another cross, painted red, again with three lines above it. He marched up the aisle—at least there were pews.

"Come on, boy, don't fall behind."

He stopped at the altar and turned to face me.

"So what do you want?"

"Like I said, I'd like to know about you and your church—"

He reached down inside his pulpit, and when he raised his arm he had a big revolver in his hand. A .357 magnum, if I had to guess.

"Don't bullshit me, Buck Reilly. You're connected to that syndicate moving in on the people here. That's what I hear."

"Hold on there, Reverend, I don't know who told you that, but—"

"Clarence Burke told me. Lives up the hill."

"Boom-Boom?"

"Said you were setting up an introduction for him—"

I held my hands up. "I'm just trying to help the Adoption AID folks find their missing people—"

He waved the gun in front of my chest.

"So you lied to Boom-Boom, not just me."

I took a step back. "I was trying to get to know you a little bit, thought you might be able to help—"

"Why would I help a liar and criminal?"

"I told Boom-Boom I was looking for John Thedford, the missing concert promoter." I paused for a beat. "I came here to get your views on the charity."

"Don't believe in it. A woman gets pregnant, she has to have the child," he said.

"What if she was raped?"

He lowered the gun. "Don't matter. God gave her a child, one way or another, and it be her job to take care of it."

"What if she had an abortion?"

He grunted. "Eye for an eye."

"So why not put the child up for adoption?"

"Same difference. That be your baby, your responsibility. You shirk what God blesses you with, you going to hell. Simple as that."

"So God thinks a mother or father should be executed—"

"Don't put words in my mouth, boy." The squint returned, which again reminded me of a wolverine. "And don't be trying to change God's will to meet your needs. You ain't shit, we all ain't shit, and God don't take no shit." His voice had a slight Germanic accent with an island finish.

Crystal said today's caller told her she'd 'eat shit' if she didn't cancel the show.

"Quite the message. And what happens to people who don't abide by that philosophy?"

"They go to hell, son. See, people today, most of 'em are selfish, self-centered, lazy. I don't care what religion they practice, if any, 'cause they all hypocrites. That whole idea of forgiveness is a license to steal, far as I can tell. Ain't nobody want to face the truth, 'cause truth's a bitch. You ignore God, you get what's coming, plain and simple."

Hellfire stood with one fist on his hip, the gun to his side, stared me straight in the eye, and spoke with absolute confidence. He never once raised his voice, but it held an authority that commanded you to listen, regardless of your opinion.

"Hellfire believes in no grace or forgiveness, that's what you're saying?"

"You catch on quick."

"So is that what happened to John Thedford?"

He took a step toward me.

"Get your ass outta here, boy. You're going to hell too, I can already tell. You got that look about you. And whether you're mixed up with that bunch or the damned mobsters, you're not welcome here."

He bumped his chest into me and pushed me back. He was coming again, so I took a backward step down the aisle. I didn't want to fight the man. He bumped me again.

"Did you call Crystal Thedford today?" I said.

"Get the hell outta here 'fore I call my boys." He lifted the gun.

I back-stepped my way down the aisle and pushed the door open with my rear end.

"Does God tell you to take his word into your hands, Reverend?"

"He's telling me to shoot your ass right now if you don't get off my property!" His lips were peeled back, showing stubby teeth. He pointed the massive revolver at my head. "Get out!

The door slammed in my face and I heard the metallic sound of the ancient lock click. So much for asking him to call me a taxi.

I started down the road, breathing deep to slow my heart rate and process his statements. Boom-Boom obviously told Hellfire about me. Could Boom-Boom be the kidnapper? Could the kidnappings be his way of gaining leverage in whatever this crime war was that's brewing? Hellfire mentioned his boys, too, and I wondered whether one drove a red Cigarette boat.

The shore wasn't visible from the road, but I made a mental note to cruise the coast from the sky to see what lay around the Church of Hellfire. He might not call it that, but the shoe damn sure fit.

27

AFTER A TWENTY-MINUTE HIKE, I SAW A BLACK SUV COMING UP THE ROAD. It flew past, braked, did a quick U-turn, pulled up alongside me and slowed to my pace—all within a few seconds.

The tinted passenger window lowered and a massive black bald head peered out.

"You looking for me?" Boom-Boom. "Ready to broker the deal?"

"Just having some spiritual time."

He grinned. "Hellfire's place?"

The SUV came to a stop and Boom-Boom popped the door open. Of course there was a shotgun between his legs. I got in the empty back seat, and the same driver as last night stepped on the gas.

"How do you know Hellfire?" I asked.

The deep laugh I recalled through the stupor from last night made my toes curl.

"You ask a lotta questions, Reilly. But to demonstrate the extent of my network to you and your people, I got some information for you."

"What—"

"Not so fast, brudda, we still need to arrange that sit-down. The *quid* for the *pro quo*." He laughed. "You won't be sorry, man. We can do this together a lot easier and cleanly than if things gets hostile."

The driver turned onto the road toward Frenchman's Reef.

"I'm headed to the airport, if you guys wouldn't mind—"

"Let's go meet your people, Reilly. Right now."

"I told you, I'm working with Adoption AID." Deep breath. "Did someone grab Thedford and Mahoney as leverage for future negotiations?"

"That why you went to see Hellfire?"

The cell phone rang in my pocket.

I pulled it out: YOUR MASTER. Shit.

"Go ahead and answer it," Boom-Boom said. "Tell him I'm ready to meet, here and now." He thumped the butt of the shotgun on the floor.

My mouth was dry. The phone started to ring again and I hit the green button.

"I can't talk right now—"

"Impersonating an officer—"

I clamped my hand over the earpiece so Boom-Boom wouldn't hear Booth.

"I said I can't talk."

"White's threatening to have you arrested." He laughed. "I'm calling, Reilly, to tell you that your lady friend's now my top suspect in the disappearance of her husband."

"Are you crazy? Just because of Stud—"

"Five million dollar life insurance policy says I'm not, hotshot. Keep your eyes open and think with your big head, not the little one." He paused to make sure I appreciated his devastating wit. "I'm still assessing how this ties to Mahoney." He hung up.

Boom-Boom turned back to look at me.

"Heard something about five million dollars, Reilly. I can get you more."

I swallowed, hard. "I hear you. Why don't you tell me what you've learned? I already told you we'd work something out."

"I want a guarantee," he said. "Insurance."

My mind shot back to Booth's call. A five million dollar insurance policy? On John Thedford?

"I'll be at that concert," Boom-Boom said. "That'll put all those celebrities right in the middle, you know, in case our talks don't *go* so good."

"You help me find Thedford and Mahoney," I said, "and good things will happen."

Big yellow teeth appeared, but his eyes were slits.

"Okay, here's the skinny. Brudda from Tortola picked up the dude you looking for on St. John, few nights back."

"John Thedford? How'd he pick him up?"

"Boy got a bad ass red speed boat. Cigarette with trip 300's."

"Where'd they—"

"He's a boat for hire, used him plenty times myself. Said he dropped the dude, who was all fucked up, at another boat out in the middle of the sound. Got paid on the spot in cash, but he don't know shit. People approached him at the bar on Soper's to make the run. Just business. Said he didn't know the dudes."

We were down in Charlotte Amalie now, driving up through the hordes making their way toward the cruise ships, when I smelled something not unlike burning rope. Boom-Boom had lit a monster blunt. He passed it to the driver, who pulled on it with Olympic strength, then tried to hand it back to me.

"Not today, fellas," I said.

"Suit yourself, but you owe me now," Boom-Boom said. "I want that meeting."

"Fine, but I need to know where Thedford is, Mahoney too. Otherwise it's just gossip. Did the same guy pick up Mahoney on Peter Island?"

"'Brudda with the boat didn't know shit about no actor getting kidnapped."

"So what's his name, the guy with the red boat?"

Boom-Boom turned back to look over his shoulder, smoke streaming from his nostrils.

"That's it for now. You set the meeting or I'll be at the show this weekend, don't forget it." He stared into my eyes. "And if things don't go good, there'll be a whole bunch of other famous people in trouble."

Boom-Boom gave me a long, hard stare. I held his eyes but had my hand on the door handle. I'd jump if that shotgun budged off his crotch. By the time he turned back around we were at the General Aviation building.

I got out. Fast.

"This weekend, Reilly. I'm counting on that meeting. And if things get ugly around here with your boss, I'll find you first."

28

WITH THE PRE-FLIGHT CHECK COMPLETE, I REREAD THE LETTER FROM THE FAA for the umpteenth time. Had they transmitted this to all the local authorities? Would Commissioner Duncan Mather of the Royal Virgin Islands Police Force really allow me to make a water landing in the BVI?

Only one way to find out. I fired up the Beast's twin Pratt & Whitney Wasp Jr. engines. The plane shook with the 900 horsepower from the twin radial engines. The sound and vibration stirred me to the core. Flying antique planes came with a lot of headaches, not the least of which was obtaining parts, but a thrill pulsed through me every time I cranked the Beast up. Seaplanes today were much more efficient and often faster, but they were all modified to use floats. Old Grumman amphibians like the Goose were called flying boats because their fuselages were actual hulls that sliced through the water at up to a hundred miles an hour before the physics of flight launched them aloft. It was a much more intimate relationship with the water, which I loved.

I glanced at my phone and found the same texts from Ray and Crystal: Call me.

It took one-third of the 7,000-foot runaway before the Beast was airborne and we lit out over Brewer's Bay. With my cell phone connected to my headset, I called Ray first.

He went off about the celebrities he'd met. I banked to the northeast and flew at an angle so I could view St. Thomas's mountainous region to try and find Boom-Boom's place and Hellfire's church. Ray had nothing else for me, so we signed off.

I cracked my knuckles and dialed Crystal's number.

"There you are," she said. "Have people started arriving—NO, put that over there!" Her voice boomed, but away from the phone.

It sounded like pandemonium in the background. When I told her Avery Rose declined a ride, she asked me to retrieve her from Peter Island and bring her to Jost for rehearsal. She also repeated Ray's news about demands made by Stud's kidnappers. I had trouble concentrating—the five million dollar insurance policy and her silence about her relationship with Stud were bugging the hell out of me.

There weren't many dwellings in the mountainous area, but I flew with purpose until I found the old stone house where I'd been delivered to Boom-Boom. It was bigger than I thought, with two wings—a fortress surrounded by sheer rock cliffs and dense jungle. Several people emerged from the woods to peer up at me. The black SUV was parked next to the house.

I banked to follow the road down and spotted Hellfire's church. Behind the woods at its back, I was surprised to see three other buildings.

Could John or Stud be in one of them?

Below all that was a path that led down to a dock. No boat, but direct water access. Boom-Boom said the red Cigarette rendezvoused with another boat in Pillsbury Sound to transfer Thedford. Could that boat have come to this dock?

I vectored west and dialed Harry.

"I thought you'd forgotten about me," he said.

"Sorry, Harry. I guess it seems like I only call you when I need information these days. But with those, ah, sixty three companies—"

"Back to sixty four. In fact, your being in the Virgin Islands inspired me to acquire a telecommunications firm based in Roadtown, Tortola. And I much prefer your calling for knowledge than money, dear boy. But we are overdue for a social evening."

Got to love Harry.

"So when I called you a few days ago, I know it was a really broad question, but did you have any luck?"

He chuckled. "Yes, well, I did query Percy's accuracy in noting your inquiry. What he relayed to me was that you wanted to know if there were any radical groups so opposed to the adoption of children that they'd go to any length to prevent its becoming more commonplace."

"I'd say Percy nailed it."

"I was able to research through G&M, our security consultancy in Manhattan, and they did produce a list of rather disjointed possibilities, several pages in fact—"

"Tell you what, Harry, I'm in a major hurry here, so why don't I mention a few things and see if any match what your group discovered?"

"Spot on," he said. "Whenever you're ready."

"The obvious ones would be radical pro-life or pro-choice elements," I said. "But rogue abortion clinic bombers and in-your-face reproductive rights groups? Abduction, blackmail, and torture don't seem to fit their platitudes."

The sound of paper rustling came through the phone.

"Hmmm...it says here...yes, G&M concurs with that line of thought."

"So another one I've come across is a religious zealot who calls himself Reverend Hellfire. Anything on him?"

A brief rustling this time. "I'm afraid not, but if he's a lone wolf, it's unlikely we would have found him."

"How about international opposition. Anything on that?"

More crackling of pages. "You can find opposition to nearly anything, but groups targeting adoption don't come up specifically. However, when you factor in religion—"

"Stud Mahoney's kidnappers have demanded that prisoners be released from Guantanamo," I said.

"So there you are. An obvious connection. Muslims oppose adoption."

"Could it really be Muslim extremists? They get blamed for everything these days." I sighed. "Anything else on the international front?"

"You also have the overseas export of children, a.k.a. adoption, recently virtually outlawed by the Russians. But unfortunately the picture becomes quite muddled when you examine the broader perspective."

With Tortola now close, I asked Harry to keep digging and promised to call again later.

Muddled indeed.

29

THE FLIGHT FROM ST. THOMAS TO BEEF ISLAND, THE SPIT OF LAND connected to Tortola where the international airport is situated, would be over in moments, but I had a few things I wanted to check first. At an altitude of 3,000 feet I could see every island in the BVI, big and small. The sky was partially clear, but the large cumulous clouds that had been building all day rocked the Beast with serious turbulence.

Somewhere down there were John Thedford and Stud Mahoney. I hoped they were still alive—and that I'd find them before it was too late. Or before Boom-Boom's threats to bring trouble to Adoption AID came true, which amounted to the same thing.

As Tortola grew larger ahead of me I added flaps and pointed the nose of the Beast toward its west end. The harbor there was where the ferries docked and boaters passed through Customs, but across the harbor was an island officially named Frenchman's Cay but known as Soper's Hole.

I buzzed over Soper's and focused on the boatyard and marina where Pusser's and the Blue Parrot bars were located. I saw several large catamarans but no red-hulled Cigarette. I circled south, over Pillsbury Sound, and scanned the harbor again—nothing aside from some damn nice cruising ships.

With Tortola ATC barking in my headset, I continued north over Cane Garden Bay. I glanced over at Jost Van Dyke to the west, noting the concentration of white dots—boats in Great Harbor where Foxy's was located—and vectored east around Guana Island, Great Camanoe, and Scrub Islands, adding flaps as we circled.

I straightened out toward Terrance B. Lettsome Airport and touched a third of the way down the 4,500-foot runway. I taxied along toward the FBO, where I was directed to park the Beast on the tarmac, just before the private aviation building.

The trip had been too short to process all the beauty I'd observed along the way: the brilliant turquoise water, rugged rock outcroppings, white strips of sand, and red terracotta roofs dotting green hills. Nothing replaced the feeling I always got when soaring above the islands, all of which I knew by name. It imbued my soul with a sense of peace that calmed the fears I had in coming here.

With my flight bag over my shoulder and the letters from the FAA and FBI in my breast pocket, I was as ready as I'd ever be to go through Customs. Not just because it was a mind-numbing process, island time being especially prevalent where bureaucrats reign, but because it was Tortola.

The line was short and it only took a few minutes before I handed over my passport to the blue-uniformed agent who looked as if he'd fall asleep if left alone for more than a minute. He glanced at the passport, then my face, then back to the passport photo. Okay, so I hadn't updated it post-e-Antiquity, but it's still me.

His fingers dragged over the keyboard. He stopped typing, glanced up at me again, looked over his left shoulder toward a closed door.

"Hang on a minute," he said.

I watched him walk to the door, knock, glance back at me, then enter the room. My gut twisted tighter with each moment that passed. The customs agent came back out followed by a woman with two gold stripes on her epaulets and a scowl on her face. A moment later, the door that led outside to the street opened up and two armed police officers entered the room—headed straight for me, of course.

I swallowed.

"Charles Reilly, III?" the woman said.

I nodded.

"Gentlemen, please escort Mr. Reilly to holding room one."

The policemen, who now stood on both sides of me, each took one of my elbows and turned me toward another door.

"What's this about?" I said.

No response.

"Commissioner Mather's expecting me," I said.

Still nothing.

The door opened to a short hallway. A painted number 1 adorned a gray metal door with a massive lock and steel bolt fixed on the outside.

Crap.

Was it because of the seedy appearance of the Beast? All of the drug and weapons smuggling in the area? Or because law enforcement tends to be paranoid about amphibious aircraft?

"Please take a seat," one of the policemen said as the other officer closed the door. The sound of the locks being secured didn't help my stomach. "Empty your pockets, please."

"What's the problem, officer?"

He gave me an impatient nod and I began to empty my pockets. Wallet, Chapstick, wad of paper with the schedule for Ray and Lenny's pick-ups. I felt the phone in my breast pocket. Just then, the policeman's cell phone rang. He stepped back to answer it and turned away for a moment.

I pulled out my phone, scrolled down the saved numbers, found the one I wanted, and hit SEND. I placed the phone on the table and covered the screen with the wad of paper.

The officer turned back around.

"Welcome back to Tortola, Mr. Reilly." His British accent was anything but welcoming. "There's a warrant out for your arrest."

"For what?"

"The murder of Stanley Ober."

Shit. Crap.

"I was released—the judge threw the case out—"

"You were ordered to remain on-island, but you disappeared."

"That's crazy! My attorney—he said I was free to go."

Officer Robertson, according to the gold nametag, held up his right palm.

"Save it for the magistrate, Mr. Reilly."

I slumped into the metal chair, which was bolted to the floor.

Dammit!

Officer Robertson scooped up my possessions and knocked twice on the door, which opened slowly. He exited without a glance back.

I slumped forward and took my face in both hands. When your only hope is T. Edward Booth, you know you're in deep shit.

Next Time Skip the Reunion

30

After being handcuffed and taken by van over the bridge to Tortola and through the hills into Road Town, I was back in the same cell where I'd spent a month nearly four years ago. Time hadn't been kind to either of us: the 8' x 10' cut stone chamber smelled even worse of piss, vomit, and feces than I remembered. The cell walls were scarred with more graffiti, the toilet in the corner was plugged up with more of the previous occupants' detritus, and the flicker of the lone fluorescent bulb was already driving me crazy. As for me, last time I was here I was still wealthy, still married, still at the helm of e-Antiquity, and had a flock of attorneys fighting to gain my release.

I lay back on the hard bunk and looked up at the window, a foot-square slash in the two-foot-deep wall. At least I could tell it was still daytime. Avery Rose would expect me at Peter Island, and Crystal Thedford would await us at Jost. Good luck to them, since I was at the mercy of the local court system. Customs processing at the airport might be on island time, but due process here was glacial.

Footsteps sounded outside my door, followed by the clank of the locks. In stepped none other than Officer Bramble, fists on his hips. His belly was bigger but he seemed shorter than I remembered.

"King Charles, back where you belong."

"The judge threw this out—"

"Shut up. When I saw you on TV in St. Thomas, I reissued the warrant and reserved your room here."

"That murder charge was bullshit. I'm here to help the Adoption AID people with their show on Jost Van Dyke."

"Ha!" Bramble cried. "Assuaging years of guilt with charity work? That's funny, Reilly, almost Dickensian. Now you're just another broken-down has-been cluttering up my islands with get-rich-*again* schemes. I'm so sick of you people. Americans and Down-islanders make a fortune hauling drugs while arms merchants peddle stolen guns to thugs and gangs that litter our shores with innocent victims. Pathetic." He paused, the sneer on his face as vitriolic as I remembered it, if not worse. "And now you're a charter pilot *and* salvage hunter! Here to help a charity try to change the world—"

"What are you doing to find John Thedford? Why are you wasting your time with me when you should have every available man out looking for him?"

"We're looking for the actor—"

"And never mind about Thedford?"

Bramble held his stare, but there was something different in his eyes. A flicker.

"I want to call my attorney!"

He laughed. "You got the money for an attorney?"

"What am I being charged with!"

"Now who be da King, huh?"

"I did nothing but help Stanley Ober—"

"I don't give a rat's ass about him."

"The Adoption AID people need me—"

"They're the reason you're here." He reached for the door.

I sprang up from the bed as he slammed the door shut.

"What am I being charged with, you miserable piece of shit!"

I paced the cell so fast I was practically running in circles, jumped over the toilet, screamed at the top of my lungs. I knew none of it was any use, but I was boiling mad and seething with frustration—jailed, kept from doing my job, no resources to fight back.

Finally I slumped against the back wall, where I slid down to the concrete floor. I sat with my head low and listened to the sounds that came through the window. I heard laughter and imagined Bramble leaving the building for home, thoroughly pleased with himself. I sat there for what seemed an hour.

"Charles Reilly, you in there?"

I jumped up. "Who is that out there?"

"Zachary," the voice said. "Zachary Ober."

Zachary *Ober*? What the—

"My father was Stanley Ober, the man who sold you the fake information about the Indian treasure."

Oh sweet Jesus, now what?

31

"I NEED YOU TO HELP ME FIND THE TREASURE," ZACHARY SAID.

"There was no treasure. Your father sold me a bogus map then got himself killed, which is—" I started to say it was why I was back here in jail, but Bramble said I had Adoption AID to thank. Why?

"My father was an immoral man," Zachary said. "He said if you sell something once, you'll eat a fine meal, but if you sell things again and again, you'll eat abundantly." He sighed. "I'm sorry for what you've been through, King Charles—"

"Forget King Charles, call me Buck if you don't mind. I'm broke, stuck in a piss-coated jail cell, and nobody even knows where I am. I'm more like a jester than a king."

I laid my head against the cold stone below the window.

"We can help each other—"

"How can you help me? Are you a magistrate?"

"I drive an ambulance, but I—"

For some reason his answer set me to laughing. I slid back down the wall again and sat on the floor.

"I'd pretend to be sick so you could rescue me, but Bramble wouldn't give a shit."

"When I heard on the scanner you were arrested, I came right over. It's a sign, I'm certain. You can help me find the treasure."

"Not if I can't get out of here. And I told you, there *is* no treasure."

He was quiet for a moment. I wondered if he believed me.

"Why'd you get arrested, anyway?"

"That's a damned good question, Zach."

Silence followed. Street noises, cackling birds, bleating goats, distant voices filled the void. I jumped up.

"You still out there, Zachary?"

"I'm here, um, Buck."

"Listen, if you make a call for me, we can talk. Will you do that?"

He was quiet so long I thought he'd left.

"Buck, I believe you could help—"

"You get me out of here and I'll listen to whatever you want to say. I can't promise I'll be able to help you, but I promise I'll try. Okay?"

He agreed and I repeated the number I now had memorized. He didn't have a pen, but after three tries he could repeat it back to me. He promised to call when he got home.

"I'll be waiting for you when you're released," he said.

"Last time I was here for a month, so don't hold your breath."

A crack of thunder was followed by what sounded like a torrent of rain. Zach must have fled, as he no longer responded to my calls. Along with the rain came the fetid smell of manure. The goats I'd heard earlier grazed in a field behind the jail, and I remembered from my last stay that every time it rained the stench of goat feces lasted until the heat of the sun evaporated the moisture.

Night brought vivid dreams that woke me in a sweat, grateful I couldn't remember them. The sound of the rain had ceased, the smell of dung worse than I remembered. In fact, it smelled as if the goats had been throwing up booze.

I rolled over and realized why.

A drunk was passed out on the floor near my bunk. I couldn't believe I hadn't waked up when they threw him in here. A pool of vomit circled his head, and had I not heard him breathing heavily I might have thought he'd drowned in his puke. He faced away from me, so all I could see were rows of untended dreadlocks spread out like snakes from Medusa's scalp.

I curled back into a ball, closed my eyes, and next thing I knew it was dawn.

When I glanced at the floor, the drunk was gone—

"Good morning," a voice said.

I leapt to my feet to find the man who'd been passed out on the floor standing by the window.

"Sorry if I woke you," he said. "I been trying to wash this stench off me."

Nothing like a toilet bath to start your day.

"You was sawing same major lumber, man," he said.

I looked at my new roommate's face and did a double take.

"Hey, aren't you—"

"Diego sends his love."

It was Brass Knuckles, the Rasta who'd cold-cocked me at the Beach Bar on St. John.

"I'm here to deliver some information. Diego heard you was here because Bramble be up to some tricks."

I crossed my arms.

"We're at war." His voice dropped. "That big international syndicate moved in and killed some of our men…." His chest heaved once and he caught his breath. "Blew up Diego's boat, fired shots at his house from a helicopter, stole his car."

"When did this happen? I was just in St. Thomas—"

"Yesterday afternoon." He slumped over. "They grabbed Spice… my friend."

Dreadlocks?

"The guy with you at the Beach Bar when we, ah, met?" He nodded. "He okay?"

"No idea, but hope so," he said.

"You say it's an international syndicate?" I thought back to my conversations with Lieutenant White and then Harry. "From where?"

"We don't know, but they big—went after everyt'ing all at once. Arms trade, bitches, gambling, drugs—"

"Boom-Boom?"

His brow furrowed. "Yeah, him too, same shit—shot up his compound, took some of his men. Pretty fucked up."

Silence followed as his eyes grew distant.

"So why'd you come to see me?"

"Diego needs you to get him out. He's stuck in Fish Bay. The syndicate has people at the ferry and the marinas that'll shoot him dead. He needs you to fly into the bay by his house and pick him up."

I stared at him. "I can't exactly walk out of here."

"You'll get out."

I bit the side of my lip.

"Have you heard anything about John Thedford?"

His expression compressed into a thoughtful scowl, then he shrugged.

"Could be, or maybe that actor. We heard someone be holed up in a private villa on Guana Island."

"There's a hundred-grand reward for Mahoney," I said. "If you have news on him go get him yourself."

"Call the cops? Nah, man, not me—and Diego ain't calling no police neither. But we'll take half the reward money if you collect. After you fly us outta here."

I ran my fingers through my hair and rubbed my eyes.

"I don't care so much about the actor, I'm looking for—"

"That red Cigarette boat, right?" he said.

I sat up straight. "How'd you know?"

"You texted Diego."

"What about it?" I said.

"You gonna pick Diego up at Fish Bay?"

"If you get me what I need."

What I didn't need was to be smack in the middle of an organized-crime war.

He shrugged. "Baldwin outta Marina Cay. Keeps that sweet red boat over on Scrub Island. Too pussy to work for us, but he do this and that for others."

Damn! I'd flown right over Marina Cay and Scrub Island on my approach to the airport.

"Baldwin, huh. You know his first name?"

"Nah, mon, but everyone call him Baldy. He run the marina there. Got that boat from a DEA auction on St. Thomas couple of years ago." He laughed. "Won't be long 'fore they take it back, soon as Baldy get busted running shit around the islands. But we heard he be working for this new syndicate, so he might be dead 'fore you get to him."

I let this sink in for a minute.

"Any chance Baldy might have taken Thedford to Guana Island?"

"Could be." Brass Knuckles nodded vigorously, which made his dreadlocks jump. "So when you get out, Diego be waiting. So make it soon."

My under the radar network was under attack and falling apart, but at least it had delivered some information.

"Now I got to get outta here."

"Thanks for the visit."

He walked straight to the door and beat on it, hard, with the palm of his hand. He yelled something unintelligible and beat on it again. The door opened a minute later, and the guard looked in and smiled. They exchanged garbled conversation, then Brass Knuckles walked out without looking back.

I jumped up and tried the same thing, beat on the door hard and yelled, but nobody came.

32

My ass grew numb sitting on the cot, so I did an isometric-aerobic workout that soaked my already soggy shirt with more sweat—no climate-controlled comforts here in the jail. As the hours passed I felt myself descending into the mental numbness that comes with incarceration. Not that I had much experience with anything beyond the month I spent in this cell four years ago, maybe a few days here and there, but it was the same every time. After the initial anger and outrage fade, you become sluggish and enter a semi-hibernated state to survive the anguish of confinement.

I didn't know how my former partner had handled nearly two years in jail, so far. I'd be a basket case. Last I heard Jack had another year to go before he'd be eligible for parole. My brother and I had helped support the Dodson family while he was locked up. Jack could have dragged me down with him—and my brother, too, since he inherited the wealth my parents gained when I warned them to sell our stock. Jack wasn't the only one who hid assets as e-Antiquity free-fell into insolvency, but the cash he stashed was a lot more obvious than the maps and background information I had spirited away.

I heard a noise—the slide of the bolt and keys jingling in the lock. The heavy door slid open. Three men stood outside: a guard, Officer Bramble, and another man who was vaguely familiar—the court magistrate who released me last time.

"Charles Reilly, III," the magistrate said. "Do you remember me?"

"Of course. You released me last time because you knew I was innocent—"

"Hardly innocent," Bramble said.

"Why have I been arrested?"

"There's a crime war going on in your islands, Reilly," Bramble said. "I assumed you were part of it."

"I'm here to help an Adoption AID charity concert on Jost Van Dyke. The head of the nonprofit, John Thedford, disappeared several days ago—"

"Also in the USVI," Bramble said.

"My sources say he was taken by a man named Baldwin from Marina Cay aboard a red Cigarette boat. Have you heard that, Bramble? Or do you give a shit?"

Bramble took a step toward me. The magistrate stepped between us.

"That's enough of that!" This to Bramble, who looked ready to cold-cock me.

"Marina Cay's in the BVI, in case you forgot," I said. "And Stud Mahoney was last seen on Peter Island, also in the BVI—"

"*Our* investigation," Bramble said, "shows him leaving on a private boat with his lady friend after they checked in—"

"A red Cigarette, by any chance?"

Bramble's eyes narrowed as he rubbed his chin between his index finger and thumb.

"And what do you mean, *your sources*? You got a license to be investigating here in the British Virgin Islands? Or are you connected to one of the gangs in the USVI?"

"Or the FBI?" the magistrate said.

Had Booth interceded on my behalf? The call I made from the airport when the officer confiscated my possessions may have connected after all. Or had Zach Ober reached him?

The magistrate stared at me, waiting for an answer.

"What am I being charged with? Or is this just another case of police brutality—"

"You're a *common* criminal, Reilly!" Bramble said.

The magistrate literally shoved him aside.

"There's no charge, Mr. Reilly. You were detained due to an outstanding bench warrant dating back to when you departed Tortola without appearing in my court for official release."

"That's it? You kept me in here overnight, interrupted my... investigation—"

"You're no law enforcement officer!" Bramble's face was so red I thought his head might explode. "You're a phony and a punk!"

"Enough!" the magistrate said.

"I'm walking out of here right now," I said. "You've held me without cause—"

"Not until you pay the fine!" Bramble said. "That bench warrant's been outstanding for three years!"

Damn. I didn't have much cash, but...

"My FBI credit card is in my wallet," I said. "Feel free to charge the fine."

Bramble's face turned chalky mocha. The magistrate held both hands up, palms out.

"The court waives the fine, Mr. Reilly, and please accept our apologies for the treatment you've received here."

I held my breath. The moment was so good I almost didn't want it to end, but I needed to get out of here before I went too far.

Then I remembered *why* I was here.

"I came to Tortola to meet with Commissioner Duncan Mather—"

"What for?" Bramble said.

"That's enough, Kenneth!" The magistrate turned to me "Was he expecting you?"

"As a matter of fact, he was. If you can retrieve my personal effects, you'll see a letter from the United States Federal Aviation Administration providing me with authority to land my plane in USVI waters. There's another letter, from the Special Agent in Charge of the South East Region and Caribbean Basin for the FBI to Commissioner Mather, respectfully requesting the same consideration be provided by the British Virgin—"

"Absolutely not!"

"Officer Bramble!"

I took in a deep breath and let it out slowly, looking from Bramble to the magistrate.

"This request is to assist both the U.S. and Royal Virgin Islands Police Force efforts to locate missing and kidnapped United States citizens," I said in the lowest voice I could muster.

Piling it deep now, I had to bite my lip to keep a straight face.

"I will speak with Commissioner Mather myself, Mr. Reilly," the magistrate said. "You can assume your request will be granted—"

"Aboard that piece of junk airplane?"

"Not another word from you, Officer Bramble. Last warning. Mr. Reilly, is there a number where Commissioner Mather can reach you if he has any questions?"

I gave him my number, and just to turn the knife one more time recited Booth's number too. The magistrate led the three of us out of the cell, Bramble shaking his head but finally silent.

What had been one of the worst, most frustrating nights of my life had turned into one of the most enjoyable mornings in recent history. Not that I had time to gloat. I collected my possessions, got my passport stamped, and allowed the magistrate to make copies of the two letters, which he then scrambled off to present to Commissioner Mather after apologizing yet again.

I tried to bolt for the door, but Bramble blocked my path.

"A lot of people getting hurt in your islands. All the trash getting swept up."

After the battle we'd just had in the cell, his smile stopped me in my tracks.

"That make you happy?" I said.

He bit his lip as if he was trying to hold something back—then winked at me and sauntered away. Whistling.

What the hell?

33

THE HEAT HIT ME IN THE FACE LIKE A SUCKER PUNCH. I SQUINTED INTO THE sun and felt like I was in a kiln. Outside, policemen were coming and going, chit-chatting and loitering, none in a hurry. I doubted they felt any urgency to find Stud Mahoney and assumed John Thedford wasn't on their radar at all.

My cell phone came to life when I thumbed the power button.

Ten missed calls. Crystal had called six times, Ray—

"Mr. Reilly, can I speak with you?"

I recognized Zachary Ober's voice, but had yet to seen him in person. He was dressed in a uniform, had a gold tooth in the center of his smile, and tight-cropped hair. Tall and lanky, he reminded me of Kobe Bryant. I spotted his ambulance at the end of the lot.

"Did you wait out here all night? And remember, it's Buck."

"I called that number you gave me, okay? Agent Booth never answered."

"Then how—"

"I called Michael Bush, the magistrate who was just here. He's my girlfriend's uncle."

"You got me out?"

"I just let him know you were here and that you were either with the FBI or helping them." He winked and the gold tooth caught the sunlight.

Wow.

"Thanks, Zach. Can you give me a ride to the airport in that thing so we can talk? I'm way behind schedule."

"Sorry, Buck, no rides allowed. I could lose my job." He pursed his lips, crossed his arms. "I know my father ripped you off. He was a thief. I'm sorry. But he wasn't totally lying. There *is* a treasure out there—"

"Zach…how can I put this? I'm really not equipped to mount a salvage operation these days. I told you, I'm broke. Bankrupt. e-Antiquity is history, okay? Again, I'm grateful for your help, but I need to get caught up on this Adoption AID concert—"

"The one on Jost Van Dyke?"

"Yeah, you know about it?"

"I'll be there working, in case anyone gets injured," he said. "But I'm kind of interested in the subject anyway."

"Why's that?"

"I was adopted by my father. His sister was my mother, but she never cared for me, so he raised me." Zach's voice dropped. "He may have been an immoral man when it came to being a thief, but he was a caring man too."

His words tugged at my heart.

"I need to get to my plane, Zach, so let's walk out to the road and I'll try to hail a taxi—but keep talking."

"Long time ago, in the early 1800's, there was a big riot on-island when a rich plantation owner killed one of his slaves—man named Prosper."

I looked both ways up and down the road. Deserted.

"Why'd he kill him?"

"They said it was because he let a mango fall off the tree and hit the ground. Word spread through the West Indies and slaves began to rebel, give their owners big trouble, so the court did what had never been done before. They convicted the plantation owner—hung Arthur Hodge right over there behind where the jail stands today."

Zach was pointing over to the field where the goats grazed in tall grass. Something about the story stirred a memory, but I couldn't nail it.

"It was a big step in the move toward emancipation here in the islands," he said.

"Convicting a plantation owner for killing a man over a fallen mango?"

"That was the official story." The gold tooth again glistened. "Prosper was a distant relative of ours, great-great-great uncle. One of his women, well, down the road she told the truth behind the murder."

If I hadn't already been hooked, the mischief on his face would have done it.

"Mr. Hodge's plantation made rum, and he was a rich, rich man. He was also a miser who didn't pay his expenses, didn't trust nobody, and treated his slaves real bad—had as many babies by the females as he could because he was too cheap to pay for slave labor. Everybody hated him." He smiled again. "Old Hodge hid all his gold in rum barrels, and the story was that Prosper found the gold and stole it."

My old treasure-hunting instincts fired right up. This was an entirely different story from the one Zach's dad had told me when he sold me the map. And this kid oozed sincerity.

"Keep going," I said.

"So Prosper, before he got killed, drew a map showing where he buried that gold on the old plantation estate."

I held a palm up. "Look, I don't have the money to buy any more maps."

"I'm not selling any, Buck."

His smile was either the best con I'd ever seen or the real deal.

"Story goes that the old barrels—"

"*Barrels*?"

"—were filled to the top with gold coins." He paused. "Right, three fifty-gallon barrels."

My mouth hung open while I tried to do the math—

"The gold's in a place where I can't get to it, but you, with your reputation as an international archeologist—"

"That kills it," I said. "The only doors my reputation open these days are jail cells, trust me."

"But you could advise me on how to get onto the Hodge estate!"

Hodge. That's what I recognized.

"Do you know a guy named Valentine Hodge?" I said. "Old guy, drives a taxi?"

"Sure, I know him." His face had turned serious. "He's a relative of Arthur Hodge, the plantation owner."

"Valentine's black—"

I stopped, remembering what Zach had said about Arthur Hodge and his female slaves.

Zach watched the penny drop, then said, "He's a distant relative."

Valentine was an old friend from back when I spent time down here on e-Antiquity business. He used to drive me everywhere. Even better, Zach had his phone number. When I called he said he'd be happy to come pick me up. When I said I'd been at the jail, he laughed and said he wasn't surprised. Nothing like old friends to keep you humble.

"Listen, Zach, your story's intriguing," I said. "Maybe when I'm done helping with the concert we can talk more about it, but I'm up to my neck in this situation right now."

His eyes dropped to the pavement.

"The concert promoter disappeared—last seen on a red Cigarette boat out of Scrub Island or Marina Cay owned by a guy known as Baldy Baldwin." I paused. "Ever heard of him?"

"No, but I can ask around."

I gave him my cell phone number just as Valentine pulled up.

"Please don't mention the gold to him, Buck."

"I understand. Don't worry. And call me if you get a line on Baldwin."

"I'll see you at the concert, and we'll talk afterwards," he said.

"Right."

The maybe-con artist, the drug smuggler, and the arms merchant. I should flip a coin to see who's likeliest to get me killed.

34

"King Charles! Back on-island, back in jail." Valentine Hodge's bright smile lit up the dark interior of his old Ford Crown Victoria.

"Seems I get arrested wherever I go."

Valentine let out a deep laugh.

"You know what they say, karma's a bitch."

We caught up. I was surprised to hear he now had four great-grandchildren.

"So why was you in jail?" he said.

"That old son-of-a-bitch Bramble's still got a grudge against me—at least that's what I thought it was, but… do you know him? Is he on the up and up?"

"Don't really know him but I could ask around."

Valentine drove, not too slow, not too fast, just steady and straight. I'd forgotten how old he was, but he still looked good. I told him about the Adoption AID mess and the disappearances, neither of which were news to him.

"Do you know a guy named Baldwin from Marina Cay, drives a fancy red Cigarette boat?"

"Baldy? Shoot, Buck, he's one of my nephews. I got thirty-seven nieces and nephews now. He in some kinda trouble—again?"

I swallowed. "I'm not sure, but he was paid to snatch John Thedford on

St. John and apparently delivered him to somebody who's been trying to put a stop to this concert."

Valentine shrugged. "That sounds like Baldy. His father weren't no better. Always looking to make fast money. I seen that red boat of his and knew it was only a matter of time till he got himself arrested for something."

"I'd like to talk to him, find out who hired him and if he has any idea if—where Thedford is."

"I can find out where Baldy is. Can't promise he'll tell you squat, though."

As we passed over the Queen Elizabeth II Bridge onto Beef Island and the airport, Valentine whistled.

"Tell me you ain't flying that plane there, are you?" He pointed toward the Beast. "Land that thing in the water, you'll go right back to jail."

"The magistrate's supposed to square it with Duncan Mather—"

"Dunk's my son-in-law, heck, I'll call him myself."

I smiled for the first time since seeing Bramble's expression when he thought I was FBI. Valentine pulled up in front of the airport terminal and I had my hand on the door handle, ready to jump.

"What do I owe you for the ride?"

"Forget it, man. Give me your phone number. Something tells me I'll be seeing you again, real soon. I just hope it's not back at the jail." Again with the brilliant smile.

"Me too, brother. Me too."

35

THE BEAST ROARED DOWN THE RUNWAY HEADED DUE EAST. RATHER THAN pulling back on the stick to gain altitude, I kept low and headed straight to Marina Cay, then banked to starboard over Scrub Island. I spied the fuel dock and marina. I kicked down on the pedals and banked to port, which spun the Beast on its wing, a few hundred feet over the big Marriott and private villas behind it.

No red boat. Damn!

Would Baldy agree to talk to me, or just disappear?

We gained altitude and banked south. I had a lot of people to catch up with and only moments of flight time to Peter Island. I removed my headset and grabbed the cell phone.

"Buck, where've you been? I've been worried sick!"

"Sorry, Crystal. I was arrested at Customs on Tortola—"

"Arrested!? Why, what happened?"

"Old e-Antiquity loose end. No valid charge so they let me go this morning with a gazillion apologies. I'm headed over to Peter Island now. Is Avery Rose still there?"

"Yes, she said she'd wait for you. But, Buck?" Her voice dropped. "There's been more bad news. Stud Mahoney's kidnappers have raised their stakes, again. And they mentioned John this time."

Uh-oh.

"What did they say, and how was it relayed?"

"They called one of the networks, CNN, I think. They were furious their demands hadn't been met. They increased the number of prisoners they wanted released from Guantanamo and raised the ransom to two million dollars for Stud—"

Her voice broke. I wished I could see her face, but she sure *sounded* cut up.

"What about John?"

"They said he would…die…if the show…wasn't cancelled," she said between sobs. "The show's… tomorrow night. "Everyone's here—"

"So the same people that have Stud also have John?"

It took her a few moments of whuffling before she could speak.

"I assume so."

"Did they make the demands at the same time to CNN?"

"Oh, no, the man called me again on my phone about John, right after the broadcast. They have to be connected, don't you think?"

The mystery within the mystery, I wanted to say.

"What about the police, they given you any updates?"

"A senior agent from the FBI was here to ask questions. He wasn't very friendly."

Booth. Investigating his theory about Crystal.

"How did that go?"

"He asked a lot of questions about the phone calls, then he wanted to know about our marriage, whether John was faithful… whether I was…." She was sobbing again.

"Did he have any news or updates at all?"

It took a moment for her to catch her breath.

"Only that they had all law officers mobilized in both the USVI and BVI. He asked a lot more questions about Stud, but…"

My knuckles were white on the wheel. I waited, but she was done with the news.

I said I'd be there after I collected Avery Rose, then we disconnected. I'd been played for a fool before, and while I had a hard time believing she was involved, I had to face the fact that she could be. If she was innocent,

Crystal was damned if she cancelled the show and damned if she didn't. Would John Thedford really be released, either way? What if he was already dead? What if Baldy's job was to throw him into Pillsbury Sound, not to transfer him?

What if Booth was right?

Peter Island grew larger ahead of me. Avery Rose wasn't the only reason I was headed here, but for now I had another call to make.

"So you managed to get out of jail?"

"No thanks to you, Booth. Didn't you get my call from Customs?"

"I did, but you're off the case. I can't afford the negative baggage that follows you like a caboose."

I hesitated. "Fine with me—"

"I'm disconnecting the phone and cancelling the credit card." He paused and I glanced at the fuel gauges. They were half-full. "And no more water landings. I'm telling the FAA to revoke your privileges."

"What the hell? I still have a job—"

"Not for me you don't."

Good thing there was little air traffic as I sat there with my mouth agape. What crawled up his ass?

"But I found the name of the guy with the red Cigarette boat—"

"There is no red boat, Reilly—I said you were done! I don't want to hear—"

"What, my leads? What the hell's with you?"

I could hear him gnashing his teeth.

"Damn gang war. People disappearing, getting killed—"

"What's that have to do with me?"

"No more questions. Like I said, you're through."

The line went dead.

Already well past Peter Island, I initiated a long slow turn to the west, then scanned the horizon for planes and the water for boats. I had to get my breathing under control.

Now what?

Since Peter Island was private and didn't welcome boaters, there was little traffic. I spotted a long beach on the northwest coast, the water a deep blue that faded quickly to turquoise close to the beach.

With my headset back on, I flinched at the scream in my ears.

"Grumman Goose, Grumman Goose, return to St. Thomas approach, Grumman Goose, do you read me?"

I pulled the headset back off. Damn.

Was I about to commit yet another offense that would put me back in jail?

One last look around. No boats, private or police.

I smiled.

They'd have to catch me first.

36

The Beast splashed down with authority into the mild chop. As much as I missed Betty, I once again appreciated what a couple thousand extra pounds will do for stability.

I feathered the props and alternated throttles between the two engines to aim us toward the channel markers that led to the beach. The wings seesawed, and each float alternately skimmed off the surf, but once my course was set the Beast sliced through the water like the regal old yacht she was at her core. People had emerged from villas, the restaurant, and cabanas on the beach to watch us approach.

Since Peter Island was private, there shouldn't be any BVI police here to arrest me for making a water landing. Of course, there could always be an over-zealous security chief looking to make points with Roadtown. Even if the magistrate or Valentine Hodge had spoken to Duncan Mather, I had no signed piece of paper from them, and thanks to Booth the one I had from the FAA was no longer valid.

Once through the channel markers, the water color abruptly turned lighter, so I pulled back on the throttles. The draft on the Beast was about three feet, and I couldn't take any chances with her recently patched hull. Seventy-five feet or so from shore, I manipulated the throttles to spin halfway around to face into the current and reduced the power to almost nothing. I unbuckled my seatbelt, sprang from the left seat, hunched down into the crawl space—

Clunk—stars! Haste makes hurt—I'd hit my forehead on the bottom of the instrument panel. I shook it off. With the handles on the forward hatch popped free, I pushed it up and the fresh air blew my hair back. Inertia and the current had carried us starboard and we were now almost perpendicular to the shore.

I grabbed the Danforth anchor and threw it as far as I could in the direction of the current. Then scrambled back to the flight deck, glanced at the shore now fifty feet behind us, and with my hand on the throttles watched the angle of the rope, hoping the anchor would catch. This was a hell of a lot easier as a two-person job.

Snap! The anchor rope pulled taut. I reversed thrust and added power—the anchor held. Excellent.

With the side hatch open I pulled off my shirt, took the stern anchor, jumped into the shallow water, set my back against the Beast's fuselage, and pushed her straight into line with the forward anchor rope. Almost done. I splashed toward shore and extended the aft line until it ended, dropped it into the water, and shoved it into the sand with my feet

It held too.

When I turned around, what appeared to be around twenty-five people started to clap. The gold doubloon on my necklace bounced against my bare chest as I slogged toward the shore.

"My knight in shining armor," a woman said with her eyes on my abs.

"Cool plane, dude!"

"You charter that thing?"

"Is it safe?"

I ignored them, pulled on my shirt and started up the beach toward the restaurant. A man in a silk floral print shirt hair pushed through the crowd.

"What are you *doing*?" he said. "You can't just—"

"Who are you?" I pulled the soggy paper from my pocket.

"Mark Lander, general manager of Peter Island Resort. What makes you think—"

I held the letter so close to his eyes Lander couldn't read it.

"I'm assisting the FBI in the search for Stud Mahoney."

"But you can't—"

"I have permission from both governments to make water landings." This while steering him inside the restaurant.

"I've already told the authorities everything I know about Mr. Mahoney's disappearance."

"Special Agent Booth has so informed me," I said. "I just have a few follow-up questions."

He glanced around and drew in a deep breath. Not the best promo for a swanky resort, I imagined.

"How did Mr. Mahoney arrive on the island, Mr. Lander?"

"I already told… private boat."

"Did it happen to be a red Cigarette?"

"I don't know, but whatever brought him here departed immediately after dropping him and his manager off."

"Were they in one room or two?"

"One."

"Was it trashed? Did it look like there'd been a struggle?"

"Not really. The bed was messed up but nothing else."

Not what Booth had said.

"Is there any chance he could still be somewhere on-island?"

He sighed. "Our security staff did a door-to-door search, then the Royal Police did one too. Nothing but upset guests."

I tried a personal appeal.

"Look, we could really use your help and I'm sure you'd like to have us out of your hair for good. Do you have *any* idea how he may have been removed from the island?"

Lander glanced back over his shoulder in both directions.

"Not really—well, I'm not sure security has reported this back to the authorities yet, but we discovered today that one of our small rental boats is missing."

"Could the kidnappers have stolen it?"

"I guess."

"Any other guests check out around the same time Mahoney vanished?"

"No, I'm sure about that. It was later in the afternoon, our shuttle had already left, and all the other guests were present."

I let his statement sink in.

"Buck?"

I turned to find Avery Rose, smiling so big I just had to smile back. Why did it feel like we were old friends?

Lander's deeply tanned forehead wrinkled in surprise. I leaned close to him.

"If I have any more questions I'll call you."

He didn't say a word, but his mouth hung open as Avery stepped around him and hugged me.

"Sorry I'm a day late," I said.

"Yeah, thanks for leaving me stranded in such a lousy place." She winked and scanned me from my wet hair to my sandy feet. She was in beige linen shorts and an orange top that set off her fresh tan. But I knew she'd get soaked wading out to the plane.

We started back down the beach and she hung onto my arm.

"You'll have to carry me," she said.

From some celebrities this might have been condescending, but I could tell Avery thought the situation was funny. A quick glimpse back toward the restaurant revealed General Manager Lander on his cell phone, no doubt calling the police to verify my identity. The crowd from the beach followed after us, people whispering and pointing at Avery.

We walked up to where the Beast was anchored, her nose pointed out into the Caribbean Sea. It would have made a great picture if I'd owned a camera.

"I was worried you forgot about me, Buck."

"I was unavoidably detained."

I again removed my shirt stepped into the warm water and she followed me up to her knees. I turned around and bent down so she could climb into my arms. Her smile was broad, her teeth white and straight as a picket fence and her eyes darted down at my chest.

"This is the most romantic moment of my life," she said.

"Well, it's not like—"

She put her hand over my mouth as I carried her toward the Beast's open hatch.

"It's the moment, Buck. Don't spoil my fantasy, okay?"

Someone on the beach started clapping. The rest of the group picked it up, and I knew damn well somebody had to be videoing us with their cell phone. I just hoped it didn't show up on Entertainment Tonight.

Avery was looking at the Beast. "This totally reminds me of Jimmy Buffett's old plane," she said. Did she mean his old Widgeon, the one I acquired after he wrecked it off Nantucket and renamed Betty? "Too bad he parked it in his restaurant in Orlando." Ah, the Hemisphere Dancer, Buffett's Albatross.

"This is a Goose, it's a lot smaller than the Albatross. I call her the Beast. She's kind of a work in progress, you might say."

"Once you get her painted she'll be a beauty. Are you going to keep her black?"

I was up to my waist now and struggling to lift Avery high enough to stay dry and get her up near the open hatch. She took hold of the handle inside the hatch and pulled herself up.

"I haven't decided. I'm still getting to know her." I looked back to the beach and saw Lander headed our way. Time to pull the rear anchor, fast.

"Go ahead and climb in the right seat."

Once I collected the aft Danforth I dumped the anchor inside and climbed aboard. I flipped on the magnetos, batteries, pulled the chokes, and powered up the port engine, then did the same for the starboard engine.

"You can wear that headset so we can talk while in flight." I hunched down and got ready to crawl between our seats. "I need to pull the forward anchor, be right back."

My arm and shoulder brushed against her thigh as I slid between the seats, and she held it firm rather than sliding her legs to the side to let me pass. Why don't things like this happen when I have more time? I tugged slowly on the anchor rope, which drew the Beast out deeper into the channel. When the rope was nearly straight down I pulled it up fast, stowed it, closed the hatch, and scurried back into the cabin. Tight as it is between the seats, I had nowhere to put my left hand to pull myself up other than on Avery's knee.

"Sorry about that," I said.

"No worries, Captain."

As I ran through an expedited version of the take-off checklist, the cell phone rang from the side pocket next to my seat. I glanced at the screen: Ray. I didn't want to talk right now but couldn't afford to risk missing any important updates.

"Where are you, Ray?"

"What happened to you last night? We were on St. John like you said, but you never posted."

"I had a little diversion but I'm back on track."

"What was her name?"

"Funny, Ray. I'm just leaving Peter Island, headed to Jost Van Dyke—"

"We're back on St. John." His voice lifted. "Lenny's in love with Faith Hill—"

"Ray's got man-love for Brad Pitt!" Lenny's voice boomed in the background.

I checked my watch. "I'll meet you at the Beach Bar tonight—and, Ray? I need you to make a call for me."

I shoved the throttles forward, which pushed Avery back in her seat. I finished with Ray, disconnected and took in a deep breath. The day was half over and I still had a lot of water to cover. The RPMs climbed steadily and we bounced and shimmied over the low rolling waves, jarring enough for Avery to reach out and grab my forearm. We lifted off the water and climbed at a steady rate before I banked north.

"Woo-hoo!"

This girl liked to have fun and didn't mind showing it.

Lander's revelation that a boat was missing could mean several things. I wondered if Booth knew—but he'd fired me, so screw him. We climbed to a thousand feet and I had an exchange with Air Traffic Control out of Tortola, who again demanded I steer toward St. Thomas or return to Beef

Island. I explained that I had permission from the FAA to make water landings in the USVI and that the same permission had been allowed by Duncan Mather of the Royal Virgin Islands Police, but they said he had no jurisdiction over BVI airspace. Made sense, but there was nothing I could do about it now. I was admonished not to make further water landings before I shut my radio off.

Avery gave me a wide-eyed stare.

"You really are a cowboy, aren't you?

"Hi-ho, Silver," I said.

37

We circled Jost Van Dyke once at a thousand feet so I could survey the harbor, then descended and set down just outside of Great Bay, where the boat traffic was far heavier than around Peter Island.

"I wish I could make an entrance like this at my concerts," Avery said.

There was a clear path toward the dock near Foxy's, which is where I had us pointed. The admonitions from Air Traffic Control had me fidgeting in my seat. There was a police station on Jost, and busting an outlaw seaplane pilot would be a good way to gain recognition. And with a gang war raging back in the USVI, law enforcement would be super sensitive right now.

As we glided up toward the dock I cut the power, then scrambled under the instrument panel, again brushed past her leg, popped open the bow hatch and tossed a line to the young boy who stood there. He wrapped it around a cleat a third of the way down the dock. I jumped out with another line, wrapped it through a ring on the Beast's tail, and tied it off on a cleat at the end of the pier.

Avery had opened the side hatch and stood there smiling. Her black hair blew in the breeze but she did nothing to keep it in place, and it struck me again that she was more laid back than most celebrities I'd known. I extended my hand—she took it and leapt toward me. I caught her in a brief hug before I set her down on the dock, giggling like a teenager.

"You sure know how to show a girl a good time, Buck Reilly—"

"Yes, he does," a voice came from over our shoulders.

I turned. I was surprised to see Crystal standing there, more surprised by the *really* dark circles under eyes. She must not have slept in days. I gave her a hug.

"Are you okay?" I said.

She gave me a slight nod, then stepped around me.

"Hi, Avery, I'm Crystal Thedford. So glad you're finally here."

Avery's smile looked a bit forced, which made me uncomfortable.

"This is my assistant, Scarlet," Crystal said. "She'll help get you situated with rehearsals."

A tall mid-twenties brunette stepped forward from behind Crystal and offered a crisp handshake to Avery, then me. She fit the description of the woman Captain Jeremy described as being on the beach when he met John Thedford.

Avery looked at me. "Are you taking me back to Peter Island tonight?"

"I don't—"

"We've made arrangements for you here," Scarlet said. "There's a private party for our whole group after rehearsals at Soggy Dollar around the corner at Great White Bay—private villas there for the evening. If you'd rather return to Peter Island, we can have someone take you over." She smiled. "Now if you'll come with me, I'll introduce you to everyone."

Avery surprised me with a quick hug and peck on the cheek.

"Now I see why you're not interested," she whispered.

I wanted to set her straight, but finding the right words would take some thought and she was already following after Scarlet. I scanned the beach, then out to the horizon—no police. I spotted a small group of picketers down near Foxy's but couldn't read their signs this far away.

"Everything okay with those folks?" I nodded toward them.

"They fight more among themselves than with us." Crystal attempted a laugh. "I keep them plied with Foxy's painkillers and daiquiris."

"Any of them given you the impression they might know something about John's disappearance?"

She shook her head. "No, and believe me, I've asked them a million questions. They're passionate about their positions but none have made threatening comments about John or Stud." She took in a deep breath. "All the news has been about the kidnapper's demands and speculation about Stud, and if it's mentioned at all, John's disappearance is characterized as him leaving St. John drunk after a party and presumed drowned."

So much had happened since I last saw Crystal. I hadn't told her about the red Cigarette boat or its captain, not wanting to share my concern that Baldy might have dumped John into Pillsbury Sound on the off-chance that Booth's theory about her involvement was right. His revelation about Crystal's past relationship with Stud also sealed my lips.

"This must be the charter pilot you said is helping you, Crystal." An older, rotund man dressed in slacks and a pressed tropical shirt walked up to us.

"Yes, Viktor, this is Buck Reilly." Crystal turned to me. "Buck, please meet one of our board members, Viktor Galey."

We shook hands, but I continued to look past him down the dock.

"Former treasure hunter, isn't that right, King Charles?" Galey said.

That got my attention.

"Many of your discoveries were quite amazing." He had a slight accent, from where I couldn't tell.

"Those were good times," I said. "What business are you in, Viktor?"

"Petroleum, natural gas and mining, but I have several other diversions as well. Like you, I made my fortune hunting for treasure—just different kinds."

"And of a more sustainable variety," I said.

He nodded. "The global downturn ruined many an entrepreneur." Crystal had mentioned a billionaire on her board, I figured this must be him. "Thank you for helping to look for John. It seems the law enforcement agencies are focused elsewhere."

"Buck's been a big help," Crystal said.

Movement along the shore caught my attention. A police car had pulled up on the road behind the beach.

Damn!

"I've got to go," I said. "Viktor, nice to meet you." I felt the sudden urge to warn them. "By the way, as busy as you've been you may not have heard, but there's a turf war going on over in the U.S. Virgins—"

"Special Agent Booth from the FBI has informed us of these matters," Galey said. That accent—European?

He smiled and turned back down the dock.

"Why do you have to leave so soon?" Crystal said. "I haven't even told you the latest—"

I pointed toward the policeman who now stood outside his car, speaking into his radio and looking at us.

"Approval for my water landings has been revoked—"

A siren sounded in the distance, behind us. I swung around to see a flashing light on a small police cabin cruiser as it rounded the western tip of the bay and turned toward shore.

Crap!

I lunged for the line that held the Beast's tail. When I stood up, I saw that Crystal had jumped into the open hatch.

"What are you doing?" I said.

"Going with you. We need to find my husband!"

I tossed her the loose rope and stood on the edge of the dock, pressing against the Beast's fuselage to push her off. As the big plane began to gain momentum, I dove toward the hatch, caught hold—

My right foot slipped. My legs fell into the water. My right hand caught the bottom of the hatch—

"Buck!" Crystal grabbed my arm and pulled.

She gave me enough leverage to reach up and yank myself out of the water and on board. I scurried into the nose and released the line that held us to the dock. There goes another good rope, dammit.

I spotted the policeman from the shore now running down the dock before I pulled the hatch shut. I was more worried about the police on the cabin cruiser, since they could disrupt our take-off. That could cause us to crash or if they were really foolish, crash into us.

Before Crystal even finished buckling up I had both engines running. Reverse power to the starboard side combined with forward thrust to the port side spun the old aquatic hull out toward the open sea.

The police cabin cruiser swerved to try and impede our takeoff. I adjusted our course to the west, but a ferry coming in from the USVI forced me back toward the cruiser. Our speed was impacted by the changes in direction—and the cruiser was now dead ahead, its red light flashing atop its bridge.

"Buck, what are you—Buck! That boat!"

My grip was so tight on the wheel my fingers ached.

The police cruiser wasn't budging!

"Buck!"

I glanced at the speed indicator. We were still shy of takeoff speed.

"Dammit, girl, go-go-go!"

At seventy miles per hour we closed the gap quickly. I couldn't risk changing course at this speed. With only about forty feet to spare, the police finally hit the gas and tried to get out of our way.

The Beast broke free from the water—

And the police cruiser cleared the float under our port wing by a hair. Well, maybe a foot, but it was way too close for comfort.

Crystal had both hands over her eyes as I banked to port and saw two policemen in the cabin cruiser shaking their fists at me.

Adios, boys!

38

WE WERE HALFWAY TO ST. JOHN BEFORE CRYSTAL SPOKE.

"I got a package delivered to me at Foxy's—it must have come off a boat, so I have no idea who delivered it." She reached into the pocket of her shorts and pulled out a Rolex watch. "It's John's. I gave it to him for our fifth anniversary, just last year."

My stomach dropped. "Was there a note?"

She unfolded a piece of crumpled paper as if doing it pained her fingers, then passed it to me.

YOU CANCLE THE SHOW OR THE
NEXT BUNDEL WILL HAVE HIS HEAD

Black magic marker. Blocky capital letters. Cancel and bundle both misspelled.

"Maybe you *should* cancel, Crystal. Not the most convincing threat, but that could be because they want to throw us off, in which case they're serious and it's not worth risking John's life. I have to say, I'm not at all sure his fate depends on this concert, but…"

"I agree—to both sides of your argument." Her voice was a whisper. "Guess I'll cancel—how can I continue if there's a chance they might kill him?" A bitter laugh. "Here we are trying to support women, help adoptees, expand choice, and what? Extremists would kill us for *trying*?" Her voice rose to a near scream.

"Crystal—"

"Is our world that fucking twisted?"

I was pretty sure she'd once faced an unplanned pregnancy herself, but her emotion was so real I just couldn't buy her involvement in John's disappearance, kidnapping, murder, whatever the hell it was. Stud Mahoney bugged the hell out of me, but my mind was compartmentalizing the two events. At least I knew this wasn't rational.

"So what did Special Agent Booth want with you?" I said.

She turned to look out the side window.

"To ask about the threats we'd received."

Screw it.

"And what about Stud?"

She turned to face me, her eyes scanning mine.

"You know, don't you?"

I held her gaze.

"I told him all about my past with Mike—that's how I knew Stud." She pressed her fist against her lips. "I'm sorry I didn't tell you. It's just that I didn't...I couldn't...hell, I should have." A tear dropped down her cheek. "We were together just as his star was rising, and when it rose big-time, he changed. I moved out when he was in Spain filming a movie. He was crushed—he tried everything to get me back. That's when I went to D.C. and met John."

"Rebound?"

She bit her fist. "I don't like to be alone... but I don't... I mean I love John."

"Did he know?" I said.

"Not until after we were married. And when we came up with the idea for Adoption AID, John contacted Mike and asked him to participate. I was so angry at him. And now they're both missing and I can't help but think it's my fault." The tears started up. "But I don't understand *why*!"

My throat had gone dry.

"Are you going to leave me too, Buck?"

Determination pulsed through my veins. Whether the Adoption AID concert went ahead or not wasn't my concern, but I decided once again that I'd do everything possible to help Crystal find her husband.

And her ex-boyfriend.

"Let's wait until we land, see what we can find out before you make your decision, okay? Maybe we can use the concert to draw out the kidnappers—we have no assurance they'll cooperate if you do cancel."

Jaw tight, eyes blazing, she said, "Let's find these bastards."

I felt a jolt of electricity pass between us that sat me up straight.

Damn. Suspicion had been an ally when it came to corralling my thoughts about Crystal Thedford. Now I'd need to rely on self-discipline.

Double damn.

I BEGAN A LONG SLOW CIRCLE AROUND WESTERN ST. JOHN, LOOKING FOR A good place to land. Great Cruz Bay was filled with boats. We flew over Rendezvous Bay to Fish Bay, where I spotted the compound that belonged to Diego Francis. We continued to bank over the green wilderness of the Virgin Islands National Park, over Cinnamon Bay to Trunk Bay, and continued west.

I followed the shipping lane that led straight into Cruz Bay, added flaps after a few miles, turned onto a base leg and minutes later a final approach. Had Booth contacted the FAA yet?

When we touched down I realized that my headset had been quiet. No air traffic controllers freaking out, no demands that I divert to St. Thomas or Beef Island.

As we taxied on the step toward the beach at Cruz Bay, a small black helicopter rounded the western point from the direction of Caneel Bay. It was headed straight toward us and buzzed past at high-speed, right over the Beast. I could clearly see two men: one was the pilot, the other held binoculars aimed right at us. They didn't circle around but continued past. I remembered Brass Knuckles's report of Diego's compound getting machine-gunned from a helicopter.

I had a feeling I'd seen that chopper or maybe one of the men before but I couldn't remember where. I'd call Booth and mention it, but the phone was probably disconnected by now, and he didn't want my help anyway.

The Beach Bar was up ahead on the right corner of the thin sandy strip that separated Cruz Bay from the Caribbean Sea—

What the hell?

The beach was packed with people all the way around the bar, several hundred of them at least.

"What's going on here?" Crystal said.

I killed the engines and was out of my seat before the props quit turning.

"Let's find out," I said.

39

WITH THE BEAST'S AFT AND STERN ANCHORS SET IN THE SOFT SAND IN front of American Watersports, Crystal and I waded to shore. Billy Hartman, at his usual corner of the patio restaurant, agreed to keep an eye on the plane and said he'd advise security to watch it overnight. He was half in the bag, but he'd been right about the red Cigarette so I figured I could trust him to follow through.

The sound of live music increased in volume as we walked down the beach. Everybody in the crowd seemed to be having a good time

"Who's playing?" I asked a cute blond in a bikini perched on some lucky guy's shoulders.

A big smile. "Scott Kirby, Thom Shepherd, and Matt Hoggatt!"

"Shoot, I knew that," Crystal said. "They told me they were doing a show here on St. John."

"Are they part of Adoption AID?"

"Matt has a few step-kids and has friends performing, and the others wanted to support the effort."

We meandered through the crowd and caught a glimpse of Scott, Thom, and Matt set up at the far end of the bar. At the moment they were singing Thom's song "Texas Girls." As much as I'd have loved to kick back, have a cold Carib, and enjoy the show, the clock was ticking.

I scanned the crowd. There had to be nearly a thousand people on the beach, packed into the bar and out on the road behind the stage.

Crystal grabbed my arm and pulled me deeper into the crowd, toward the bar—I spotted Ray, wearing a big loopy grin, Lenny next to him chatting it up with three smiling lovelies. Figures. Conch Man was comfortable on either side of the bar.

It took a few moments and a dozen screamed "excuse me's" to reach them, but when we did, Lenny interrupted whatever spiel he'd been spinning to give us a big smile and a high-five.

"About time you guys showed up!" Ray yelled.

"Brother Buck!" Lenny's bright white teeth gleamed. "And sister Crystal. Welcome to the party, y'all! If these dudes are rocking the ladies this good, I can't wait to see what happens at the show. Ha!"

Crystal's smile was on the tepid side, but her eyes were still sharp.

I leaned in to shout in Ray's ear. "Did you get a hold of—"

"Right over there." He pointed across the bar.

It took a moment, but déjà vu struck me when I spotted Brass Knuckles in the same spot I'd seen him a few days ago. He'd cut his dreadlocks off. His eyes were locked on mine and he seemed oblivious to the music and scene playing out around him. There was no sign of Diego Francis.

The song finished and Scott Kirby announced they were taking a break. In the vacuum that followed, I leaned in close to my two friends from Key West. I felt Crystal push up against me.

"Did you talk to that guy?" I nodded toward the other side of the bar, but Brass Knuckles was now pressing through the crowd, glancing at me.

"Yeah, he didn't say much, only that he wanted to talk to you," Ray said.

"Bad-looking mother," Lenny said. "The hell you want with him?"

"More like what he wants from me," I said.

"You're late," Brass Knuckles said. "Diego's been waiting for you. He don't like to wait, especially under the circumstances."

"As you recall, I was held up in Tortola."

"Diego's down the beach," he said. "Let's go."

"I'll be right there, just give me a second with these guys."

Guys like Brass Knuckles don't respond well to people countering their orders, because they're under orders themselves. His eyes narrowed to the point I wondered how he could see out of them.

"I *said*—"

"Look, friend. I'm the one who suggested we meet, got it? So give me a couple minutes and I'll be right there." I stood square to him, loose, ready to deflect whatever he threw at me. But after a brief stare-down, he turned away.

"The hell's that all about, man?" Lenny said. "What kind of shit you into now?"

"You don't even want to know, Lenny."

Ray was no longer smiling. "What's the plan, Buck?"

I let out a long breath. "We need to flush this situation out. As of now, there's a whole bunch of theories as to who might be opposed to Adoption AID, but little more than that." I swallowed. "I need to meet with these guys to see what they've found out, but they're up to their eyeballs in… a competitive beat-down—"

"The gang war we been hearing about?" Lenny said. "That dude ain't exactly a Good Samaritan type, man."

"You three discuss the final logistics for tomorrow afternoon, while I—"

"I'm going with you—"

"No, Crystal—you need to help these guys hold things together and let me see what I can learn, okay?"

It was the first time since I'd known her that she gave me a fuck-you look. And for that, I liked her even more.

Down the beach I found Diego smoldering in an open-air restaurant, flanked by Brass Knuckles and two empty chairs.

"Nobody keeps me waiting, Reilly. I'll stuff your ass back in that trunk and take you on a one-way trip to Fish Bay."

"Nice to see you too, Diego. How's business?" I glanced at Brass Knuckles, who gave me his best scowl.

"I need you to get me out of here." Diego delivered this statement in a quiet yet chillingly clear voice.

"I can do it but not quite yet, Diego. I'm sorry—"

"Sorry?" His mouth twisted into a sneer. "I'll pay you, big-time. I've got crates of cash and—"

"Not until the day after tomorrow." I nodded toward Brass Knuckles. "And not unless the information he gave me amounts to something."

Diego sat back and looked me up and down.

"You haven't been over to Guana Island yet?"

"Haven't had the chance—"

"That's your own fool fault. I delivered. In my business I produce the goods, and my clients pay. What about Baldy Baldwin?"

"I'll help you the day after tomorrow, Diego. All the shit will hit the fan when this concert goes forward, and the only way I can find that woman's husband is to be there and hope to see something." My voice was nearly a whisper.

Diego rubbed his cheeks and closed his eyes.

Brass Knuckles leaned forward, ready to clobber me if his master gave him so much as a wink. At this point, I really didn't care. I'd been cold-cocked, hijacked, arrested, imprisoned, threatened at gunpoint *and* knifepoint—

Knifepoint—that's it!

The face I saw holding the binoculars when the helicopter flew over us—it was Slicked-back! The guy who'd tried to grab Crystal in Key West in front of the Casa Marina Hotel.

"Want to hear something funny?" Diego said. "I like your conviction. Most guys'd jump at the money and ditch the honey. But I still need—"

I stood up and the chair's legs screeched on the concrete floor. "Like I said, Diego, I'll keep my word if your information's helpful. Otherwise, good luck with your new rival."

Diego's stare was a slow burn.

"I'll have people at that concert, Reilly. And I'll make damn sure you'll be here when I need you." His head twitched like a pit bull with somebody's leg clenched in its jaws. "We have a deal." He stabbed a finger at me, started to walk off, then turned back. "Remember, I'll be watching you."

I almost laughed. Like he thought I was going to forget that?

40

I WENT TO THE BEACH BAR AND FOUND MY LITTLE THREESOME TALKING WITH Scott Kirby and Matt Hoggatt.

"Buck Reilly, sure," Matt said. "Jimmy's mentioned you."

Scott gave Crystal a hug, said he'd see her tomorrow on Jost Van Dyke.

"And I heard you rocked your debate, Lenny," Kirby said.

"Should of been there, man," Lenny said. As they walked away, he turned to me. "What the hell we supposed to do now, man?"

"Don't be hung over tomorrow," I said. "You two have to get all the talent to Foxy's, per the schedule."

I couldn't think of anything else—fatigue hit me like a sucker punch. Last night in jail, all the running around, the dead ends, everyone wanting a piece of me… I was out of gas. Crystal's eyes sagged, and the circles under them made her look like a zombie.

"I'll try to save *some* energy for tomorrow," Lenny said.

"I'm asleep on my feet, so I won't be worth a dime if I don't get some shut-eye," I said.

We rode in the back of the open-air truck taxi without saying a word. Once at the Westin, we were told the hotel was full. Crystal asked for a cot to be sent to her husband's room which she had kept in the hope that he'd show up, then walked out of the lobby without waiting for an answer. I caught up with her.

"Sorry, Buck. I'll sleep on the cot."

We disagreed about that all the way to the room and I decided I'd go back and sleep in the Beast. When we entered it she became very still and just stood at the opened door, staring in. John's briefcase was in sight, and I assumed his clothes still hung in the closet.

Damn. I hadn't even thought how she might react to seeing all that.

"You okay?" I said.

She let out a long breath and continued into the room.

"It's just weird seeing John's things here."

She sat on the bed. I felt awkward, uncomfortable. The walls moved in on me and the air seemed thick.

"I'm going to the bar for a drink," I said. "Why don't you relax? I'll come back later to say goodnight."

"I could use a shower," she said. "And I'm starving, but I don't want to go to the restaurant." Her eyes turned to John's briefcase.

"Order from room service," I said. "I'll eat at the bar."

Our eyes met and held for a second. I headed out and pulled the door closed, fast.

I needed rum. Lots of rum.

Once seated at the Tiki Bar, I drained a Cruzan on the rocks and pointed to my glass. I drained the next one the minute it came, then grabbed the bar menu.

A vibration on my hip—the cell phone. I glanced at the screen, surprised it still worked: YOUR MASTER.

"I thought you'd disconnected this phone, Booth."

"Where are you?"

"Back on St. John. And you fired me, so what—"

"Where's Crystal Thedford?"

His tone cut right through my fresh rum buzz.

"She's in her room at the Westin. I'm here at the bar. What's up?"

"Bad news, I'm afraid. Would she take it better from you, or should I take the ferry over in the morning and tell her myself?"

Shit.

"What's up?" But I knew damned well what it was.

"They found a body out in the water between St. John and Tortola. Might be John Thedford. I haven't seen him, but it can't be a pretty sight. She'll need to make the ID"

Double shit.

"No ID on the body?"

"Shot in the head and no wallet, so no, nothing."

"I'll tell her. Where is it?"

"The morgue in Roadtown. I'm headed there first thing. Can you bring her over?"

I sat up straight, my fists clenched. Dammit!

"I've requested that the body be kept as it is for forensics." He was quiet for a moment. "Sorry, kid. It's not certain, but she'll take it better from you than she would from me. This doesn't mean you're back on the case, I just need you to get her to Tortola."

I didn't ask if she was still a suspect, or about Stud Mahoney. If it was John Thedford, he was probably killed the night he was taken from St. John. Crystal was now my main priority. The concert had to be cancelled to ensure *her* safety.

A waiter came to get my order, but I handed him the menu and jumped off the stool. Exhaustion, rum, and bad news blurred my vision, but what I had to do next was clear.

Dreaded, but clear.

41

THE ROOM SMELLED OF COCONUT AND A FRUITY FRAGRANCE. CRYSTAL WAS dressed in her husband's pajamas and sitting at the desk, the contents of John's briefcase piled in front of her. My heart sank further.

A cot was folded in the corner of the room.

She offered a weak smile when I entered but must have seen something in my face, because hers kind of fell apart.

"What's wrong, Buck?"

"I got a call," I said. "From Special Agent Booth."

She was on her feet and in front of me in a blur.

"John?" Her eyes were filling. She knew.

"They found a body—"

Her legs buckled—I lunged and caught her as she fell.

"It hasn't been identified yet—Crystal? Don't give up yet."

She dropped her head on my shoulder. Tears sprang from her eyes, and her body was wracked with convulsions as I held her. She cried, hard, and clenched the flesh on my back so tight I winced though I didn't pull away. "I couldn't—wouldn't—believe this could happen."

"We don't know for sure yet—"

"How did he die?"

My neck was soaked from her tears. I couldn't help inhaling the fragrance of her freshly washed hair but felt like a creep for noticing.

"The person they found was shot."

This set her off again, wailing, sobbing, shaking. I held on to her as best I could, but gravity was winning out.

"They found him—someone— in the waters near Tortola," I said. "We'll go there first thing in the morning to make the identification."

It was as if her legs turned to jelly. All her will, even to stand, was gone. I held her up, swung her slowly around, and lowered her onto the bed. Other than trembling with grief she didn't move when I laid her down.

"Try to sleep now. We'll deal with everything tomorrow." I paused. "And don't give up yet."

She didn't respond.

I moved the pillows together, pulled down the comforter and sheet, gently lifted her into the center of the bed, tucked the covers around her. She rolled over and clutched one of the pillows in a tight embrace.

"I'm so, so sorry. Good night, Crystal."

"You're not leaving? Buck?" She reached up toward me.

"No, I'll stay."

I turned off the bedside light, and if it weren't for the open curtain there'd have been no light at all. I sat in the semi-darkness for an hour, my plan to return to the Beast to sleep no longer appropriate. I opened the cot between the other side of the bed and the sliding door out to the balcony. Crystal, thank God, had succumbed to exhaustion. Her head was on the pillow facing me—her eyes were closed, she wasn't crying or quivering, and her breathing was steady. I hoped she'd sleep straight through the night, because tomorrow would likely be hell.

Once I drew the drapes, the room was pitch black. I slid my shirt over my head, dropped my shorts, and crawled into the cot. It had been a grueling two days before I had to watch a woman I cared for reduced to a catatonic heap of grief. I wasn't under the covers five minutes before I was as dead to the world as my roommate.

42

I DREAMT OF THE JAIL IN ROADTOWN. BRAMBLE WAS THERE, GOADING ME, then he morphed into a guy with dreadlocks who had brass knuckles, only it wasn't Brass Knuckles, it was—

I sat up halfway, an arm raised to defend, or fight.

"What—"

"It's me."

Crystal?

She'd crawled onto my cot.

"Hold me, John," she said.

I felt her skin against mine. She had no clothes on—

"Crystal," I said. "It's me, Buck—"

She placed her hand over my mouth.

"Hold me...please. Just hold me."

What the—oh, God, no...

I turned onto my side. Our bare chests came together. Crystal buried her head in my neck. Her warm body squirmed in even closer. I tried to lie still, but my mind spun. Maybe she was dreaming, delirious—she'd called me John.

But she was kissing my neck now, and my body started to respond as she worked her way up toward my mouth.

She wanted to make love—to her husband?

I was ready—my body felt as if every fold of skin had pulled taut, I was *so* ready. I ran my hands up her bare back, pulling her toward me—

What the hell are you doing?

John Thedford might still be out there. And one of us—more likely, both of us—would be regretting this tomorrow, whether he was or not.

I pulled her in tight. She tried to move her arms around me, but my gentle yet firm embrace pinned her arms. I slipped my hips slightly away so she couldn't feel my response.

"Buck—"

"Let me hold you, Crystal. Just hold you."

My whisper was met with a brief struggle. She whimpered, but I was doing everything possible to keep this delicate wall I had erected—ugh, bad word—to just focus on holding her, nothing else. After a minute, she melted in my arms. Her warm flesh, firm yet buttery soft, pressed against mine. It would be so easy to give her what she wanted—but not like this.

After a while her breathing slowed to a rhythmic pace. She was asleep, her head nestled on my shoulder, but my heart continued to pound like a snare drum.

I lay awake for an hour while she clung to me, and gradually I was able to roll over onto my side without waking her. She had used my name, so she wasn't delirious. She spooned me, and as I drifted toward sleep my mind zigged and zagged through scenes sparked by the heat of our bodies pressed together. Finally, all thought eased to a deep blackness and I slept more fitfully than I had all week.

A PINK LIGHT IN MY EYES BROUGHT ME INTO THE MORNING. MY EYELIDS fluttered and I realized my face was inches away from a gap in the blackout curtains, the rising sun shining bright on my head. I had no idea of the time—

Memories of last night jolted me into full consciousness. I rolled slowly toward the center of the cot and felt nothing but springs pressing up through the cheap mattress.

Crystal was gone.

I sat up. She wasn't in her bed.

On my feet, I found the bathroom door open and the room dark.

I noticed the sliding door ajar. I pulled my shirt and shorts on, pushed my fingers through my hair, and slid the door wide.

"Good morning." Crystal offered a contrite smile.

"Did you get some rest?" I said.

She nodded her head slowly. Her feet were propped up on the railing and she was sitting back, staring into the blue sky and crowded harbor beyond the beach.

"Sorry for last night," she said.

"Don't be sorry. I hope—"

"I know it was foolish, but at the time it's what my heart, and hell, my body wanted me to do."

I smiled. "Yeah, well, my heart and body were right there with you."

Her lips bent into a brief smile.

"Let's forget it, all right?" she said.

There was no embarrassment in her eyes, and I realized all over again what a complicated woman she was, flaws and all.

We discussed the logistics of the day. She didn't think there was any way to cancel the show at this point, given that all the television crews and talent were already on Jost Van Dyke. She had no intention of going there herself but asked if I could help her assistant, Scarlet, handle the situation after we went to Roadtown to meet the authorities and identify John.

"If it's him," I said. "They're not certain, remember."

I sent a text to Ray and Lenny and asked them to meet us on the beach at Cruz Bay so I could fill them in on what had happened and devise a plan to handle the post-concert departures.

I found a cab outside of Reception. When our eyes met, I could see the sadness, the emptiness I'd never seen in her before. From all she'd described, her relationship with John had been happy, and they'd changed their lives to pursue a shared dream.

The morning sun was bright, but the air was still cool. We rode in silence, seated close to each other.

We wound down toward the water, went around the square, and pulled up in front of the ferry dock. I paid the driver and we got out and walked toward the beach. The Beast remained at anchor amidst the American Watersports fleet, but Billy Hartman was nowhere in sight. Neither was any security.

"Buck, over here!"

I glanced up to the restaurant above the seawall and spied Ray and Lenny seated at a table. Crystal stopped in her tracks.

"I'll wait here, okay?"

Ray was wearing the same outfit as the night before, and Lenny's eyes were puffy slits. So much for not being hungover today. Lenny's gaze was fixed on Crystal.

"Why'd you wake us up so early?" Ray said.

Lenny nodded toward the beach. "Why's Crystal blue?"

I glanced from Ray to Lenny.

"The police found a man's body with half his head blown off. They think it's her husband."

Ray winced and Lenny's eyes bulged to capacity. I filled them in on the details and told them to get to Jost Van Dyke. One way or another, today would be the day when everything came together. Or went to hell.

They followed me down the steps and took turns hugging Crystal. No words were spoken. None would help.

She and I walked to the end of the beach. The Beast was anchored seventy feet off shore, just past the American Watersports fleet. As we trudged out into the water I realized the plane was askew in the surf. The starboard wing hung lower. My stomach dropped. In an amphibian, that was often a sign it had sprung a leak. And if that were the case, we might not be doing anything other than baling her out. Crap!

When I arrived at the hatch, the air froze in my lungs.

The lock had been tampered with. Fucking Billy Hartman!

I glanced back at Crystal. She was oblivious, wading toward me, her mind far away. Had the Beast been booby-trapped? Maybe a hole punched through the floor? I popped the hatch—

"About fucking time you showed up."

My mouth dropped open.

"Get in here and crank this bitch up, I got places to be."

Boom-Boom was in the starboard rear seat with a shotgun pointed at my head.

"What's wrong, Buck?" Crystal had stopped ten feet behind me.

"Who's that?" Boom-Boom said.

I still hadn't found my voice.

He leaned out, the gun still pointed at me.

"Got a lady friend with you, huh, brudda? Good for you." He waved the gun. "Come on honey, let's get on this old piece-a-shit so your boyfriend can get me outta here."

Crystal stared at him, her mouth wide open.

"Leave her alone, Boom-Boom. I'll take you wherever you want to go, but she's got enough problems—"

"Problems? You don't know shit about problems—and man, was I wrong about you. You just a broke loser who ain't connected to shit. This group that rolled into the islands is heavy, man. My people been disappearing left and right. My whole organization's gone to shit."

Crystal's face shifted from surprised to wild-eyed as she slogged toward us as fast as the thigh-deep water allowed.

"Did you kill my husband?"

"Whazzat she saying?" Boom-Boom's brow furrowed. "Kill who?"

Crystal had nearly reached us.

"Did you kill my husband!"

I grabbed her around the waist as she tried to push past me.

"Crystal! Stop—"

"You better calm her ass down, Reilly, or I'll pop her right here and now."

I tried to hold her, but Lord, she was strong.

"That son-of-a-bitch killed John!"

"What the fuck!" Boom-Boom eased back inside the plane, the weapon pointed straight at us. "I ain't killed shit, least not yet, but you better shut your damn mouth or that's gonna change."

"Crystal, stop, please! If he wanted to hurt us, he'd have already done it." I held her in a bear hug. "Listen to me, he's a drug smuggler. He doesn't care about adoption!"

She finally stopped struggling. We were both soaked from wrestling in the surf.

"*Was* a smuggler," he said. "But I got one last run to make, 'cause they took all my cash."

Crystal collapsed in my arms.

"Give me a hand, Boom-Boom," I said.

I lifted her toward the plane, he reached out and grabbed her beneath the armpits to haul her inside. She was nearly dead weight. I helped push her up into the hatch, where he laid her down in the rear seat. I pulled myself aboard. The gun was resting against the cabin wall, and he must have read my mind because he snatched it up.

"We're on our way to identify her husband's body," I said.

"You lied to me, Reilly. Said you could hook me up with those assholes."

"I told you I'd help you if you came up with anything that helped me find John Thedford. Alive."

"That's one of the reasons I'm here, brudda." He nodded toward Crystal. "If there's a reward, then I got some intel for you."

I knelt down and fastened Crystal's seatbelt.

"I said alive, Boom-Boom."

"But even if he's dead, well, wouldn't you like to catch the motherfuckas who killed him?"

Crystal's eyes suddenly cleared and she sat up straight.

"Damn right."

Boom-Boom smiled. "Thought so."

I climbed into the left seat. Halfway through my pre-flight checklist, Boom-Boom slid into the right seat next to me.

"You ain't interested in what I got to tell you?"

"You told the Royal Police?"

"I ain't going to no police station, brudda." He reached into one of the pockets of his cargo shorts and removed a baggie from which he pulled out a fat blunt. "These murdering bastards is after my ass—hell, I had to take the public ferry to St. John!"

I fired up the engines and the Beast roared to life. I checked the fuel gauges—which were low—and the charges on the batteries, then glanced back at Crystal. Her head was against the seat and she stared ahead with faraway eyes.

Boom-Boom pulled on the spare headset and lit his doobie.

"Slide that window open," I said. "What's your information?"

"I heard some Russian dudes grabbed your boy. In fact, they may be the same motherfuckas that destroyed my business."

"Russians? What about Baldy—"

"They hired Baldy to make the snatch then met him for the trade."

"Trade?"

He rolled his eyes. "Money for the dude, brudda. Hell you think?"

What the— If it was a Russian cartel that had moved in, it was because of the shipping lanes and all the drug and arms trade passing through here. What would that have to do with adoption? Did Booth know all this? I powered on my phone to text him but after a couple tries realized it was dead—disconnected.

Prick!

"Buckle up, we're headed out."

Boom-Boom exhaled a plume of smoke.

"Haven't told you where we're going yet."

"We're taking the lady to Tortola," I said.

His smile caught me off guard. I suddenly felt like Little Red Riding Hood.

"Perfect, Brudda. Now wasn't that easy?"

Something told me nothing about this day would be easy.

43

THE TENSION INSIDE THE BEAST ON THE WAY TO BEEF ISLAND WAS SO THICK it felt as if we were under water. Crystal sat in the back with her eyes closed, Boom-Boom watched my every move. He smelled like week-old sweat, had bags under his eyes, and his normally eight-ball-shaved head had a crown of stubble. For now he was getting what he wanted, but what would happen after we landed?

He caught me staring at him. "You do anything stupid when we land, what boys I got left'll find you and your lady friend, and it won't be pretty. Know what I'm saying, brudda?" He turned the barrel of the shotgun toward me from where it rested between his legs.

I get it, asshole.

The brief flight took us back around Marina Cay. As I focused on the runway beacon at Beef Island, I glanced north toward Guana Island. Diego had been urging me there since yesterday, but with John likely dead, I wasn't doing anything until we saw his body.

Once Air Traffic Control gave me the go-ahead, I set the Beast down hard, which jarred Boom-Boom and jerked Crystal up straight in her seat.

"Remember what I told you," Boom-Boom said.

"I really don't care what you're doing here," I said. "Just leave the lady alone."

"Noble motherfucka, aren't you?" He smiled again. "And all I'm doing here is picking something up. Then you're running me to St. Croix."

I started to respond but bit my tongue.

The Beast settled into an open spot in front of the private aviation terminal. I shut down the power, turned off the batteries, and locked the windows.

"I won't be long," Boom-Boom said.

"This may take a while—"

"The lady can go by herself, you need to fly my ass to Christiansted."

"Not happ—"

"I got somebody waiting." He glared at me. "If I don't show, he got his orders, *brudda*."

I unbuckled and pushed past Boom-Boom. Crystal's eyes were full of tears, but she was first out the hatch. Outside, I took both her shoulders in my hands.

"Are you going to be okay?" I said.

"You're coming with me, right?" Her watery eyes were wide.

I swallowed. "Of course."

We started toward the terminal.

"Reilly?" Boom-Boom's voice came from behind me.

I asked Crystal to wait, then jogged the fifty feet back to the plane hoping against hope she could hold it together. I noticed a baggage handler pushing a large covered cart toward the Beast. There was no other plane nearby, so he had to be on the way to mine.

"Where the hell you going?" Boom-Boom said.

"I'm taking her to get a taxi, all right? Relax." I nodded toward the rapidly approaching baggage cart. "What the hell's in there?"

"My salvation."

With that I hustled back to Crystal, who was staring toward the terminal, her face like chalk. I opened the door to the small building—

Special Agent T. Edward Booth jumped up from the couch and threw down a copy of *People* magazine.

What the hell?

"I've been waiting for you." His blue blazer and khakis looked like he'd slept in them. He stepped forward and extended his hand. "I'm sorry, Ms. Thedford."

"I tried to call you, but my phone's dead," I said. "Are you here to give us a ride?"

Booth's mouth twisted into what passed for a smile at Crystal.

"I've got good news. The body the Royal Police found is not your husband."

Crystal's hand shot up to cover her mouth but the fast intake of breath was still audible.

The air froze in my lungs.

"The deceased was a black man. Gang-banger from St. John."

Booth's smile made it clear he was oblivious to the pain he'd caused with the false alarm.

"John's still alive!" Crystal shouted. She jumped up and down, then lunged into my arms. "John's still alive!"

"Well, Ms. Thedford, we're really not sure where—"

"He's still alive, Buck! We can still find him!"

My heart lifted at the tears of joy springing from her eyes.

"What do we do now, Buck?" Crystal said when she'd calmed down a smidge. "I need to get back to Jost Van Dyke! Everyone there'll be worried sick—can you take me there now? Please?"

"Sure—"

"No water landings, Reilly."

I glared. "Give me a minute with Agent Booth first." I took him by the elbow and steered him back into the waiting area. "How the hell could you think a dead black guy was John Thedford?" I said.

"Take it up with the Royal VIPD, it's their fault—"

"You said a gang-banger from St. John. Any ID?"

"Worried it's a friend?" I just stared at him. "Guy named Derek "Spice" Jones, part of Diego Francis's gang."

I felt the blood rush from my face. Spice was Brass Knuckles's friend. I thought of what Boom-Boom said about Russians—damn! What the hell was Boom-Boom loading into my plane? With Booth right here!

"Do you know this is a Russian cartel that's moved in—"

"I told you to drop this."

"—and John Thedford was grabbed from St. John by—"

"That's enough, Reilly!" Booth glared at me, his eyes like black beads. "This is too big—I can't have you free-lancing through the middle—"

"You have me do the dirty work with Crystal, then cut me out again?" I worked up my best glare. "Oh, I get it! The path to glory's opened up and you don't want anyone—"

"Cease and desist or you'll be arrested, I'm not fucking around!"

"Unbelievable." I pivoted on my heel and started toward the door.

"I'm serious, Reilly! We have an operation going—"

I stopped, dug into my pocket, and threw the dead cell phone at him.

"Go to hell, Booth!"

With that I pushed the tinted glass door opened and stomped toward Crystal on the tarmac. Then stopped cold.

44

BRAMBLE STOOD IN THE SHADE NEXT TO CRYSTAL, AND HE LOOKED ANYTHING but contrite. My stomach flopped as I looked past him toward the Beast. There was no sign of Boom-Boom, but the baggage cart was uncovered, empty and abandoned by the plane. They'd already loaded the contents?

I tried to swallow, but my mouth was stone dry.

"The hell're you doing here?" I said.

Crystal's eyebrows shot straight up and she slapped a hand over her mouth.

"Talking to the nice lady, *King* Charles. Bold of you to return here after those water landings."

"I have permission—"

"Not any more you don't. The FBI said you was no longer on their team."

"FBI?" Crystal said.

"Go on out to the plane, Crystal. I need to speak with the good officer for a moment."

She didn't move for thirty seconds, staring me straight in the eye. Was it that I'd given her a brusque order, or was she afraid I'd do something foolish?

She stormed off, and I again wondered where Boom-Boom was and what he'd put in my plane.

"I been playing you like a yo-yo, Buck Reilly. Flying back and forth like a dog chasing his own fool tail." The squint in Bramble's eyes matched his sneer.

"Do your people go around misidentifying dead bodies for fun?"

"Shit's going down, asshole. You want to help that pretty lady, best thing you could do is take her home before you both get hurt."

"What the hell's that supposed to mean?"

Then it hit me—Bramble must be on the inside with the Russians. Adrenalin exploded in my head.

"If I find out you're a part of all this you'll—"

"Shut your trap, boy. You say any more you'll *wish* you were in jail."

What the hell am I thinking? God knows what's inside my plane, aside from one of the most notorious drug smugglers in the Virgin Islands. And I'm going to pick a fight with a dirty cop in the middle of it all?

We stared at each other, my tongue burning with the acid of constraint.

"You got it, Officer. I'll be on my way now." I gave him a two-finger salute off my temple, then turned and walked as casually as I could back toward my plane. I damned sure didn't want him following me back there.

"I mean it Reilly! Get out of my islands, or you'll wish you had!"

I kept walking. As I turned toward the Beast's open hatch, I glanced back. Sure enough, Bramble stood with his fists on his hips, watching me.

I peeked inside the plane. Three burlap bales, each the size of a steamer trunk, were piled high behind the back seats.

Had to be weed.

Crystal gave me a pinched-lip stare from the back seat. I couldn't blame her. Boom-Boom sat up front, the shotgun pointed toward us.

"What was that about?" she said. "And what's in these burlap bundles?"

"It's a long story." If I shared my concerns about Bramble with them now, Boom-Boom might jump out and shoot him.

I glanced back at the bales—and the smell hit me, hard. Had to be five hundred pounds of the stuff.

"Let's go," Boom-Boom said.

Multiple deep breaths did nothing to check the speed of my heart.

"Crystal, I'm going to get you to Jost Van Dyke, but first we need to make another stop, okay?"

She just looked at me with the same expression that had crossed her face when I barked at Bramble. I strapped in up front.

"Christiansted, brudda. Chop-chop," Boom-Boom said.

I pulled the chokes, primed the engines, and fired them up.

And to think I could have been camping out in the Marquesas all this time.

I taxied out into traffic and waited for a Delta 737 to amble its way up to the head of the runway. The roar was deafening when it started forward, even though I had my headphones on. Once it was airborne ATC told me to proceed, and within a minute the Beast lifted off over Beef Island.

We lit out over Marina Cay and I banked to the south. Christiansted, St. Croix, was about a thirty-minute flight, dead ahead.

But that's not where I planned to go.

Once up to 1,000 feet, I banked hard to port. Boom-Boom grabbed the instrument panel in surprise.

"Hey, what the hell're you doing? St. Croix's that way." He pointed with his thumb to the right.

"That's the next stop. Right now I need to follow up on the lead Diego Francis gave me."

"That piece of shit? The hell you talking to him for?"

Guana Island was ahead. It looked like a giant triangular insect with big pincers on the top. The mountains that filled the southern land mass dropped down to a flat area with beaches on both sides and a saltwater pond in the middle. Brass Knuckles had said there was a small private beach on the northwest inside edge of what I envisioned as the top pincer. Were he and Diego were still alive, or had they too disappeared at the hands of the Russian cartel?

There was a person—no, two people below on the small beach, a man and a woman.

My palms got clammy. After everything Crystal and I had been through, all that mattered now was the truth. And there was only one way to find out.

I banked again and added flaps. We set down in the two-foot waves, just north of the far tip of the island. I hoped the hill above the private beach would muffle the sound of the Beast on our approach so the people at the villa didn't have time to react.

"This better not take long," Boom-Boom said.

"This is probably nothing," I said, "but there's a chance it could be either of the missing people, John Thedford or—"

"Stud Mahoney? Motherfucka's the baddest-ass in movies, man. Makes those old timers like Sylvester Stallone and Bruce Willis seem like pussies." Boom-Boom sat up in the seat and was now staring out the windshield. "Plus there's a big reward out for him."

"This should be the private villa up here. At least that's what Diego Francis told me." I sighed. "Only thing is, it could also be where the Russian mob is holed up."

Boom-Boom scowled. "If they're here…"

"Here's what we're going to do," I said. "When we go around this point, I'm going to turn in toward shore and get as close as I can. There's no pier here, so I need you to jump out and scope the beach and villa out while I set the anchors. Can you do that?"

"Stud Mahoney was kidnapped, man. If it was by the same Russians fucking with me, these dudes'll have guns."

I nodded down toward his lap.

He held up his shotgun. "I only got four shells."

We rounded the point, and thank God the water remained dark blue. I checked the trees and the spray on the water for wind, taxied a little further south, then pressed down on the left pedal. A moment later we were pointed toward the white sand beach. The chairs that had been occupied when we flew over a minute ago were now empty.

"Get in the back and pop the hatch."

Boom-Boom dragged his shotgun through the cabin. I heard a click, and a rush of salt air blew through the plane. I added manifold power and jockeyed the rudder to turn the port hatch toward the shore.

"Go!" I yelled.

To my surprise, he was out the door in a flash and up to his chest in water with the gun over his head. Then again, the guy was a smuggler. He'd probably flown into worse situations.

I didn't want to take time setting the anchors, so I revved the power and beached the Beast in soft sand. Crystal jumped into the water, I followed after her. Her expression was hard—she knew what we might face, but she was ready to go. We swam the remaining distance and arrived at the sandy beach just as Boom-Boom emerged from the foliage between the beach and the villa, which from here looked like the epitome of luxury.

"See anything?" I said.

"Couple people ran into that house when I got to land."

"Did they have guns?"

His mouth twisted. "Nah, man, looked like tourists. Dude and a woman. Scared shitless."

"Let's check it out anyway."

"What do we do?" Crystal said, her voice hushed.

"Find some answers."

45

WE CREPT UP PAST THE BEACH AND DOWN THE MANICURED PATH, HESItated, then listened for what might await us at the villa. Birds chattered, the breeze blew through palms trees—

THUD!

Boom-Boom swung the shotgun around, right past my head.

I crouched into a purple bougainvillea and waited. Nothing. I crept back down the path, stubbed my foot, and nearly fell over a fat green coconut. It had to be the source of the noise.

I kicked it off the path and returned to Crystal and Boom-Boom, still hunkered down.

"Damn coconut."

We continued on toward the villa. No lights were on and the curtains were drawn. Not exactly heavily fortified—or captors lay in wait inside and would pounce if we got too close.

Once at the front door, we stopped, and both Crystal and Boom-Boom turned to me.

"Now what, brudda?"

"Hide that gun so we aren't arrested if this is a false alarm," I said.

I reached up and knocked hard on the door.

A lengthy pause stretched out with no response.

A quick try of the handle revealed the door was locked. To the left was a steep rock incline the villa was built into. No passage in that direction, so I pushed tropical foliage aside and crept through the bushes along the front of the house. Around the corner was a landscaped patio with a bubbling hot tub. There was a sliding glass door but the shades were drawn.

The door glided open. A muffled shriek—I burst through to see a man in an orange Speedo dash from the room. A tousled pretty woman about my age, wrapped in a towel, rushed toward us with a ceramic pitcher raised high to strike.

I ducked and blocked the downward arc of her arm. The pitcher flew from her hand and shattered against the wall—

Another shriek from the adjacent room.

"What do you want!" the woman said. "This is a private villa—I'll give you all my money!"

My heart raced, Crystal's face went death-sheet white, and Boom-Boom jumped inside with the shotgun.

"Shut up, bitch!"

To my surprise the woman lunged at him, fists pounding on his raised forearms. Boom-Boom dropped the gun, she dove for it, I stomped my foot down on the stock and pinned it to the terracotta tile.

Crystal shoved the woman, who stumbled over a table. Boom-Boom grabbed the gun.

"Where's my husband!?" Crystal shouted.

"Husband?" The woman rolled off the ground to jump up in our faces. "What fucking husband—get out!"

Again came a shriek from the other room.

I pushed past the tigress and found a man curled up in a ball on the sofa in the next room. He'd covered himself in pillows that quivered like Jell-O.

This guy who reminded me of a rabbit wasn't John Thedford. The exposed legs and arms clutching the white cushions were mahogany tan, and his hair was dark brown—not blond.

Boom-Boom rushed in after me with the woman hanging onto his back. She jumped between me and the man cowering in the couch.

"I said get out!" she yelled. "This is none of your business—"

I yanked a cushion from the man—who shrieked, yet again—and my eyes bulged when I recognized him. Gasps erupted in stereo behind me.

"Stud Mahoney?" Boom-Boom's voice got higher with each syllable.

"We'll give you our money—she has jewelry!" Stud's eyes widened. "Crystal?"

"The *action* star?" Boom-Boom said.

"What have you done, Mike?" Crystal said. "What the hell's going on here?"

"It was *her* idea. My manager!"

"Shut the hell up you dumb Polack!" the woman said.

"I don't understand," Crystal said. "Why did you—where's my husband?" Her voice had dropped to a whisper.

"Who the hell're you?" the woman said.

"Crystal Thedford," Stud said. "My ex fiancée."

"What?" Boom-Boom and the manager said at once.

"What the fuck's going on, Mike?" Crystal said. "Or do you only go by Stud now?"

"Back off, honey, you had your chance," the manager said.

Just then Stud Mahoney, née Mike Kuznewski, jumped up from the couch.

"You rescued me! That's it, you saved me—the reward, you'll get the reward!"

"You supposed to be a badass, man—what the fuck?" Boom-Boom had the look of a six-year-old who just caught his parents hiding Easter eggs.

Bile surged in my throat.

"You have a new movie coming out next month, don't you, *Stud*?"

He straightened, puffed up his chest, and cocked his shoulder forward.

"That's right, third in the Brock Blade Navy SEAL series."

The manager rolled her eyes.

I gritted my teeth.

Crystal sprang forward and punched him in the nose. The blow buckled his knees.

"You son of a bitch! My husband's been missing for days—and this is a...a publicity stunt!"

Stud clutched his face. Blood dripped down his chin.

"You broke my nose!"

I grabbed him by the arm, yanked him upright, and pulled him toward the door.

"Let's go, *Dud*, time for your curtain call!"

"Wait!" the manager shouted. "You'll get the reward! The studio will pay—"

"Damn straight they will," Boom-Boom said.

"But that won't stop the FBI from throwing your meal ticket in jail," I said.

"Bastards." Crystal's voice had dropped to a hiss.

All the attention that could have been focused on searching for her husband had been directed toward this guy. Unbelievable.

Stud pulled his arm out of my grasp and turned toward Crystal.

"Paybacks are hell," he said.

Boom-Boom kicked Stud in the rear end.

"Shut the hell up, fool. Get your ass out to that plane before I shoot you." His head snapped toward the manager—co-conspirator—whatever the hell she was. "And you say another word, I'll throw your skinny ass out that piece-a-shit plane. Now move it, I got business on St. Croix!"

We marched out of the luxury villa. Empty champagne bottles, dirty dishes, and tabloid magazines littered the tables. It was all I could do to not pound Stud Mahoney into a pulp.

I turned around and found Crystal crying, her face in her hands.

I wrapped my arms around her. What a miserable twenty-four hours. I held her while she shook. Once she stopped crying, she pushed my arms away and took long strides toward the door.

"Goddamn crummy stupid sons of bitches," she said.

I couldn't have said it better myself.

46

BOOM-BOOM COCKED THE SHOTGUN.

"Take my ass to Christiansted, man!"

I glanced into the back of the plane. With eyes as kind as a vicious dog's Crystal watched over Stud Mahoney and his manager, who were buckled into their seats whispering. No doubt concocting a story to explain their disappearance.

"You hear me, brudda?" Boom-Boom was back in the co-pilot's seat, twisted toward me, a hand on his shotgun. "You need to take me to St. Croix, *now*."

"As much as I want to get you and your cargo off my plane, we're going to Jost Van Dyke first—"

"Look, motherfu—"

"*You* look!" I glared at him. "We have two very important situations at hand here. One, the asshole movie star who conned the world and who has every law enforcement agency in the Virgin Islands looking for his lying ass, and two, Crystal Thedford, whose husband is still missing, and the rest of Hollywood and Nashville awaiting her return to commence their charity concert." I took a breath. "Not to mention television networks here to cover the event, who'll go apeshit when we show up with Dud McPhoney."

Boom-Boom stared at me.

"Why don't you stay here on Guana Island and get one of your buddies to come pick you up?" I said.

"'Cause I don't know who's left or who I can trust."

"Then hang on."

I shoved the twin throttles forward and the Beast leapt ahead like an Olympic sprinter out of the blocks. What sounded like a shriek rang out from the cabin. Crystal rolled her eyes.

"What the hell am I supposed to do with these bales when the police show up at your plane, huh?" Boom-Boom pumped his thumb toward the back of the plane.

"Throw 'em overboard, I don't care." But I did. What if Bramble *was* waiting on Jost Van Dyke? Or Booth? If they found those bales, I'd be toast. "Better throw them out now, we could all get arrested—"

"Ain't happening, brudda." He lifted the gun. "This is all I got left."

Son-of-a-bitch!

Just as the Beast broke free from the water's grasp, I spotted two helicopters speeding toward us out of the west.

Uh oh.

"Christiansted!" Boom-Boom pointed the gun at me.

"You shoot me, we crash," I said.

He turned the gun back toward the others in the cabin. His stubbly bald head glistened with sweat, and his eyes were cold. Nothing about him quivered as he stared at me.

"Grumman Goose, Grumman Goose, do you read me?" a voice sounded in both my and Boom-Boom's headsets.

His eyebrows arched. "Don't answer."

"Grumman Goose, this is Sikorsky N1960, flying straight at you out of Tortola, Grumman. We have a report that you rescued Stud Mahoney and have him on board your vessel, copy?"

What the—how would they know that?

I glanced into the back. Stud's manager was whispering into her cell phone. The helicopters blew past us on both sides, each with cameramen hanging out of open doors. She smiled and pointed them out to Stud.

She'd alerted the press!

"The hell do they want?" Boom-Boom said.

The choppers spun back around and gained on us. I had the Beast flying at low speed, still unsure of our destination, so they cruised right up on our starboard side, one behind the other, cameras trained our way. I heard laughter in the cabin: freaking Stud Mahoney waving from his window like a victorious warrior returning home.

"Hey, cut that shit out!" I yelled.

The manager gave me a thin-lipped smile.

"You'll be a hero." She squinted, then reached backwards and patted the top burlap bale of reefer. She smiled again.

Perfect.

"What the fuck?" Boom-Boom said.

He held his hand up between the window and his face to try and hide from the camera. I wasn't as lucky. They'd check on the Beast's N-number and have the name of Last Resort Charter and Salvage before we landed—and if the press knew of the "rescue," so would the police.

"We're screwed now, *brudda*," I said. "We can't go to St. Croix, and you can't toss those bales without it being captured on film!"

"Come in, Grumman Goose," the voice came again.

"You going to answer them?"

I added power, pulled back on the yoke, and tried to lose them with altitude. Jost Van Dyke was already in view. If I ran for it, my radio silence and the fact that we had the missing movie star on board could lead to an aerial version of the O.J. Simpson Bronco chase. As focused as the Royal Virgin Islands Police and FBI had been on finding Stud, there had to be a mad scramble going on right now—

I felt a tap on my shoulder. Crystal handed me her phone. A text appeared on the screen: "Tell Reilly to bring Mahoney to Jost Van Dyke. I'm waiting. Booth."

My sigh was lost to the noise of the twin Wasp engines.

"What's that?" Boom-Boom said.

I held the phone up for him to read.

"Who's Booth?"

"He's the head FBI agent for all of South Florida and the Caribbean, that's who."

Boom-Boom's shoulders sagged.

"The hell we gonna do now?"

Damn good question.

The once Dutch island grew in front of us as my mind sought options. Rescued movie star or not, those bales were inexplicable. And that shrew of a manager would damn sure use them against us.

They say necessity is the mother of invention, but in our case, innovation was the *brudda* of desperation.

I pushed the yoke forward.

"The hell you doing?"

Using Crystal's phone, I dialed a number.

"Obeying the FBI." I winked at Boom-Boom. "What choice do we have?"

Confusion dawned on his face for the first time since I'd known him.

47

AS WE CLOSED IN, WE COULD ALREADY SEE THE HEAVY BOAT TRAFFIC AIMED at Jost Van Dyke. It came from all directions: sailboats, power boats, cruisers, ferries, sloops, fishing boats, everyone ready for the all-star concert. I glanced back at Stud Mahoney—his smirk reignited my desire to punch his lights out.

I wouldn't exactly call what I'd initiated a plan, but I hoped it would buy some time. We passed by Sandy Spit, the small island between Tortola and Jost Van Dyke. It was also the place where Crystal and John hatched their plan for this concert. Would he be missing now if they'd never set foot on that pink-sand oasis?

I added fifteen degrees of flaps and the Beast began to descend. We carved a sweeping turn around Georgy Hole Point and straightened out, aimed into the heart of Little Harbor.

"Missed it by one, brudda," Boom-Boom said. "Great Harbor's the next bay over." He pointed toward the steep wall of green vegetation that made up the western edge of Little Harbor.

"I know."

He nodded and glanced back out the window. Say what you will, but guys like Boom-Boom knew how to think on the fly.

"Why're we landing here, Buck?" Crystal shouted. I lifted my headset off my right ear.

"Too much traffic in Great Harbor."

With our airspeed down to a near stall, the helicopters caught up and flanked us. We set down in the middle of the harbor, which was largely unoccupied. The plane slowed in the aquamarine waters, came off the step, and settled into a nice taxi toward the western corner of the bay.

"Sidney's Peace and Love?" Boom-Boom said.

I nodded. "Do me a favor and get up in the nose, open the hatch and ready the line. We'll tie up at their dock."

"The cops'll just drive over here from Foxy's."

Rather than respond I watched the point, feathered the props, and further reduced power as we glided toward the dock in front of Sidney's. A large man stepped out onto the dock just as Boom-Boom grumbled and squeezed below the instrument panel to do as I'd asked.

A boat sped around the point, slicing through the water like a sailfish. The narrow beam, high speed, and three men on board had me holding my breath. The boat slowed and settled into the water fifty yards away.

Ray Floyd waved from the bow.

Thank God.

Back in the cabin, the woman with Stud Mahoney glanced again at Boom-Boom's bales of grass. There was no back-down on her face.

Yeah, bitch, I get it.

Crystal, on the other hand, was frozen in her seat. With her husband still missing, the concert upon us, and the bogus kidnapping, our landing in this strange location had her paralyzed.

"We're going to be okay," I said. "Ray and Lenny are here with Captain Jeremy, and they'll run us over to Foxy's. The police are there, and with Stud found, they'll double their efforts to find John."

She looked up into my eyes. A sneer twisted her lips as she glanced back toward the actor and his manager.

"Assholes." Her voice was a whisper.

"Now that this is over," Mahoney said. "I'll do what I can to push the cops to find your husband—"

"Spare me," Crystal said.

"You keep our secret, and you guys can have the reward from the studio," the manager said. "And we'll keep your secret."

"What secret?" Crystal said.

The woman pointed toward the bales, just as the side hatch popped open. Lenny Jackson's big grin instantly lightened the mood.

"Goddamn, Buck! You rescued Stud Mahoney! Son of a bitch!"

"He's a hero all right!" Stud said. "All of them are."

"Man, the cops and press are going crazy on the other side of that hill. Let's get your asses over there. . . ." Lenny's smile faded as his eyes caught the bales. As a native Conch, he was no stranger to square grouper, as marijuana bales are referred to in the Keys.

The sound of the helicopters that hovered above us made Lenny flinch. Stud Mahoney jumped up from the seat, ran his fingers through his hair, and leaned out of the hatch. He looked up and waved toward the cameras, laughed and pumped his fist in the air. His manager followed but took measures to hide her face.

Crystal unbuckled.

I took her shoulders in my hands. "This isn't over yet, Crystal. Don't give up, okay? When we get over to Great Harbor the press and police will focus on Stud. I don't really care what their story is because I still have to find John."

Her eyes softened. Tears welled up that blurred the soft amber of her irises. My mind shot back to the early morning hours. My heart held as much regret as it did peace at my decision. Right or wrong, I was still here for her now.

"You focus on herding the celebrities," I said. "I'll circle the wagons and see if there's any news about John."

She took a deep breath, stood, and planted a long kiss on my cheek. My eyes closed for a second, then she was out the hatch.

Could I pull a rabbit out of my hat?

Hell, I didn't even have a hat.

Adios to Jost

48

THE SALT AIR STUCK TO MY SKIN AS WE RACED ACROSS THE WATER TOWARD Great Bay. The helicopters circled above and I imagined their footage was live on networks all over the country.

Boom-Boom had stayed with the plane, but I insisted on locking it up. We skipped through the bay and dodged boats. Word had spread fast, even for the coconut telegraph. My stomach turned.

Police boats cleared a path and we pulled up to the pier outside Foxy's, greeted by numerous uniforms both medical and law enforcement. Amongst the faces was Special Agent T. Edward Booth, no doubt pissed that Stud had been rescued outside his jurisdiction. Closer to the front was Zach Ober in his EMT uniform, his gold tooth reflecting the sun.

The far end of the pier was a mob of cameramen and broadcast equipment awaiting the opportunity to swarm the movie star, get the scoop on what happened and how he'd been rescued. I was curious to hear what their story would be, but given the cargo still on my plane, my lips were sealed.

As soon as the rope was thrown down from the dock, they descended on us, with Stud lifted up on several sets of shoulders. As soon as his manager was off the boat I nodded to Jeremy, who yanked the throttles into reverse and backed away.

Booth pushed his way through the throng around Mahoney and waved at me.

"Reilly!"

I pointed toward Foxy's.

Jeremy navigated through the anchored boats and got us all the way to shore, where he spun the boat around and let the surf carry us in until we settled into the soft sand. Nobody met us, which was fine by me.

"Look at that dude," Lenny said. "Stud Mahoney! I can't wait to hear how you saved his ass."

I knew I'd need to bring him and Ray up to speed, but that could wait. I jumped onto the sand, then helped Crystal off the boat.

"Remember what I said, okay? I'll find him."

We locked eyes for a moment before she turned and hurried toward the headquarters for the concert. Ray and Lenny jumped onto the sand and watched her walk away, then I filled them in on the situation with her husband.

"You sure he's alive?" Lenny said.

"No."

"You sure we can find him?" Ray said.

"No."

Before they could ask me another question I didn't have an answer to, I heard somebody shout my name.

"Yo, Buck Reilly, nice entrance!"

Diego Francis stepped out of a weather-beaten shack adjacent to the beach, behind one of Foxy's bars. Brass Knuckles stood beside him. I felt a grin on my face, although I wasn't sure why.

"You found him on Guana Island like I told you, right?"

"Where can we talk?" I said.

Diego jerked his head toward the square building he'd just come out of, away from the crowd that had swooped in on Stud.

"Foxy's office," he said.

I spotted Booth's blue blazer.

"I'll meet you inside," I said. "I need to talk to someone first."

Diego followed my gaze and his eyes bulged. He hustled out of sight. Ray and Lenny followed after him, along with Brass Knuckles.

"Where the hell did you find those two?" White spittle was caked in the corners of Booth's mouth. "Every asset…in a five hundred mile radius… has been searching." He took in a deep breath. "And your band of misfits shows up with the prize!"

"What did Stud and his manager say?" I said.

"Some bullshit story about them overpowering two guys, jumping off a boat, swimming to Guana Island, and finding an empty villa to hide out in. Then you found him by chance when you were having engine troubles—"

"Ha! That's good—"

"So what *did* happen, hotshot, and why would they lie?" Booth mopped his sweaty forehead with the sleeve of his blazer.

I bit my tongue.

"Well?"

"All I care about right now is where can we find John Thedford," I said. "Do you have any news? And I don't want to hear that everyone's been focused on finding that weenie." I jerked a thumb towards Stud, still holding court. "And what's the deal with the Russian cartel?"

Booth's hesitation was all I needed—he wasn't going to tell me a damn thing. Time was of the essence, so I decided to come clean. I core-dumped information from all of my meetings, including Hellfire, Boom-Boom, and Diego Francis, the syndicate moving in—

"What the hell were you thinking?"

"Put it to you this way, Booth. It was Diego Francis that pointed me toward Guana Island—"

"Francis had Mahoney?"

"No, but he had better intel than you and all the rest of these cops put together—at least until they came under attack themselves. What can you tell me about that?"

"Those favors aren't cheap, so you better watch your *own* ass." He glanced around. "Some of the Royal Police seem to be less than trustworthy too."

"So I've noticed."

"And I told you to forget about the Russians—"

"While all the locals get kidnapped and murdered?"

A smile tugged at Booth's lips.

"Cleansing process," he said.

Stud swept passed us to enter Foxy's bar area, where we could hear him being appropriately greeted by some of his Hollywood brethren. It was obvious the show hadn't been cancelled, so would John's abductors' make good on their threat?

"Reilly! Don't drift off when I'm talking to you. Have you learned anything else that could help us find Thedford?"

"So now you're interested?"

He rolled his eyes. I decided to come all the way clean.

"It was Boom-Boom's people who told me the Russians grabbed Thedford."

"Why the hell would they care about a charity concert for adoption?"

"You're the intelligence czar, you tell me."

He shook his head. Something seemed to click in his eyes. What?

"We're *way* out of our jurisdiction here—"

"*We*?" I said.

"I meant the FBI, smartass." His teeth were gritted. "But leave the new crime boss to me, Russian or not. The Royal Police and the BVI government are already pissed—"

"I don't give a shit—"

Loud and tinny, The Star Spangled Banner's first line burst from Booth's blazer. He reached in and grabbed his cell phone. He checked the number, hesitated, and pressed END.

"Shouldn't you take that?" I said.

"You know what I'm curious about, Reilly? Why was Crystal Thedford with you when Stud Mahoney turned up? Like maybe they had all this planned—"

"Don't even go there, Booth. You saw her earlier today, you know how upset she was."

"But how did you find—"

"I told you, Diego Francis clued me in."

"For all we know her husband's hiding out at some other resort, and this is all for ratings," Booth said.

I'd never admit to Booth that I'd wondered the same thing, but if that were true, Crystal deserved an Oscar for Best Actress.

Booth scurried off in search of quiet place to return the call to his handlers. Knowing him, he'd already taken credit for the recovery of Stud Mahoney. I walked in the opposite direction, and just as I was about to enter Foxy's office, a dark figure jumped out of the dense brush. My heart double-clutched.

It was Boom-Boom and his trusty shotgun. He glanced around in all directions. "No more bullshit, Reilly. You're taking me to Christiansted, now."

"We're having a meeting here in the War Room to try and figure out what the hell's going on. Come on, join—"

"I got no time for this shit!"

"One of your friends is in here," I said.

I opened the door and Boom-Boom entered first.

The sound of multiple guns being cocked and the ear piercing sound of people shouting sent us both diving for cover.

49

"THE HELL'S THAT BUTCHER DOING HERE?" DIEGO SAID. HE HAD A Kimber 1911 .45 pointed at boom-Boom's chest. Brass Knuckles had a Mac 10 aimed at our faces.

I tried to speak, but only a bleat came out. I swallowed dust and cleared my throat.

"Relax, he's with me."

"Like I give a shit?" Diego said. "Motherfucker's cost me a lot of money—for all I know he's connected with the bastards who killed some of my people—"

"Killed my people too, brudda," Boom-Boom said. "We both been squeezed out."

A slow smile crossed Boom-Boom's face. He sat up, shrugged, and reached a hand into his shirt—

Diego thrust his gun forward. "Unh-unh!"

But Boom-Boom had already pulled a fat blunt from inside his shirt.

"Let's have a toke, brudda." Boom-Boom lit up and passed the blunt to Diego.

"Guys?" I stood up. "Now that Stud's been found, the show's going forward—"

Diego pointed his gun at me. "Only reason I'm here's for you to fly my ass out—"

"Not before me," Boom-Boom said.

The shriek of what sounded like a wounded animal turned all our heads. After a pause it sounded again, closer to the shack. We all looked at each other.

The door flew open and Crystal Thedford ran in, carrying a small box. Her face was bright red and she was crying so hard she wasn't making a sound—until another shrill wail erupted.

"Crystal!" I grabbed her and held her by the shoulders while she shook. Another shriek filled the room as she expelled every bit of air from her lungs.

"What's wrong?" I said. "What's in—"

"They're killing him!"

The box shook like a rattle as she jerked it up.

Ray Floyd must have wet himself after the guns came out, because I smelled urine. Lenny was peeking up from behind a chair. Boom-Boom and Diego looked relatively unfazed—and why not? They had the weapons, and they had a fresh buzz.

I caught Crystal and half carried, half dragged her to the chair Ray was crouched behind. She collapsed into the seat and clenched her fist between her teeth. Somehow the box wound up in my hands—I was surprised at how light it was.

"Open it up, man," Diego said.

I pulled the lid open on what I realized was a fast food hamburger box.

Another shriek from Crystal while I was flinching myself from the sight of the contents.

It was a finger with a ring on it.

"That's John's wedding ring!"

I wrapped an arm around her shoulder and pressed my jaw next to her soggy cheek.

"What's in the box?" Ray said.

"Crystal, listen to me," I said.

She continued to wail.

"Crystal!" I shook her. "This must mean that John's still alive! Okay? If it's his finger—"

"Finger!" Ray squealed.

I kicked him. "Then that's more like a serious message. Was there a note?"

Her hand shook like a Parkinson's victim as she reached into her pocket and removed the crumpled paper. I unrolled it, surprised that it was on linen—high quality stationary. The note was brief and in blocky letters:

LAST WARNING, STOP PARTY OR
HE IAT SCHIT FOR ALWAYS!

"What's it say, man?" Lenny said, his lips curled at the sight of the finger caked with dried blood.

I read it aloud, paused on the misspelling, then read it phonetically. "Eat shit?"

"They gonna make him eat shit?" Brass Knuckles said.

Crystal moaned. Diego jerked his head around and glared at his lieutenant, who held his palms up and stepped back.

"It's like some kind of bad translation," I said.

"From Russian, maybe?" Boom-Boom said.

The linen stationary wasn't the size of a typical letter, and I noticed the top had a jagged edge. It had been torn. Had there been a logo on top?

Scarlet, Crystal's assistant, came running into the shack. She glanced around at the unsavory group, then gently urged Crystal forward.

"Don't give up, okay?" I said. "I've got all these guys here to help me find John. They're not pretty but they're connected."

She pushed past me without a word and walked out of the shack. Scarlet gave me a sidelong glance and a raised eyebrow, then she too brushed past me. My hands clenched into fists. I felt helpless—and worse, useless.

"Ain't looking good for her man," Diego said. "These people ain't fucking around, whatever it is they want."

Boom-boom blew out a ring of smoke. "Telling you, brudda, I heard the Russians had the dude, so maybe—"

"Same bastards that wiped us out?" Diego said.

Both men looked at each other, then me.

"As in the Russian mob?" Ray said.

I felt a pressure building inside me that threatened to explode. I couldn't just sit in here.

"I need some air—be right back."

I stumbled outside and slammed the door.

"Buck!" Ray and Lenny called out, but I was already jogging toward Foxy's.

The bar was crowded and the energy palpable. Uniforms and familiar faces from the silver screen, CD covers, book jackets, and the nightly news clustered in groups, laughing, talking, and milling about. But there was no sign of Booth.

Of course as soon as I need him, he's nowhere to be found.

Dammit!

I slumped onto a bar stool and covered my face with both hands. My skin was gritty, my hair slick, my shirt pasted to my back.

I'd failed Crystal. The whole event, for that matter. If it went forward John Thedford would be—

"Hey, good-looking," a familiar drawl sounded behind me.

I glanced over my shoulder.

Avery Rose. Short shorts, tight tank top, snakeskin boots, straw cowboy hat with black hair down to her shoulders.

"Can a girl buy you a drink?"

"Thanks, Avery, I'll take a rain check."

She put her hand on my shoulder and squeezed. A pleasant, relaxed feeling moved all the way to my feet—

An idea popped into my head and I got off the stool, fast.

"Whoa, cowboy!"

"I'd much rather take you up on that offer, Avery—but later!"

I raced back to the shack—empty. Where had everyone gone? My flight bag was on the floor and Crystal's phone was still inside. There was only one battery bar lit. I punched in the New York phone number.

"Harry Greenberg."

I explained what had been going on since we last spoke.

"I saw you on television after rescuing the actor, dear boy. Quite dashing. Too bad e-Antiquity isn't still traded, the stock would have soared."

I almost smiled. "So of all the groups we discussed before, it seems the Russians have jumped to the top of the list."

"Makes sense. They're highly liquid, ruthless, and would logically go after the shipping routes for illicit goods in the islands."

"But *adoption*, Harry?"

"Not directly, perhaps, but the oldest—well, the *second* oldest criminal profession is the flesh trade. The Russians are big into that now, probably the biggest, and from what my people tell me their mafia was behind the Russian government's abolishing overseas adoption."

"But why?"

"Supply and demand, dear boy. People always pay more for scarce items. Babies are no different. From what you've told me of Adoption AID, their goal of making adoption more accessible would be a direct threat to the Russian's move to increase demand and control the market. American babies only account for a small fraction of all adoptions, and that likely won't change—"

"Unless Adoption AID succeeds."

I let our conversation and speculation sink in.

"One last thing, Harry?"

"As usual."

I swallowed. "Just to try and confirm that the Russians are behind all this, can you have someone check a translation for the phrase 'eat shit?'"

Harry asked me to repeat it, so I spelled it the way it was written on the note. He promised to call or text me if he learned anything. I thanked him, asked him to note the number I'd called from, and hung up.

Russian flesh trade? Really?

50

DOWN THE BEACH WAS HELLFIRE, HOLDING UP A SIGN AMIDST THE OTHER protestors. It was too far for me to read the placard, but he was moving funny—dancing? Yes, with a young woman who also held a sign.

No way he was involved with cutting John Thedford's finger off.

"Reilly!"

Booth pushed his way through the party atmosphere and made a beeline for me. Hundreds if not thousands of people had arrived on Jost Van Dyke now that the start of the show was just hours away. The harbor was full, the bar was packed, and people everywhere were blissfully unaware of Crystal's pain or John Thedford's minced finger. Stud Mahoney's resurrection couldn't have been better timed.

"What's this I hear about a severed finger?" he said.

"The final warning, Booth. None of the law enforcement efforts have produced a thing, and if the kidnappers are for real and the show goes on tonight, John Thedford will be killed."

Booth looked to the left, then the right. His eyes were pinched, his lips pursed, and he had a tic in his cheek I'd never seen before.

"I tried to have it cancelled." His voice was a whisper.

"*Tried*?"

"I demanded the concert be cancelled but your lady friend said no and the television network pulled rank on me and contacted the Director." He swallowed and pressed his lips together.

"Crystal said no?"

"Wants to do it for her husband, no matter what. The damn media says this show's going on, dead promoter or not."

I almost laughed at the thought of Booth's being muscled out by a woman and a few TV executives, but this was bad news. It eliminated whatever urgency there might have been amongst the collective law enforcement agencies to find Thedford.

"Yo! Buck!" a voice called out from the water.

I turned toward the voice—and in the dim light of dusk saw a red Cigarette boat rumbling into the harbor, its triple monster engines vibrating and spitting water into the air.

Baldy's boat.

Valentine Hodge was at the helm. He steered the Cigarette toward the end of the dock and waved me over. Just past him was another boat heading out to sea—it was a sleek, blue-hulled speedboat, and with all the boats coming in, it was the only one leaving. I couldn't make out the name, but the typeface looked familiar. There were two men in matching blue shirts and an old bald guy who stood facing back toward the island. He looked familiar, but in the fading light I couldn't make him out. I turned back to Booth.

"If the show's on, you better keep an eye on those celebrities," I said. "If the kidnappers realize Thedford's expendable, they may up their ante."

He hesitated only a second, then ran back toward Foxy's.

I headed for the dock. I passed Hellfire on the beach with his followers, but they'd leaned their signs against palm trees and settled into a party atmosphere. Past them, up on the road, were Boom-Boom, Diego, Lenny, and Ray—almost jogging parallel to me, away from Foxy's.

I called out with a shrill whistle and they hustled toward me as I reached the dock, which had so many boats tied off it looked like a hundred-foot-long mother hog nursing swarms of piglets. I looked out to open water. The speedboat was now a blue speck moving at high speed out of Great Harbor.

"Everyone's given up on finding Thedford," I said. "If the kidnappers are serious—"

"I'd say that finger in the burger box qualifies them as serious," Lenny said.

"—he'll be dead in a few hours."

Boom-Boom held his hands up and turned his head at an angle.

"Told you, brudda. It's the Russians. In fact, me and my friend Diego—"

"Friend?" I said.

"Merger." Boom-Boom smiled. "Bruddas vs. Bolsheviks."

"Perfect," I said. "Come on, we've got some news out here."

I jogged toward the end of the dock and arrived just in time to catch a line from Valentine as he squeezed between two boats. My old friend might be ancient, but as a native of the BVI, he'd been traveling these waters his entire life.

"You find Baldy?" I said.

"Who're your friends?" He wasn't smiling.

"These guys have been helping me search—"

"They're hoodlums," he said, "some of the worst in the islands—*your* islands."

He wasn't whispering, and he clearly had no fear of these men. He stared at them a long moment, then finally stood up. I helped him off the boat and onto the dock.

"My legs mighty stiff," he said.

He glanced toward Foxy's and raised an eyebrow at the hordes of people crawling over the dirt road and beach on their way to the main event.

"Where'd you find the Cigarette?" I said.

"Soper's Hole." He shrugged. "Keys were in it, so I figured I could strand him over there and come find you."

I smiled. "You think he'll stay there?"

"Not for long."

"What do you mean?"

Valentine pointed at the horizon. The moon was now in view above the water. It looked huge now that the sun had nearly set.

"Full moon," he said. "Baldy never misses the full moon party at the Bomba Shack. Sells mushroom tea, gets tourist women all trippy and takes 'em down the beach for funnin.'"

Light was fading fast. "Can you get us there in the dark?"

"Shoot, boy."

Right. I smiled and turned back toward my team of misfits. Moment of truth.

"You guys ready for some action?"

Boom-Boom and Diego looked at each other, then turned back to me.

"If Baldy can lead us to the Russians," Diego said, "we're in."

"Long as my shit's safe in your piece-a-shit plane, damn straight, brudda," Boom-Boom said.

"Right." I said. "Here's what we're going to do."

51

VALENTINE NAVIGATED BY MOONLIGHT SO BRIGHT IT SEEMED LIKE SILVER daylight. Ray and Lenny remained on Jost Van Dyke in case celebrities needed to be shuttled off later, but it would have to be by boat since Lenny had spotted the bales in the plane. His political aspirations and Ray's spastic colon made them risk averse. They had no intention of going near my old Goose.

Once we cleared Great Harbor, Valentine pressed the throttles down and the Cigarette surged forward. Whether it was from the wind or the thrill of driving the water rocket, my octogenarian friend smiled. The rest of us were pressed into our seats and holding on for dear life as the boat cut through the water and roared like the start of the Indianapolis 500. The dark hulk of Tortola filled the western horizon, with only a smattering of lights on the otherwise colorless silhouette. Valentine didn't need lights, and he didn't need GPS. He knew every road, hill, and contour on his native island, so he aimed the Cigarette toward Capoons Bay, the location of the Bomba Shack. The moon had risen well off the water now and lost that *trompe l'oeil* effect when close to the horizon. The night was clear, warm, and would have otherwise been a wonderful one for Adoption AID.

The armada of lights coming toward us from other boaters on their way to Foxy's left me hollow. Not for me, but for what Crystal must be feeling with her show going forward while her husband was being diced up. I wondered if she felt a twinge of guilt at *letting* it go forward, but Crystal was Crystal. If the price of realizing hers and John's dream was his being tortured and killed, so be it.

I was surprised at the sudden glow cast off the white beach of Sandy Spit ahead. The moon's brightness should draw Baldy to the Bomba Shack. Every muscle in my body felt knotted as the zero hour for the concert got closer. We had to find Baldy and get a lead to Thedford before the show started, and the burden was on me. That's all there was to it.

The North Shore of Tortola consisted of several wide and loosely defined bays. Capoons Bay was in the middle, and as we got closer to the island, Valentine steered us hard to the south. After running in that direction a few minutes, I tapped him hard on the shoulder and leaned in close—

"Where're you headed?" My words were lost into the roar of wind.

He squinted at me and shook his head. I yelled my question again.

He pulled back on the throttles and everyone fell forward out of their seats.

I pointed east. "The Bomba Shack's that way—"

"We go straight there, Baldy'll see us and know to skedaddle," Valentine said. "He ain't stupid and you can't hide this devil machine."

"So what's the plan?"

"My car's over at the West End ferry dock." Valentine smiled. "We can sneak in from the road a lot easier."

With that, Valentine jammed the throttles forward. After we passed the western tip of the island, he again cut the wheel and aimed us between the mainland and Little Thatch Island. Just past that, the bars, restaurants, and marina of Soper's Hole lit the southern area of the bay.

"What makes you so sure Baldy wouldn't still be at Soper's Hole?" I said. "Wouldn't he be trying to find out who stole his boat?"

Valentine shook his head.

"Didn't steal it. Left word with the dock boy I was borrowing it. Good or bad, everybody knows me on this island, so no way I could sneak off with the boy's boat." He shrugged. "Anyways, he knows the police been looking for him, so not like he was gonna call them."

Once past Soper's, I spotted a dark silhouette in the back of the harbor—the big blue yacht I'd originally seen days ago in Charlotte Amalie.

We pulled up to the ferry dock. There was a ferryboat at the pier along with a few boats and some dinghies, but not a soul in sight. The Customs office was closed.

Once the Cigarette was tied up, we assembled on the dock.

"I'm gonna miss that boat." Valentine laughed. "First time I driven one in twenty years."

"Now what?" I said.

"Let's go find Bomba."

Bomba, the shack's proprietor, was a recluse of a man but also a native, so hopefully he and Valentine were friends. Hell, they were probably relatives.

Valentine's Crown Vic was on the street in front of the Customs office.

"Makes us look like cops," Boom-Boom said. His teeth gleamed in the moonlight.

Valentine fired up the v-8 and popped it into gear. The tires chirped as we set off for the north shore.

52

Cars were parked well up the road before the Bomba Shack was even visible. Valentine parked at the end of the line.

"What's the plan, Buck?"

"You point Baldy out, I talk to him." My palm was sweaty on the door handle, and adrenalin pumped into my system like floodwaters through a New Orleans' levy. Less than an hour before the concert was set to start.

From the back seat I heard a clip being ejected from a gun, then shoved back in.

Diego grinned. "I'm not so popular over here."

Boom-Boom pulled a long black knife from inside his shirt.

"Me neither, brudda."

Valentine craned over to look at me in the passenger seat.

"Fuck-up or not, Baldy *is* my nephew, Buck. Don't nobody hurt him."

"We need answers," I said. "We're out of time."

My stomach rolled. Guns, knives, smuggling, kidnapping—I needed to raise my charter rates.

"Let's go," Diego said as he popped open the doors.

From inside the waterside party spot, a throbbing bass rattled my head. Several dozen people were packed around the bar, on the beach, in the street.

The full-moon party was in full swing.

"Bomba normally stays on the other side of the road," Valentine said. "Let's check with him first."

It had been years since I'd been to the Bomba Shack. It hadn't weathered well, but given the big crowd, its popularity had only increased. We crossed through the chain link fence, where Bomba's old abandoned Cadillac sat engulfed in weeds. I nearly tripped over the sculpture of a crazed-looking dog painted in psychedelic hues and perched at the gate as if to ward off evil spirits—or to greet those embarking into the world of mushroom tea-tripping. Either way, the ceramic mutt sent a bad vibe dancing up my spine.

Just ahead, Valentine hugged a man slightly younger than himself but heavier, sitting in the shadows under a broad Tamarind tree. They spoke in hushed tones, and the old man, who I presumed to be Bomba, glanced at Diego. His eyes grew wide—then he spotted Boom-Boom and did a double-take. Valentine was talking, but it didn't look like Bomba was listening. He nodded toward us and said something I couldn't hear. After another moment of hushed conversation, Bomba nodded again and slipped back into the shadow of the Tamarind's broad reach.

"Baldy's here," Valentine said. "Inside by the bar, buying tea for the ladies. Knew he would be."

"Time to find out who been raining hell on us," Diego said.

"I'll get him," I said.

"No, Buck, Baldy see you he'll get trippy," Boom-Boom said. "I know him and owe him some money, so I can get him outside, then we can talk."

"What if he takes off?" I said.

Diego laughed. "Where to? You got beach in both directions, 'less he got another boat out there."

My heart rate escalated along with the bass beat. After everything that had gone down so far I didn't want to trust the success of this moment to Boom-Boom, but he did have a point. I glanced both ways up and down the street.

"Valentine, why don't you go get the car. If we need to take him out of here, we will. Diego, you go down to the far side of the bar by the beach in case he takes off—"

"He ain't going nowhere, Buck," Boom-Boom said.

"I'll get the car," Valentine said. "Remember what I said about not hurting him, eh?" He left without looking back.

I rubbed my palms together. "All right, let's do it."

Boom-Boom walked toward the bar like Moses parting the Red sea. Locals who must have recognized him stepped back on either side of him. Tourists didn't know who he was, but his size, bald head, and serious expression made them step back too. He disappeared inside. To my surprise Diego walked down the road like I'd asked, so I went around the other side of the bar toward the beach.

A commotion sounded from inside Bomba's. A woman shrieked.

A blur shot out the side of the building—it was a man running up the beach.

I took off after him in a sprint. A group of women jumped as I passed. One of my boat shoes flew off—I stumbled but kicked the other up in the air and kept going.

Baldy wobbled as he ran, but he was still fast. I high-stepped it over the hard-packed sand with my fists pumping and quickly gained on him.

As I closed in he turned. Stopped, reached into his belt—

I leapt. He froze. I wrapped him around the chest like a linebacker and drove him down. Baldy squirmed as both of us rolled in the sand. His elbow caught my jaw.

High school wrestling moves still came as natural as flying the Beast. I spun behind him, twisted his shoulder down—

"Aaagghhh!"

Anger burst inside me, and within seconds Baldy's shoulders were pinned beneath my knees.

I tried to catch my breath. Boom-Boom and Diego moved in.

"What you want with me!" Baldy choked out. He reeked of booze.

"Who…the fuck…are you working for!" I said.

"Can't…breathe," he said. "You on…my chest!"

I got off him and stood. Baldy sat up and wrapped his arms around his knees.

"This is fucked up, man, what the hell you guys want?"

"We need information, got it?" Boom-Boom said.

"About what, man? I ain't done nothing against you guys! I ain't crazy!"

His eyes were bloodshot. I looked right into them.

"That guy you grabbed on the beach in St. John a few days ago—"

"What the—whatchu talking 'bout, man?"

"Don't fuck around, Baldy!" Boom-Boom said. "Those mudda-fucking Russians moved in hard on our shit!"

Down on one knee, I leaned into to Baldy. He was shaking, his eyes darting back and forth from me to Boom-Boom to Diego.

"We know you picked up John Thedford on the beach in Cruz Bay. What did you do with him after that?"

"I don't—man, I'm not—"

Diego leaned down and pressed his Kimber .45 into Baldy's forehead.

"Sons of bitches killed Spice, now talk!"

A small wail escaped Baldy's lips.

"All right all right, yeah, I picked him up, man, you know—but that was it. It was just a ride, I don't know nothing—"

"Where'd you take him?" I said.

Baldy cleared his throat. A shiver rocked him.

"Some dudes, man, paid me cash—they found me at Marina Cay that day—then they met me between St. John and Tortola that night, man, that's it."

I took his shoulders in my hands, gripped them hard.

"What do you mean, that's it? *What's* it?"

"They gave me the money and I gave them the dude—he was drunk and didn't know shit, thought I was his ride or something—"

"Who were the people that hired you?"

"Fuck man, I don't know—"

Diego pressed his gun against Baldy's head.

"Locals? White? Black?"

"White dudes, man, funny accents and shit. Paid me cash, in Euros—"

"Were they Russian accents?" I still had him by the shoulders. "What kind of boat were they in?"

"I don't know, man, serious—the boat?" His eyes rolled. "Blue, sleek little bitch. Fancy, you know? Nice wood and shit—"

I shook Baldy's shoulders and he refocused on my face.

"How big was the boat?" I said. "Did it have a name?"

"Blue boat...pretty, man. Name?" He paused. "Ah, yeah, some kind of foreign name I think, like that soda drink, I don't know—"

I shook him again. "What was the name?"

"I'm not—ah, what was it? Something like that soda—Not Pepsi, you know? Like Shasta, or something—"

Shasta? Why does that—

A bolt of lighting erupted inside my head and I leapt to my feet.

"*Shashka*!"

Baldy held a hand up in front of his face, the moon over my shoulder all but blinding him as he looked up at me.

"Yeah, that's it, man."

I rubbed my hands over my face. Several days of beard dug into my palms. I pictured the speedboat leaving Jost Van Dyke when Valentine arrived, the fat man looking back toward shore, and finally realized who it was. The boat he was on was the same color as the *Shaska*, too.

"You figure something out?" Boom-Boom said.

"Afraid so," I said.

"The hell's that supposed to mean?" Diego said.

I spit sand from my mouth.

"Because it's worse than I thought."

Viktor Galey.

53

BACK IN VALENTINE'S CROWN VICTORIA, WE RACED TOWARD THE WEST END ferry dock. The air was thick, the air conditioning not much help.

"That big-ass boat?" Boom-Boom said.

"It's called a yacht, young man," Valentine said. "Big difference."

My mind bounced back and forth as I pondered whether I should call in the Royal Virgin Island's Police or Booth. I decided against it. I knew my favorite FBI agent had little or no pull in these islands, and I didn't trust Bramble. There was maybe thirty minutes before the concert was scheduled to start.

Shashka. Even sounded Russian. I checked Crystal's cell phone—a text from Harry Greenbaum: "Eat shit has no direct translation, but the spelling you gave me, when checked phonetically, sounds close to *ischezat* in Russian, which means 'to disappear.' Does that help?"

Unfortunately it did.

"I'm used to taking risks, man, but this is crazy," Diego said.

"Gotta be a bunch of guns on there," Boom-Boom said, "we'll need to be super stealth. Maybe they got some of our men hostage too."

Diego shook his head. "Ain't nothing left to lose at this point."

"We'll have the element of surprise," I said.

"You some kind of James Bond or something, brudda?"

I shook my head. "Just an adoptee trying to help these people change the world."

Diego's grimace-smile bent his lips. "I just want to kill some Russkies."

We drove in silence down the dark, winding road. As we began the descent from the hillside toward West End, I again reached for the nearly dead cell phone.

"Buck, that you?" Ray said.

"Things about to get started there?"

"Pretty soon. It's insane."

"We have a pretty good idea where John Thedford's being held, if he's still alive."

Silence on the other side of the phone made me check the battery. A red light blinked.

"Ray, you still there?"

"Just waiting for the other shoe to drop."

"How's Crystal?"

"Haven't seen her—she's locked up in Scarlet's room. Your friend Special Agent Booth's running around like Mother Hen, forcing himself on the talent with promises to protect them. He'll be glad to get your news—"

"Keep him out of it."

Again the silence.

"I need you and Lenny to be ready to head this way in the Beast—"

"What about the contraband?"

"Forget that!" I paused and looked at the others in the car, all of whom were staring at me. "Listen, I don't know what we're going to do yet, but we're going to find some way to get on that boat and rescue Thedford."

"And fuck up some Russians," Boom-Boom said.

"What boat?" Ray said.

"The big blue yacht that's been back and forth between St. Thomas and Tortola all week. My guess is it's owned by Viktor Galey, who must be connected to the cartel that started the gang war—"

"Russian cartel?" His voice climbed a couple octaves. "You and what army?"

I glanced back at my cohorts. "Suicide Squad, Virgin Islands division."

Diego rolled his eyes.

I explained to Ray where the yacht was, told him to grab Lenny and anyone they could rally who could get there quick aside from Booth and the local police.

"We'll need the help."

"You're crazy, Buck!"

"So I've been told—" The phone emitted a series of quick beeps. "Ray? The battery's dying—"

Silence.

"Ray?"

Dead.

I asked Valentine for his charger but it didn't fit Crystal's phone.

"So what makes you so sure they on that yacht, man?" Diego said.

I told them about seeing the speedboat leaving Jost Van Dyke long before the start of the concert with Viktor Galey on board, a billionaire industrialist and a member of Crystal's board.

"I'm not sure of his nationality, but he had an accent. And that blue color? I'm sure it matched. At least, I'm gambling on it."

"*We're* gambling on it," Diego said.

"And if not, we crap out," Boom-Boom said.

"Here's the deal," Diego said. "Any weapons worth grabbing on that boat, I get 'em—"

"*We* get 'em, brudda!" Boom-Boom said.

"The only thing we're getting off that yacht is John Thedford, and we'll be damned lucky if we get that far," I said. "Boat that big will have a big crew."

Now down near the water, I could see the Customs building up ahead. Valentine parked the Crown Vic and we piled out. I checked my watch: nearly ten o'clock. It had been over five hours since the finger arrived in a hamburger carton on Jost Van Dyke. Urgency built up inside me like a bicycle tire pumped to its breaking point.

"You guys wait here," I said. "I'm going to look around."

The moon provided plenty of light. But if there was a lookout on the yacht, this was one of the places they'd be watching, so I crept around the building. The ferryboat and the red Cigarette were there, a few pleasure craft, dinghies—what's that? Two down was a 30-foot cabin cruiser with a stripe on its hull, a flag billowing in the light breeze, and VISAR painted on the wheelhouse. Virgin Islands Search and Rescue.

A glance in both directions—what did I expect? Nobody's here but Reilly's Renegades.

I climbed over the gunwale. There were no keys in the ignition and the cabin was locked. Damn. There were a couple unlocked drawers in the cockpit. Inside were charts, a radio, and binoculars. I scanned the yacht end to end with the binoculars. Low light on the rear deck—red light. It would allow those on board to see out while making it hard for anyone to see on board.

The only person I could spot was on the fantail, holding what looked like a machine pistol.

54

"THE HELL TOOK YOU SO LONG?" DIEGO SAID.

"See anything?" Valentine said.

"There are dinghies with motors and oars."

"What's wrong with that speedboat we came here on?" Diego said.

"Too risky," I said. "They'd recognize it from when Baldy dropped Thedford."

"You know how much shit I could transport on that yacht, brudda?" Boom-Boom rubbed his palms together. "Paybacks are a motherfucka."

"What can I do?" Valentine said.

I handed him the binoculars.

"Keep an eye out. If you lose us, just watch the back end of the yacht. If you see anything happen or hear shooting, call in the cavalry."

"What cavalry?" he said.

"Ray, Lenny, the Virgin Islands police—here, let me give you this one too." He entered the numbers I recited into his phone's contact list.

"What's the name?" he said.

"T. Edward Booth. Special Agent in Charge of Florida and the Caribbean Basin for the FBI—"

"What the fuck?" Diego said. "You got his number memorized, man?"

"Long story, trust me—"

"I don't trust *nobody*—why you think I'm still alive?"

I drew in a long slow breath. My recon of the yacht's silhouette had also revealed the shape of a helicopter—the same one that buzzed me and Crystal yesterday in Cruz Bay. If we were detected, our getaway would be… tough.

Boom-Boom lit a blunt, and ganja smoke burned my eyes.

"Let's go," I said.

We walked down the dock toward a dinghy. My idea for a cover, if questioned, was that we were sailors heading back to our boat. There was one near the *Shaska* that was dark.

Diego had his Kimber .45 in hand. That and Boom-Boom's knife were our only weapons.

"Let's roll," Boom-Boom said.

I pulled the handle on the engine and it fired right up. Boom-Boom untied us and we idled out into the black abyss of the harbor.

"If it looks hopeless we won't try it," I said.

"Shut up and drive," Diego said.

I turned my eyes toward the ship. The moon lit the harbor with a wide, brilliant silver splash across the black water.

The smell of gasoline made me sit up straight.

I glanced around and hoped it was in the water—no, a thin spray of gas was spewing from the fuel line where it connected to the engine and had made a puddle in the bottom of the dinghy by the transom.

Shit.

"Lose the doobie, Boom-Boom, we got a gas leak back here."

The only response was a flash of sparks off the joint's tip when he flicked it.

All eyes were on the massive yacht that grew larger every minute we drew closer. She was huge, one of the biggest I'd ever seen. In the daytime she was midnight blue, sleek, wide and long. By night, she eclipsed everything behind her.

How many people would it take to crew that ship? Would they all be armed? Maybe some were real sailors, unaware they were in the employ of the Russian mob.

Yeah, right.

A sudden dizziness made me drop the motor's handle and put my hands on the gunwale. The dinghy slowed. Boom-Boom and Diego turned back to me with eyebrows raised. I grabbed the handle again and the dinghy jerked forward. Our lack of plan, frontal assault, and limited armaments had me unconsciously holding my breath.

What the hell *was* the plan?

Maybe it was the smell of gas, or the disorientation caused by driving in the near darkness, or our steering straight toward a no doubt heavily armed billion-dollar yacht with an unknown number of hardened criminals aboard, but… When the odds are so stacked against you, ignoring that reality can sometimes provide the boldness to try for a miracle. Not the kind of odds I wanted to risk my life on, but as we closed in on the yacht, the question became moot.

A man appeared on the bow of the *Shashka*, the black shape of an assault rifle in his arms. I tried to swallow, but the cottonmouth and stench of gasoline caused instant reflux. Diego nodded toward the guard on the bow.

I raised a casual wave and never looked up, continuing down the length of the ship about 75 feet off its port side, headed toward its stern. Sailors returning from a night at the Bomba Shack, that's what we were. Certainly not three fools plotting to board the monster ship in an attempt to attack the Russian mob and free the captive they'd been torturing all week.

Once amidships, I killed the motor. The side of the ship went nearly 60 feet straight up to the top, but there was a lower deck thirty feet above the water. I hoped the guard on the bow hadn't alerted his associate on the back end of our presence. I took one of the oars and started to paddle toward the rear of the dark monster. Boom-Boom caught on and grabbed the other oar. The water ahead was lit up and I realized they had lights on under the waterline.

Of course.

If we were discovered, we'd say the engine failed. If they threatened us—

"What's the plan?" Diego whispered.

I nodded toward the back of the yacht. It was the logical place to try and board, but with the water lit up—

In the darkness I spotted a white line hanging down the side of the ship from the lower deck above, not more than ten feet above the water. From that lower deck the superstructure tiered down toward the back of the yacht, with what I assumed to be three different deck levels.

"Psst!"

They turned toward me. I nodded toward the rope.

"Paddle over there."

From the bow, Boom-Boom switched sides and turned us toward the yacht. If they had radar or any other types of perimeter alarms, we'd know soon enough. I pitched in with deep thrusts into the black water, which produced a swirl of phosphorescence around our paddles, and in what seemed a long couple of minutes we zigzagged our way up to the hull of the yacht.

Next to it, I felt infinitesimal.

"Now what?" The urgency in Diego's whisper made it clear he thought I was nuts.

"See that rope hanging down from the second deck? If I get up on Boom-Boom's shoulders, maybe I can reach it and climb up. You continue toward the back. When the guard sees you, steer close and if he says anything, chat him up for a minute."

"Can you climb that fucking thing?" Diego said.

"We're about to find out."

55

TWENTY FEET UP THE WALL OF FIBERGLASS I KNEW I'D MADE A FOOLISH DECISION. My palms oozed blood and my arms weighed a hundred pounds each. I focused on my breathing and tried not to flop against the side of the ship.

A flashback to reruns of Batman my father used to make me and my brother watch when we were kids. This looked a hell of a lot easier on TV.

One hand after the other…

My hand slipped. I slid—my toe caught—I stopped. I held my breath.

A glance down spied my right big toe clutching a piece of black metal trim.

With the rope wrapped around my forearm, I rubbed a blister-bubbled palm against my sweat-soaked shirt and risked a glance all the way down. The dinghy, which now looked tiny, had just entered the radius of light that emanated from beneath the ship.

I sucked in a deep breath—I was behind schedule. I gritted my teeth and renewed the ascent.

One hand after another…come on, Batman…one hand…after…the other.

So focused on each inch of ascent, I was surprised when the rope turned at a ninety degree angle below the railing—I'd reached the top. I glanced up and down the walkway. To the left were stairs going up. To the right was about a twenty-foot straightaway that dropped off in what I assumed were more steps.

No people. My arms shook like a luffing sail in a twenty-knot wind as I pulled myself up over the edge. I lay flat on the teak deck for a moment. The sound of my heart throbbed in my head, my hands were raw meat, my legs wet spaghetti. A voice sounded below—

Shit!

I got up off the deck, rushed ahead in a crouch, and found stairs down toward the back. I descended into darkness. A line of soft lights were imbedded in the outer edge of the deck, and what had appeared as dark blue fiberglass along the side was actually glass tinted the same color as the hull. Perfect. For all I knew, I was being watched right now as I ran down the stairs toward another straightaway that again dropped into oblivion.

I hadn't heard any more voices, but I assumed—hoped—it was the guard on the back calling out to the dinghy. And that it was only *one* guard.

The closer I got to the rear deck, the brighter the red light became.

"Stay back!" A voice ahead sounded.

I stopped so fast I slid on the wet teak.

Another voice responded from below, but all I heard was "brudda."

Boom-Boom.

"No closer!" the man on the deck said.

Hunched over, I crept up to the corner. A sentry in black was peering over the edge. He held a machine pistol behind him so they couldn't see it from below. A quick glance around revealed he was alone.

The distance was about fifty-feet—

"I said get back!" The guard swung the gun forward.

I rushed toward him, and halfway there it occurred to me I needed a plan. On a table ahead of me was a silver thermos. I grabbed it as I hurried past, making a metallic scrape. The guard half-turned as I closed the distance—

"You want some weed!" Boom-Boom bellowed from below.

Apparently he did, because he turned back as I lunged forward and beaned the side of his head with the thermos.

The guard's legs buckled. As he fell toward the edge of the deck he pulled the trigger on the gun and it exploded into the night with a flame a foot long. I grabbed the gun while he kept going, fell the twenty feet and made a large splash ten feet away from the dinghy.

Boom-Boom and Diego stared up at me, their eyes bathed in the brilliant red light I now stood under. Boom-Boom held up both hands, palms up, and shook his head. They paddled toward the dive platform on the bottom deck.

The sound of an alarm broke the silence.

So much for our plan to be super stealth.

56

BOOM-BOOM AND DIEGO TIED THE DINGHY OFF AND SCRAMBLED ABOARD. A shot sounded from below. Diego raised the Kimber and fired a round inside the boat.

Shit!

More alarms sounded.

Boom-Boom looked up at me— the crazy son-of-a-bitch was smiling!

"Find the dude!" he said.

He then lit his lighter and tossed it back into the dinghy.

WHOOSH!

A fireball blew me back on my ass.

I got to my feet and ran toward the salon door, which was tinted so dark I couldn't see who or what was on the other side. I glanced at the gun still in my hand. Last thing I wanted to do was shoot someone.

The salon door opened automatically when I approached it. There was nothing inside but a few muted lights which reflected off of chrome-framed contemporary furniture, glass tables, chandeliers—

A door opened ahead at the top of a stair, and four men dressed in black and carrying guns ran out. They hustled down the steps without even looking my way. I swallowed to force my heart down out of my throat. There was shouting below but no more shots.

I entered the hallway and peeked around the corner where the men had come from—and found yet another hallway. Damn this boat was big!

There were only kitchen and food storage facilities in this corridor, so I continued down and turned toward the outside of the ship. In that hall were six doors, one after the other. I tried the first one—unlocked, so I pushed it open and pointed the gun inside. It was a cabin with four bunks, all empty. I repeated the same maneuver in the next three rooms with the same result. The fact that I'd found four rooms with twenty empty bunks told me what we were up against.

Two doors left. I opened the next one—a crewman inside was reaching for the handle. In the second it took him to grab at his shoulder holster I dove into him and rammed his body hard against the wall.

"Ooph!"

He kneed me in my quadriceps—just missed my balls.

His elbow swung up. Stars erupted when he connected to my nose. The pain squeezed a few tears out of me. He squirmed and I crunched him into the wall again, then pounded him with uppercuts. He deflected them. I caught his chin—his legs buckled.

A left cross finished him. I caught him so his body didn't make a thud on the teak floor.

My breath was ragged, but with alarms and gunfire sounding I didn't bother to tie him up. I glanced both ways down the hall, then hurried to the last door.

Please be the one!

I jiggled the handle—locked. A muffled noise came from inside. I held my ear to the door, hoping I might be able to hear something above the sirens—

"What the hell's going on?" a voice said.

"Are you John Thedford?"

I pressed my ear up against the door again.

"Yes, it's me!"

I stepped back, kicked the door hard, and it flew open. I fell inside.

Thedford—I recognized him from the photos—was handcuffed to a railing with his hand wrapped in gauze.

"I'm Buck Reilly, I've come to get you out of here."

"Buck who?"

"Doesn't matter." I took hold of the metal railing the handcuffs were attached to and pulled. "I'm a charter pilot hired by your wife."

He was pale and his leading man features were a bit worn, but his eyes were alert.

"Some charter pilot."

I jumped to the other side of the railing and tried to leverage it at another angle—nothing!

"I've tried everything to pry that—"

"Cover your face!" I said.

He leaned back as I pointed the machine pistol toward the bolts where the rail was attached to the wall. I squeezed the trigger and the gun jumped in my hand to the sound of an ear-shattering *crack*.

Wood and metal flew in all directions as the burst of lead splintered the wall and fitting that secured the railing. It came free and John Thedford wasted no time jumping up and sliding the handcuff over the now loose end.

"Son of a bitch!" he said. "I thought I was a goner."

"Let's go!"

I looked down the hall in both directions and saw nothing. The alarm was deafening. I imagined twenty-plus men surrounding Boom-Boom and Diego—

"How many police are here? You have a helicopter or boat?"

I paused. What was I going to tell him? My mind processed options like a high-speed slot machine, but every thought came up lemons and bananas.

"Stop right there!"

We spun around to find Viktor Galey behind us. He held a large automatic pistol pointed our way. I lifted the machinegun toward him.

"Viktor?" John Thedford said.

"Buck Reilly," he said. "You've officially become a pain in my ass."

"Viktor—what the fuck's going on?" Thedford's face bunched first in confusion, then anger.

"Galey's a Russian mobster," I said. "Your vision for an adoption revolution threatens his plans to manipulate the supply and demand of infants—"

"You had them cut my finger off?"

"Better let us go," I said. "We're not alone and the authorities are on their way."

He turned the gun toward Thedford's chest.

"I heard you were prone to exaggeration, Reilly. Drop the gun and go into the next room there," Galey said.

I lowered my weapon. "Are you familiar with Diego Francis?"

He paused. "Local arms conduit into Mexico and South America. Now out of business and on the run for his pathetic life. What about him?"

"He happens to be below deck."

Galey eyes widened, if only for a moment.

"He's got enough explosives to sink this tub."

"You're bluffing."

"How many kids would you have to peddle to cover the cost of this yacht?" I said. "Worthwhile trade?"

He stared at me. His radio crackled. Indecipherable words were spoken. I hoped it wasn't a report that the two men had been captured, or worse, killed.

His lips pursed and he let loose a torrent of verbal ass-kicking into the radio.

Russian, another language I didn't speak. But I was fluent in body language, and when a bead of sweat ran down his temple, I felt a surge of adrenalin.

Then I realized he must have demanded backup.

A gunshot sounded. Galey whipped the radio down and lifted his weapon to John's head.

"Contact your associates and have them surrender or he dies! Now!"

"Cant." I pulled out my phone, pushed the on button. Nothing happened.

"Battery's dead."

"What kind of commando are you!?"

"If I don't meet them on the fantail in five minutes they'll blow this beauty up," I said. "Be a shame, really."

"You'll die before that happens," he said.

I checked my watch. "Clock's running, Galey. You might want to get outside."

"You're lying!"

Another roar of gunfire echoed through the bowels of the ship, followed by distant footsteps behind Viktor Galey.

Damn!

Galey glanced backwards toward the rush of feet.

I tried to lunge past Thedford, but he dove forward first and slammed into the Russian.

"Motherfucker!"

BOOM!

Galey's gun fired when Thedford hit him, but his arm had swung wide—Thedford drove him into the wall—and he crumpled. He was old and didn't struggle, just fell to his knees with the wind knocked out of him. The sound of footsteps was getting closer.

I kicked his gun toward Thedford, who snapped it up.

"Let's go!" I said.

We ran toward where the guards were headed when I first arrived, down into the lower levels of the ship. Thedford stuck close but to his credit ran steadily, even with the alarms blaring and his bandaged hand.

"Did you see where the launch area was for their powerboats?" I said.

"The one they brought me here on? Yeah, it's up ahead to the right."

The alarms stopped. The quiet that followed was eerie—had they apprehended the boys? Had Galey bought the lie about the explosives?

"This way!" Thedford said as he rushed down the hall ahead of me.

"Wait!"

He turned the corner and vanished.

I hurried after him and by the time I rounded the corner, he was turning left down the next hall, thirty feet ahead. I wanted to scream, but Thedford was hauling ass and I needed to catch up. I rushed up to the intersection of corridors, peered right, and found nothing—

"They're up here!" an accented voice shouted from the hall behind me.

I took off after Thedford and about forty-feet up the cocoa leather-walled hallway found a door ajar. A peek inside revealed sporting equipment. I entered, gun first, and found him bent down in one of two matching, blue-hulled speedboats.

"There's no keys!" he said.

I locked the door and shoved a cart full of scuba tanks in front of it before running over to the second boat—also no keys.

I pulled up the floor mat, found nothing, checked the console—nothing. Felt around the sides of the seats, nothing!

"You find anything?" I said.

"There're some jet skis."

I jumped out of the boat—the cramped room was full of water sports equipment. There had to be…there! On the wall near the door was a gray metal box. I pulled at the handle—it was locked.

A quick aim and eruption from the machine pistol knocked the box off the wall. It fell with a clatter to the floor, its door askew. A dozen different keys were inside the box—

The door handle rattled. There was a shout—could it be Boom-Boom? A loud series of knocks, followed by pounding on the door.

I scooped up a handful of keys and tossed them toward Thedford.

"Find one that fits the boat while I try to open the hull wall."

A loud clanking noise filled the room as the men outside beat on the door with what sounded like a fire extinguisher. Next to the outside wall was a small panel with a half-dozen illuminated lights. They all glowed red.

I stumbled over a pile of swim fins and dive gear, rolled on the floor as more shouting from outside made my heart pound. At the console, each button had writing below it—in Cyrillic.

The pounding on the door began again.

I pushed all the buttons. The red lights turned green and the sound of whirring machinery filled the room. The exterior wall started to slide open.

I turned to Thedford, who held his hands up.

No keys.

57

BOOM!

BOOM!

Ziiinnnggg!

I ducked.

Someone was shooting at the hinges on the door. Bullets ricocheted around the little room.

The launch doors for the boats were now fully open. The harbor looked like an endless void lit only by moonlight shining on the scattered white hulls of boats at anchor.

I dove for the metal box, grabbed the rest of the keys, and jumped in the boat with Thedford. There was one on a small orange float—it fit the ignition!

A loud screech sounded and the door into the room collapsed in toward us, blocked only by the cart of scuba tanks.

The boat's engine fired up.

There was a rope attached to a pulley in front of the boat. I aimed the machine pistol at it, pulled the trigger, and shredded the rope—the boat slid backwards as the door into the room fell to the side. The boat splashed into the water, which muffled the sound of revving twin props.

I pulled the throttles into reverse and my rope-burned palm stuck to the handle. The boat jumped backward and water sprayed up over the transom. A man pushed the door aside and aimed a gun at us. I pointed the machine gun toward the door and fired a burst at the scuba tanks—

WHOOSH!

A concussion of air and chunks of fiberglass, loose flippers, masks, and debris blasted out through the opening our boat had just vacated.

A swim fin hit the bow of the boat with a thwack and nearly knocked me to the deck.

I shoved the throttles forward.

"Get down!" I yelled.

The bow jumped as we shot ahead. I steered us toward the yacht's fantail, searching for the boys. Galey's men ran toward the stern. I reached the end but there was no sign of Diego or Boom-Boom.

Dammit!

I spun the wheel, cut behind the yacht, and started up the port side—up toward where I'd climbed the rope—

"Reilly!"

Up above were Diego and Boom-Boom, running and waving from the top deck.

I pulled back on the throttles.

"Jump!"

Both men hurled themselves over the side and landed with huge splashes in front of us. It was a five count before they surfaced, arms waving as they swam to the boat.

WHAP-WHAP-WHAP-WHAP!

Machine gun fire slapped through the water and caught the transom of the speedboat.

The second Diego and Boom-Boom were aboard I pressed the throttles forward and the speedboat jumped ahead.

"That the guy?" Diego said.

"You see any of my men?" Boom-Boom said.

I shook my head.

WHAP-WHAP-WHAP!

I ducked. "Can you do something about that?!"

Diego pointed his Kimber up toward the deck of the yacht and fired three rounds right next to my head—my hearing in that ear instantly became a loud ring.

We blew past the stern of the yacht and I cut the wheel hard to port. A fusillade of gunfire erupted behind us. I whipped the wheel and swerved figure-S turns, hoping to evade the bullets that streaked past us.

One cracked the windshield.

"Stay down!"

I tossed the machine gun I'd taken from the yacht to Boom-Boom, who immediately returned fire. Diego held the Kimber with both hands but with the increasing distance had no chance of hitting anything.

The sound of another engine rose above the steady drone of our boat's inboard—over my shoulder I spotted the sister-ship to this one slicing through the harbor toward us, our S-turns making it easy for them to close the gap.

"Is Crystal okay?" John Thedford looked up at me from the bottom of the boat.

"Just worried about you," I said.

"Jet skis coming from the other side of the yacht! Four o'clock!" Diego pointed out to our side. A quick glance caught muzzle flashes and four jet skis.

Thedford got up on one knee, Galey's pistol in his good hand, and started firing at the oncoming jet skis.

The speedboat gained behind us. Two of the jet skis swerved toward the western point of the island to cut us off if we tried to head toward Jost Van Dyke.

Another round hit the transom and launched splintered fiberglass into my back.

"Hang on!"

I cut the wheel hard to port and dodged behind a moored line of catamarans, carving a path between them—

Whoa!

The boat came to a near stop. Boom-Boom and Diego crashed into the dashboard.

"We caught an anchor line!"

The engine whined, the tachometers surged into the red, but we went nowhere—

"Throw it in reverse!" Boom-Boom said.

The gears ground as I jerked the throttle lever backwards. The tachs redlined and I shoved it forward. The boat leapt ahead—the guys fell backward just as the other speedboat turned the corner, so close I could see the driver's goatee.

They fired at us.

The mooring lines were impossible to see in the darkness. I swerved through catamarans and emerged between them at Soper's Hole marina. Another roar exploded—a jet ski spewing gunfire was headed right at us. I pulled back on the throttle and the speedboat gained from behind—

"The hell you doing?" Diego said.

"I'm out of ammo!" Thedford yelled.

Gunfire from the front, more from behind—they closed fast. Our boat was turning to Swiss cheese.

"Reilly!" I didn't know who'd said it.

I cut the wheel to starboard, gunned it. The chase boat and jet ski were fifty feet apart, heading full speed toward each other and spraying bullets—

The jet ski tumbled. Its driver flew through the air.

"Nice move!" Boom-Boom tossed the machine gun over the side, its clip empty.

I continued in a wide circle and the chase boat followed.

I cut the wheel hard away from where the jet ski had been. The speedboat followed us.

"Watch out!" Boom-Boom shouted.

I turned just in time to avoid an anchored sloop, spun the wheel back the other way then dodged behind another. Boats were everywhere—we lost sight of the chase boat.

"Valentine, I hope you're calling for help!" I yelled toward the moon.

I was in the groove of cutting between the anchored boats, as if it were a ground course chicane back when I used to compete in Porsche Club rallies—

A flash, then acetylene agony—my left shoulder!

It knocked me sideways. A screech of fiberglass-on-fiberglass sent splinters everywhere as we sideswiped a dark green ketch.

I fell to a knee.

"Look out!" Boom-Boom said.

I spun the wheel just in time to see another jet ski streak past ten feet away, spraying machine gun fire over us as he bounced off our wake—

That face!

The jet ski driver dressed in black and soaked to the skin with his hair flying back was the same guy who tried to grab Crystal back in Key West.

My left arm fell limp. Blood soaked my shirt.

"Give me the wheel!" Boom-Boom said.

I fell onto the floor next to Thedford.

"You'll be okay." He put his bare hand on my shoulder and applied pressure. Pain surged like he'd jabbed a lit road flare in the open wound.

We flopped back and forth on the deck as Boom-Boom zigged and zagged. Nausea blurred my vision—more gunfire erupted behind us, it sounded close but my sense of hearing faded in and out.

The waves and defensive driving bounced me forward, halfway under the dash into the cuddy cabin, where I spotted a manna from heaven.

In a corner of my mind I knew I was losing a lot of blood. Hell with it—I clenched my teeth against the pain, then reached up and grabbed the AK-47 clipped to the ceiling of the small cabin.

Boom-Boom jerked the boat around like a bucking bull—I rolled and bounced between the seats until I tumbled to the transom, now peppered with holes and fiberglass hanging loose.

Boom-Boom's eyes lit up when he saw the AK-47 clutched in my arms.

"Get ready! They coming up on the right!" I peered up over the edge, surprised at our close proximity—the chase boat flickered like a silent movie between the immobile sailboats.

The chase boat turned hard and came right at us, muzzle flashes blazing. I lifted the AK-47. Another row of boats were anchored to our right creating a narrow passage.

I scrambled onto my right knee—my vision blurred for an instant—and squeezed the trigger. The Russian machine gun jumped in my arms. The chase boat was close, coming in from the right. Diego fired his Kimber—the boat veered right into my line of fire, its windshield shattered.

The boat cut right, flipped onto its side, and slammed straight into the transom of an old Grand Banks motor yacht.

WHOOSH!

The fireball blew me onto my back and the stars in the sky swirled like pinwheels.

"Yeah, mothefucka!" Boom-Boom yelled.

Our boat slowed to a stop. I pulled my knees together and lay in the fetal position. Warm water ran down my chest—were we sinking? It was sticky—

No, it was blood. Mine.

Diego appeared above me and pressed down on my shoulder, his expression serious.

I heard the gears click and we started forward. There was talking, but I couldn't understand what was being said.

WHAP-WHAP-WHAP!

A new roar of gunfire sounded and Diego fell on top of me. I tried to push myself up, but my left arm felt dead, as if I'd slept on it for a week. The puddle of blood on the deck was big, and the sound of stereo machine gun fire sounded from both sides of the boat.

My eyes focused on Thedford, who was no longer wearing a shirt—he was bent over, pressing down on Diego's blood-soaked form.

Our boat swerved from side to side. Boom-Boom was peering over the dash and looking like a homeboy in a Cadillac. The jet skis raced after us, bouncing in our wake and unable to get off a clean shot. The boat swerved to the left and I rolled over, smashing my face on the AK-47.

I tried to reach for the gun, but my arm wouldn't respond—and the effort sent electric shocks through my body.

I heard a sound—a large bird flew over us—

A bird?

I heard another roar—engines. A second dark shape swooped over us.

A roar blotted out the boat and the jet skis that had initially headed to the West End to cut us off. My eyes fluttered and my vision came into focus.

Boom-Boom was bleeding from the forehead. He was on the edge of the driver's seat, his arm wrapped through the steering wheel, bouncing in rhythm with the waves.

Was our driver conscious?

I squirmed forward, past Diego, where Thedford pressed down on his wound. He was saying something but I couldn't make it out.

"Boom-Boom, you okay?" I said.

He didn't budge. A wave of nausea surged over me.

Now on my knees, I looked over the dash—we were headed straight toward Sandy Spit, not seventy yards away.

I tried to swing my left arm, but agony tore through me. I grabbed the wheel with my right hand—thirty yards—

Boom-Boom's other arm was wrapped through the wheel's spoke.

WHAP-WHAP-WHAP!

Machine gun fire blew out the rest of our windshield.

The wind caught in my lungs as the gray boulders at the southwestern end of the island came into sharp focus. I kicked Boom-Boom loose, spun the wheel with my right hand, and the boat went up on its side before slamming back down—

WHAP-WHAP!

Our engines took a few rounds, sputtered, and cut out.

Shit!

WHAP-WHAP-WHAP-WHAP!

A cloud suddenly covering the moon distracted me from the approach of the jet ski assassins. Not a cloud—it was a plane.

A box tumbled out of the plane and hit the jet ski, which flipped. It wasn't the Beast—looked like…

Like a Cessna Caravan with floats.

The plane flew low over us. In the moonlight, I thought I saw a bald head and familiar face with a big smile.

The sound of singular machine gun fire shattered the momentary quiet, and the muzzle flash now extended up toward another black silhouette that swooped down.

Another, larger item flew out of the plane and nailed the other jet ski, which sent the driver flying.

The second plane continued over us—the Beast!

A grunt from the deck caught my attention.

"That one of my bales?"

Boom-Boom, with blood on his face and a clean groove cut down the length of his scalp, gave me a weak smile.

It was so bizarre I couldn't help laughing. It cost me spasms of dizziness and pain, but I couldn't stop.

"*Thou shalt not fear the terror by night*," John Thedford said. "Not with you crazy bastards around!"

Boom-Boom groaned. "That Psalm Ninety-one, brudda?"

"Modified version."

"One of Hellfire's favorites," Boom-Boom said.

I collapsed against the driver's seat, which was slippery with blood, Boom-Boom's and mine.

What now? The boat was shot to hell, I was bleeding out, Diego and Boom-Boom weren't much better—

I peered through the splintered windshield toward Sandy Spit.

Out of the darkness came a seaplane. It idled slowly toward us, silent on the surf like ghost ship, its lone propeller whistling like a turbocharged weed whacker.

My vision blurred again and I slipped down in the seat.

The plane, if it was real, pulled right up to our bow. Moonlight lit the pilot's face. He looked familiar, and at first he smiled but then his face turned serious. Another guy hung off the wing strut. Short but stocky, he shook a fist in the air—

In my last spark of semi-clarity, the pilot's face I imagined on the seaplane before us popped into my head.

Jimmy Buffett?

Then all went black.

58

John Thedford insisted on staying with us at the hospital, so the concert was postponed until we were stabilized and released the next day. Even the media couldn't change his mind. The delay and the shootout aboard the yacht and in Soper's Hole only increased the excitement. By show time, the crowd at Foxy's outnumbered even the wildest projections. The celebrities, be they singers, actors, politicians, judges, writers, athletes, scientists, or intellectuals, were all in top form. The television cameras ate them up, every single one, and their personal statements and support for John and Crystal's vision was broadcast on major networks worldwide.

From the side of the stage, we were as close to being a part of the show as anyone could be without actually being celebrity guests. Crystal had not only insisted we all be here, she'd had a series of padded chaise longues erected where we could convalesce, have our intravenous medicines attended to, suck on a few painkillers—the kind with nutmeg sprinkled on top—and doze between performances.

Boom-Boom and Diego enjoyed their new status. By agreement with multiple law enforcement agencies they couldn't be shown on the air, which was fine with them. As for me, after everything that had happened during the week, particularly with Crystal, I was looking to disappear at the soonest possible opportunity. But Special Agent T. Edward Booth was still demanding answers.

"You need to explain how those last two jet skis got knocked out with a bale of high-grade marijuana and a case of Margaritaville Tequila, Reilly. And how did you all get back to the hospital after getting shot up?"

In all the time I'd known Booth, I'd never seen such complete frustration on his face. I recalled the black planes swooping down and blotting out the brilliant Caribbean stars—and the face in the seaplane.

"I have no memories of the shootout, Booth. I guess losing a few pints of blood does that to you." Booth squinty-eyed me. "Any news about Viktor Galey?"

"No sign of him, but—"

"You let him get away?"

"We think he had inside help, Reilly. We lost three men—"

"Was the helicopter still there?"

Booth just stared at me, his mouth open. "Helicopter?"

I sighed.

"What about Bramble?" I said.

Booth crossed his arms. "We haven't seen him anywhere."

I feigned falling asleep until Booth hurried off toward one of the movie stars.

Jamie Foxx was talking to Boom-Boom and Diego, soaking up their stories, manner of speech, and nonchalance as if preparing for a new role. The boys were giddy at the attention, but when he caught me watching him, Diego's face turned serious.

"You still owe me for Guana Island," he said.

"And me for the Russians, brudda," Boom-Boom said.

After a long few seconds, they both burst into laughter.

Ray and Lenny had scored points for rescuing us from certain death by knocking out the last of the jet ski killers. Although their methodology had been left out of the news reports, they captivated the celebrities with their story of scrambling in the darkness with a plane full of contraband used to dispatch assassins.

Valentine Hodge regaled anyone who cared to listen with stories about the history of the British Virgin Islands, his presence adding a touch of grace and sophistication to our cast of misfits.

John Thedford had turned out to be a visionary who could kick ass. As for Crystal, well, she was keeping her distance. She'd given me a long, tearful embrace when I was released from the hospital but couldn't bring herself to utter a word. It hurt, but I understood.

For now, both Thedfords appeared calm, confident, and determined to dedicate their lives to helping adoptees, changing society's view toward women facing unplanned pregnancy, and hoping to replace the walls between the hardened constituencies of "choice" with bridges.

No small task there.

Jimmy Buffett and Matt Hoggatt were on stage, the chemistry between them entirely natural—two Mississippi-cum-Caribbean country crooners as at home in these islands as any of the natives. Since I had yet to speak to them I didn't know for sure whether or not it had been them on that other seaplane. If not, it must have been a hallucination caused by blood loss. I'm no investigator, but Buffett was known to have a Cessna Caravan with floats, and Hoggatt had been a police detective. And Booth said one of the jet ski drivers had been cold-cocked with a case of Margaritaville Tequila.

A cool breeze blew through the backstage at Foxy's as I took in the scene: the roaring crowd, the cameras, the azure sea framed in coconut palms, and the harbor filled with boats of all size and shape.

John Thedford said that lost finger or not he still believed things happened for a reason, and even derelicts like Boom-Boom, Diego, and me had a purpose on this earth.

Maybe mine had been to save his life so he could change the world.

You never know.

A beach ball flew up from the stage and Buffett swatted it back over his head. It landed right in my lap. He glanced back with that trademark smile and gave me a wink.

I heard footsteps behind me. "You ready to take me up on that drink, cowboy?"

Avery Rose. She kissed my cheek and then looked back at the stage.

"This next song is one Matt and I just wrote." Buffet looked right at me with a shit-eating grin.

Matt Hoggatt stepped up to the microphone.

"It's called 'The Ballad of Buck Reilly.'"

59

THE SUN WAS HOT ON MY CHEST AND MADE THE SKIN UNDER MY BANDAGE itch. In front of me was nothing but blue water with wispy cirrus clouds drifting overhead. The Beast was beached up near the breakwater. Sweat ran down my torso and dripped into the sand from the teak lounge chair I'd been parked in for the better part of the morning since emerging from the private villa here on Guana Island.

A periodic buzzing sound came from the tall grass behind me, or maybe it was from the villa itself. I wasn't sure and frankly didn't care. The concert had ended last night, my charter for ISA was over, and I was back on my own clock. The warm breeze rustled the grass and a feather blew across raked sand so white I had to squint underneath my sunglasses.

It seemed like a lifetime ago that I'd decided to abstain from the charter side of my business and focus again on salvage. People and their problems tended to wear me out. Hell, this time they nearly got me killed. I smiled—not that I regretted one moment of this trip.

"Buck?"

Avery Rose ambled down the path from the villa holding a tray with a pitcher of fresh margaritas and salt-rimmed glasses. She moved with the delicate care of someone who'd gone to great length to create something they didn't want to see ruined.

"I wasn't sure if you were awake." She placed the tray on a small teak table next to our chairs, bent down, and pressed her moist, full lips against mine. "You need to rest up to restore your energy."

"Indeed."

Ever fearful of paparazzi eager to spoil her public image of country innocence, she glanced up and down the private beach before sliding out of the sheer wrap that covered part of her body, leaving only a tiny bikini bottom and top that barely constrained her tanned chest.

A growing drone caused her to hesitate.

The sound grew louder, and a small powerboat rounded the long breakwater near where the Beast was beached.

"Not now," Avery said.

"They'll only be here a little while."

The boat straightened out and followed a line directly toward us before Ray cut the engine and the boat slid quietly onto the sand. Lenny jumped off the bow, pulled the wood boat ashore, grunting and cussing under his breath as he did so.

"Damn, boy, all you bastards must weigh a thousand pounds!" he said. "If I hurt my back, the people in Key West won't have the confidence to vote my ass onto the City Council."

Boom-Boom, his head still encased in gauze, stepped over the side into the water and pushed the remnants of a joint against his lips. The tip of it glowed red before he spit it into the surf. Diego, his right arm in a sling, followed—helped out by Zachary Ober, who for the first time since I'd met him was wearing something other than his EMT uniform. His gold tooth caught the sunlight like a message from the heavens. Ray Floyd stumbled over the rows of seats to the front of the boat, climbed out, picked up the rope Lenny had dropped onto the sand, and tied it to a pygmy palm on the edge of the beach.

"Why are they here again?" Avery said.

Her voice was devoid of whining or bitchiness, and I thought yet again that she was just what the doctor had ordered.

"It has to do with some history on Tortola," I said.

All five of my friends, old and new, were smiling as they stomped up the beach shoulder to shoulder, like a team of some sort.

"Let's talk about that buried treasure!" Diego slapped his good hand against Zachary Ober's back. "Hah!"

I laughed out loud. For the first time in years I was actually excited to hear those words.

"I'll pour the margaritas," Avery said.

"Sounds like a plan."

The End

The Ballad of Buck Reilly

Cunningham/Hoggatt

TALK IN: *This is the Ballad of Buck Reilly. You may have heard about him, or at least his past, because today, well, he's just trying to stay under the radar. But back in the day, he was a global treasure hunter, a regular for-profit Indiana Jones. The Wall Street Journal even proclaimed him King Buck. Of course, that was before he lost his ass...*

Buck Reilly's Just a man, Just like you and me
Gave up everything he owned to the economy
Uncle Sam took his money, lost his parents and his girl
He woke up sleeping alone one day at the south end of the world

Now he lives in the La Concha, down on Duval Street
Flying charter and salvage, to keep him on his feet
No longer burning money, just trying to stay afloat
Taking anybody anywhere in his antique flying boat

No questions asked
Especially if you pay with cash

Bahamas, Key West,
Cuba and all the rest
Of the Caribbean island chain
Buck Reilly's still trying,
Living and dying
To break a couple rules along the way
Buck Reilly, oh Buck Reilly
Fly me away

His airplane's name is Betty; she's been crashed before
Got a red float on her starboard wing and a green one on her port
Like constant channel markers, leading home or to his soul
Always headed for that treasure, that only Buck knows

No questions asked
He may be broke but hey, he's having a blast

Bahamas, Key West,
Cuba and all the rest
Of the Caribbean island chain
Buck Reilly's still trying,
Living and dying
To break a couple rules along the way
Buck Reilly, oh Buck Reilly
Fly me away

He only wants three things in life, that's true
A plane to fly, a treasure to find and a woman to rescue...

Bahamas, Key West,
Cuba and all the rest
Of the Caribbean island chain
Buck Reilly's still trying,
Living and dying
To make up his own rules along the way
Buck Reilly, oh Buck Reilly
Fly me away

CPSIA information can be obtained
at www.ICGtesting.com
Printed in the USA
JSHW082144171022
31659JS00001B/2

9 780985 442248